# PRAISE FOR ANDRÉS NEUMAN

"It is impossible to classify Andrés Neuman: each of his books is a new language adventure, guided by the intelligence and the pleasure of words. He never ceases to surprise us and is, doubtlessly, one of the most daring writers in Latin American literature, willing to change, challenge and explore, always with a unique elegance."
—Mariana Enríquez, author of *Things We Lost in the Fire*

"The literature of the twenty-first century will belong to Neuman and a few of his blood siblings."—*Roberto Bolaño*

"Andrés Neuman has transcended the boundaries of geography, time, and language to become one of the most significant writers of the early twenty-first century."
—*Music & Literature*

"One of the things I love about Andrés Neuman's work is how he restores writing as the most powerful source of knowledge. *Fracture*, this dazzling and devastating novel, is a terrific demonstration of that."
—Alejandro Zambra, author of *Ways of Going Home*

"Traversing languages and cultures, decades and generations, *Fracture* unites its many fragments to form a powerful and redemptive vision of a single, and unbroken, human life. A searching, humane, and vital novel."
—Eleanor Catton, author of *The Luminaries*

T0203275

# Once
## upon
# Argentina

## by Andrés Neuman

Translated from the Spanish
by Nick Caistor and Lorenza García

**OPEN LETTER**
LITERARY TRANSLATIONS FROM THE UNIVERSITY OF ROCHESTER

Originally published as *Una vez Argentina* by Editorial Anagrama, 2003

Revised and expanded edition published by Editorial Alfaguara, 2014

Copyright © Andrés Neuman, 2003, 2014, 2024

Translation copyright © Nicholas Caistor & Lorenza Garcia, 2024

First edition, 2024

Library of Congress Catalog-in-Publication Data: Available.

ISBN (pb): 978-1-960385-11-6| ISBN (ebook): 978-1-960385-18-5


*This project is supported in part by an award from the New York State Council on the Arts with the support of the governor of New York and the New York State Legislature*

Printed on acid-free paper in the United States of America


Cover design by Anna Jordan


Open Letter is the University of Rochester's nonprofit, literary translation press.

www.openletterbooks.org

# Once
## upon
# Argentina

*To my mother, for her four strings*

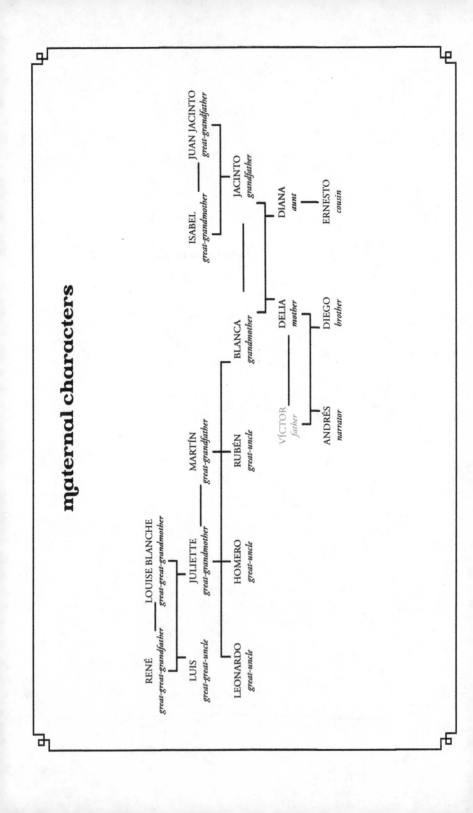

# maternal characters

RENÉ
*great-great-grandfather* — LOUISE BLANCHE
*great-great-grandmother*

LUIS
*great-great-uncle*

JULIETTE
*great-grandmother* — MARTÍN
*great-grandfather*

ISABEL
*great-grandmother* — JUAN JACINTO
*great-grandfather*

LEONARDO
*great-uncle*

HOMERO
*great-uncle*

RUBÉN
*great-uncle*

BLANCA
*grandmother*

JACINTO
*grandfather*

VÍCTOR
*father*

DELIA
*mother*

DIANA
*aunt*

ANDRÉS
*narrator*

DIEGO
*brother*

ERNESTO
*cousin*

# paternal characters

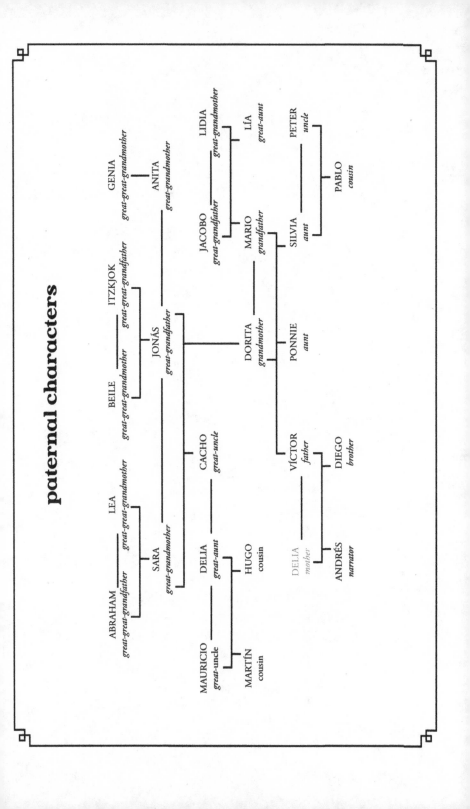

*I was told you come here and tell your story.*
MIGUEL BRIANTE


*What I have just told myself is a memory.*
ALBERT COHEN


*Your mother has a mother.*
*A country of words.*
MAHMOUD DARWISH

# 1

DO OUR MEMORIES hurt when they come back? Or do they start to heal when they return, and then we realize they've been hurting all that time? We travel within them. We are their passengers.

I have a letter and an unresolved memory. The letter is from my grandmother Blanca, its lines slightly faded. The memory is mine, although it doesn't belong only to me. Its fear is the same as always: to disappear before being told.

I'm going to travel backward.

# 2

I WAS BORN with my eyes wide open, and, unaware of the protocol, I refused to cry. The doctor held me up against the light, as if I were a sheet of thick paper. I stared back at him, with curiosity I suppose. He asked my mother what I was to be called. Andrés, she replied. Is anything the matter, Doctor Riquelme? I don't know, he said, examining me with a slight look of horror, this baby won't cry, he simply looks. Is that bad, Doctor? More or less, señora; let's put it this way: if the boy becomes too accustomed to looking, then he'll have to learn to cry.

It was a midday in January 1977. Given the political situation in Argentina at the time, Doctor Riquelme found me far too serene. Since he was averse to using violence, he began to talk to me in a kindly whisper: Andrés, Andresito, why won't you cry, eh? Just a bit. A tiny little bit. Go on, cry. My mother watched on tenderly: doubtless this was my first man-to-man conversation.

Señora, the doctor declared, this baby needs to cry right this instant, do you hear me? It's all about his lungs. What shall we do? asked my worried mother. Doctor Riquelme gestured to the midwife and then lifted me level with his forehead, squaring up to me. He encountered two round, bewildered eyes. I remained stubbornly silent. Doctor Riquelme had no choice but to yell at me: Will you just cry, damn it, motherfucking sonofabitch! Instantly, tears began to fill my myopic cat's eyes.

On the far side of the bed, next to my mother's spread-eagled legs, the midwife declared: That's that then. This boy is going to need a bit of discipline.

# 3

NOBODY KNOWS FOR certain if it was him. It may have been his father, or maybe even his grandfather. But Jacobo's surname, my own surname, was born of a deception. It's possible that, somewhere in the world, some distant relative still knows the precise details. I prefer to accept the version I heard as a child: the one that tells of a timely betrayal and sly cowardice.

My paternal great-grandfather, or possibly his father, or maybe even his grandfather, lived in Tsarist Russia. It was common for boys from poor families, especially Jewish ones, to be press-ganged into military service in regions near Siberia. So great was the terror of being conscripted, and the chances of surviving two years there seemed so slight, that many chose to maim themselves in order to gain exemption. Jacobo, or possibly his father, or maybe his grandfather, knew several youths missing an ear, hand, or eye.

But Jacobo (let's choose him—he deserves it) felt too attached to all of his limbs to contemplate such a sacrifice. So he hit on a plan that would allow him to keep his body intact without having to join the army. Did he ask for help from some distant relative to falsify his real identity? Did he bribe some Russian customs official so that he could emigrate? Or did he turn, as I once heard and like to believe, to a delinquent friend, who helped him steal the passport of a German soldier by the name of Neuman?

The only certainty is that, rebaptized in this timely way, when the First World War broke out *zeide* Jacobo found himself far from the town of Kamenetz, in today's Ukraine. Not just far away but in another world: my native Buenos Aires, somewhere I am not but where I remain. My great-grandfather saved his life by changing his identity and being reborn as a foreigner. In other words, by becoming fiction.

Following an old tradition, which nowadays seems in the realms of fantasy or taboo, the young woman Jacobo would marry was his first cousin. Great-grandmother Lidia came from Lithuania and, strangely enough, met her Ukrainian cousin in Buenos Aires. The remainder of her name was lost on the ears of a port official. There, at a desk in the Hotel de Inmigrantes, someone wrote what looks like "Jasatsca." As far as I can tell, Lidia's original name must have been something like Chazacka, which is the feminine form of Chazacky, or possibly Hasatzky. So, in part due to history, in part to chance, and in part thanks to invention, the origins of those great-grandparents is quite similar to my own memory.

*Baba* Lidia was radically thin, as if her past had consumed her present, and had sapphire eyes. Several of her sisters had died in Lithuania during the pogroms, although she never spoke about that. Before emigrating to Argentina, her childhood had been an expanse of hunger against a background of fear. Lidia had spent many winter mornings lining up for bread, which usually ran out soon after daybreak. On one occasion, she used to tell us, it had been such an effort to keep her place in the line, and the night air had numbed her muscles so completely, that when at last the bakery opened the sudden, sensual smell of freshly baked bread made her faint right next to the door. She soon came round, but by then the bread had flown out of the bakery and her dress was covered in muddy footprints.

By the time Lidia was an adolescent, her parents decided to try their luck in Argentina, a country where everybody either had or invented a family. Soon afterward, I imagine without consulting her, they arranged the wedding with cousin Jacobo.

During the early years of their marriage, Jacobo earned a living with a hat shop they set up in the little apartment where they lived. It consisted of two rooms: one for eating and sleeping, the other for making hats. Apparently back then Argentina covered everyone's needs. By avoiding all superfluous expenditures and doing without holidays for a good many years, my great-grandfather prospered, eventually becoming a textile importer. As well as being more profitable, this profession was less exhausting, as he only imported wholesale cloth. It was thanks to this second venture, I recall they recalled, that he was able to amass a fortune. Will you forgive me, *zeide* Jacobo, if I'm a little doubtful about such a stroke of luck?

My great-grandfather's frustrated vocation was civil engineering. He loved studying buildings being constructed, to watch them gradually being transformed and growing. I wonder if he saw in them a reflection of his own destiny, the patient accumulation of wealth, the source of which seems somewhat uncertain. Although his lack of studies meant he could never practice his dream profession, Jacobo managed to invest in different building projects, together with unknown partners who the family tended to blame if any venture ran into difficulties. He was always lavish with generous gifts, including several buildings he shared out among our family members, the inheritors of a legacy we are unaware of; that is, as citizens. *Zeide* also had a hand in designing the building where, years later, my grandfather Mario and grandmother Dorita were to live. He didn't have the title to any of these properties. According to him, he preferred to distribute his inheritance while he was still alive.

From the 1930s on, my grandfather Mario's childhood was far more comfortable than the hardships experienced by his parents. For some time the family lived in the residential area of Villa del Parque, in a house with a garden and a tennis court. The family moved around in an automobile, and some say they even had a *chauffeur*. Be that as it may, my great-grandfather earned the reputation of being the slowest driver in Buenos Aires: he rarely went at more than twenty kilometers per hour. Slowly does it, he would mutter at the wheel, always with a broad smile that exasperated his passengers. This manner of traveling slowly in a fast car perhaps illustrated the couple's contradictory relationship with material possessions: they wanted them, but were also embarrassed by them. By then, little Lía had been added to the family, and life became a mixture of calm and vigilance.

In my father's youth, Lidia and Jacobo lived on Calle Peña, near the corner of Las Heras and Pueyrredón. Back then my father went to Scholem Aleichem, a non-religious Jewish school my other paternal great-grandfather Jonás had helped to found. My father often used to visit them on his way home from school. The piano room with its sliding doors (walls that move!) fascinated him. The maids' quarters opened onto an inner courtyard, which meant that this part of the apartment seemed as dark and secretive as the class struggle. This was the domain of Magda, an aged Central European cook. Although it seems Magda was an excellent cook, in fact she hardly ever got the chance to demonstrate it: in a paradoxical display of authority, my great-grandmother Lidia seldom let her take her place. As if still afraid that crowds might trample on her to snatch something from her, Lidia stored her treasured belongings in small bags that went inside boxes that went inside more bags.

Apart from cooking instead of their cook, above all my great-grandmother loved to buy paintings and repair their home's electrical wiring. Whereas her husband was incapable of hammering in a nail straight, she seemed like a maintenance expert. A woman has to stand on her own two feet: she repeated this time and again to her daughter Lía, who in the end dedicated herself to medicine, as did her brother Mario. From early childhood she had been taught to drive (but not so fast, daughter, not so fast), to speak English and play the piano. My father took advantage of *baba* Lidia's love of music and often accompanied her to concerts at the Teatro Colón. Due to these night-time excursions, he became accustomed to arriving late and sleepy to the Colegio Nacional de Buenos Aires. This was when President Arturo Illia's government was allowing a certain amount of freedom, the streets were opening up, and the printed word had news. This was how, for a short while, my father experienced the sixties.

A few of Lidia's paintings came to be featured in catalogues and lent for national exhibitions. Even more surprising perhaps was the way she acquired them. Since neither her budget nor her thrifty spirit allowed her to purchase works by established painters, my great-grandmother was in the habit of visiting the youngest artists. Frowning, Lidia would enter the studio where, for example, the just-starting-out Carlos Alonso worked. Her blue-tinged gaze would flit over all the canvases. She paused at two or three. She seemed distracted, as if sniffing bread. Then she would say: This one. And they would agree on a price. This was how my great-grandmother Lidia carried off one of the few cats the maestro Alonso ever painted. The sharp-eyed feline painted in aggressive brushstrokes that watched over me as a child. Lidia also added a hen to her accidental bestiary, painted by Raúl Soldi, who years later was to decorate the cupola of the Teatro Colón, which I would so often stare at in utter boredom in my childhood.

Once Lidia visited the young Spilimbergo just after he had resigned from his job with Correos y Telégrafos. Since he needed to make some money as quickly as possible, he sold my great-grandmother a strange self-portrait in which a right hand is covering an outsized cheek. That painting, which all of us called "the toothache picture," ended up hanging on a wall in my own home. With Eugenio Daneri, who was strapped for cash, Lidia came to an unusual agreement: she promised him a monthly stipend in return for him coming every morning to paint for a while on her balcony. I imagine Daneri poking his bemused head through the sliding door and saying hello to Magda, without really understanding what she replied. I can see my great-grandmother taking the coffee tray from Magda's hands. I can see Daneri muttering sleepy thanks as he is gently imprisoned on that balcony floating like a watercolor, trying desperately to emerge from the mists of alcohol into the brightness of the morning.

Lidia's collection also included an oil painting by Raquel Forner that was part of a series on the Spanish Civil War. I have a vivid memory of that painting: snakes devouring the entrails of a decomposing corpse, while birds nest in the branches of the head. A possible allegory of the Spanish people's internecine conflict and the survival of freedom of thought. At exactly the same period that this painting evoked, the Fascist governor of Buenos Aires province, Manuel Fresco, was launching diatribes against the communist threat and creating a militarized police force similar to Mussolini's. When my father first began to take an interest in the painting, President Illia was glancing nervously over his shoulder at General Onganía, commander-in-chief of the army and imminent coup leader. Some stories change observers, but not themes.

Lidia and Jacobo had a summer house in Morón, where my father opened a large cut in his forehead trying to climb over the gate. A cut that remained as a scar which, almost thirty years later, was reproduced on my own forehead. Later they bought a new summer house in the seaside resort of Miramar, with its rhythm of beach, friends, and bicycles. It was there that my father was able to reconnect with his own father: occasionally tender, usually evasive, in Miramar my grandfather Mario relaxed and realized with astonishment how much his children had grown.

During one of those summers, Mario asked my father to keep an eye on Jacobo. *Zeide* wasn't well, and he had been forbidden to smoke more than three cigarettes a day. My father's job was to ration the stocks of tobacco, which he studiously hid and checked every morning. My great-grandfather Jacobo was only permitted a cigarette after meals or if he got carried away in some argument or other. On those occasions, my father got up solemnly, went to his secret stash, and came back proud at having accomplished his mission. It took him a good while to discover that *zeide,* in addition to the three cigarettes he accepted with a contrite expression, smoked a whole pack whenever they went for a walk: "Wait here for me, dear, I'll be right back, wouldn't you like me to bring you some candy? You're sure? Ask me for whatever you like, *inguele,* we're on vacation!"

Always with his hair oiled and a stubborn smile, Jacobo was the grandfather every child deserves. Even more than his business ventures, it could be said his true vocation was having grandchildren. His greatest pleasure came from watching them eat, from sharing their appetite. He encouraged them to order humungous desserts, and watched entranced as they devoured them. Going out for a walk with Great-grandfather Jacobo was like accompanying a white-haired child. He wanted everything, and wanted to give everything away. He had a sweet-tooth at one remove, feeding on other people's full stomachs.

Despite my great-grandmother Lidia's extreme thinness—which in her seemed almost like a matter of principle—as time went by the skin began to hang down from her arms. Without for a moment abandoning her sternly pursed lips, and after her *tsch! tsch!* protest, she would eventually agree to my father's entreaties. She would roll her sleeves up and allow him, in an act of refined cannibalism, to tug at her flaps. Even when he was married, my father continued to ask her to roll her sleeves up, and she continued to resist, knowing full well that in the end she would give in. During these visits, Lidia would talk to my mother about violins. She asked what she cleaned the bow with, where she kept it, how she changed a string. There was only one thing (apart from refusing a plate of food) that was strictly forbidden in my *baba's* home: to speak ill of Argentina. My Lithuanian great-grandmother had become a fanatical patriot. If my father complained about the country or, continuing his own parents' tradition, he bemoaned the imminent return of Perón, Lidia would frown, rekindle an ancient blue fire behind her glasses and respond: *Tsch! tsch!* Don't do Argentina down, do you hear me, this is a generous country, so be very careful, eh, don't do Argentina down.

*Zeide* Jacobo was both disturbed and bored by politics. In contrast, Jonás, my other Jewish grandfather, was a political activist. Although the two of them got on well together, they didn't have much in common apart from a foreign memory. Lacking any great topics of conversation, they compensated by exchanging gentle jokes. Jacobo would exclaim: *Vus tiste!* Jonás, you're very skinny, you should read less and eat more! To which Jonás would reply: Jacobo, *fraint*, look how old you are, at least I'm from this century! True enough, my great-grandfather Jacobo, the presumed deserter from the Russian army, was born in 1898. The same year that Tolstoy donated the profits from his book *Resurrection* to the *dujobory* sect, who were being persecuted for refusing to do military service.

My great-grandfather's life went into decline parallel to that of Perón, at a time when the Minister López Rega was alternating between astrological prophecies and organizing state crimes. On the day that Perón gave his last speech and repudiated the Montoneros, my great-grandfather was rushed to the hospital, where his son Mario supervised his final hours. A cancer victim, it was always said that the diagnosis was hidden from my great-grandfather until the very end. Considering how anxious he was about small pleasures, I suspect he knew about it from the start.

# 4

WITHOUT KNOWING, OR perhaps suspecting it, my maternal grandmother Blanca also bequeathed me her legacy. A light, burdensome legacy: the letter of her life. I once suggested she write down her memories so that they wouldn't be lost. I soon forgot my suggestion, but she didn't, and one fine day she sent me some handwritten sheets of paper: the ones I'm now holding uncertainly. The handwriting is both solemn and like a schoolgirl's: a calligraphy that no longer exists, the trace of another era. The sentences are full of whispered truths. That letter has changed my life, or at least, my obligations. Now I have to thank my grandmother by completing it.

"I'm going to try to please my beloved grandchildren by telling them my little story." That's how, like an oral narrator, Blanca begins her tale; she knows she has at least a couple of readers. The handwriting slips but she corrects herself at once, like an elderly dancer determined to stay straight despite her aching back. "I'm going to try to please my beloved grandchildren by telling them my little story. I knew both my grandmothers: one was Latin American, the other French." That is how her family novel begins, and is now traveling within mine.

Characters imagining what they remember, remembering what they imagine. Is the result true? A lie? Those aren't the right questions.

# 5

MY AUNT SILVIA and her German husband Peter ran a small bookstore on Calle Azcuénaga, near the corner with Avenida Santa Fe. Customers would come in, drink a coffee, chat to my aunt and uncle about books. Quite recently, in the back of the shop, they had burned some of the works prohibited by the Ministry of Education and Culture: anything from Freud to Fromm, Paulo Freire to Saint-Exupéry, and including Rodolfo Walsh, Griselda Gambaro, and Manuel Puig. Safer to burn than throw away, because janitors had sharp eyes and garbage could always be traced back to its owner. Improbably, my aunt and uncle's bookshop was called *Jaque al libro*, or "The Book in Check." As a metaphor that would have been a gaffe; as a real name it ended up an irony.

Following the 1976 military coup, General Videla declared that terrorists were not merely people who planted bombs, but also those spreading ideas that undermined Western Christian civilization. Hence the need to burn books, and then douse them with water to mingle the ashes: letters are hard to erase. It was rumored that, on some nights, a group of men would pile out of a Ford Falcon to ransack bookshops. And they weren't content with confiscating Marxist titles. They could also remove books on Cubism, for supposedly advocating Castro's regime, or classics like *The Red and the Black*, for containing possible anarchist messages. They could also seize the bookshop owners. Many people had heard these stories. But no one knew for sure, and, after all, why would such a thing happen to us, when we've done nothing. From one day to the next, some of their regular customers stopped coming.

Aunt Silvia, who alternated her shifts at the bookshop with occasional work as an architect, had just become pregnant. My mother, who with my father at our Calle Fitz Roy apartment had also destroyed books and pamphlets, had recently given birth to me. Exactly nine months before I was born, in the city of Córdoba, the Third Army Corps had organized a collective book burning of volumes snatched from bookshops: Proust, García Márquez, Neruda and other troublemakers were burned in their glory. In the midst of a military coup, my uncle and aunt and my parents decided to conceive children. I'm not sure whether this is a paradox. New lives were on the way and everything would get better. They believed that. They had to believe it. Until a Ford Falcon pulled up outside my aunt and uncle's house.

The following day, nobody was answering the telephone. *Jaque al libro* remained closed. When she arrived to their apartment, Aunt Ponnie found it in chaos. She saw drawers strewn around, shelves tipped over, and chairs on their backs. My grandparents Dorita and Mario were away in Bariloche. To persuade them to cut short their trip, my father told them Silvia had a problem with her pregnancy. As a father Mario pretended to believe him, but the doctor in him was unconvinced by his explanations. The couple returned from the south on the first available flight. When they reached Buenos Aires, there was still no news of her daughter or her husband.

Grandma Dorita broke down. For several hours grandpa Mario remained motionless on the sofa. My father made call after call. My mother was going to a rehearsal, she washed my diapers and chain-smoked. I still wasn't crying as I should have done.

They visited hospitals and police stations. The early morning flew by. They didn't want to believe what was happening. As the day progressed, everything seemed to be carrying on as normal. From the Teatro Colón came the sounds of the orchestra rehearsals and the muffled steps of the dancers. In Mario's hospital the sick went in and the healthy came out. In many barracks the opposite was taking place.

The next day, my grandfather Mario and my father went to see the German consul to ask him to intervene on my uncle's behalf. Schulze, Peter Schulze, they repeated like a mantra. Like everyone else, the consul promised to see what he could do. My mother went to rehearsal, still chain-smoking. My aunt and uncle had given our address as their legal residence, because they didn't yet have one of their own. But our apartment wasn't going to be raided: or was it? For no apparent reason I had a bout of diarrhea. When my mother called my grandparents Jacinto and Blanca to tell them what was going on, they sounded suspicious. Were they mixed up in something? they asked. They were not the only ones.

My father and his sister Ponnie searched through possible contacts. In one of my aunt and uncle's diaries they found the telephone number of a former Congresswoman who lived in a building close to the bookshop on Calle Arenales. This lady had three things to recommend her. She was the niece of an army colonel, a brother-in-arms of General Videla. She was probably a member, forgive the oxymoron, of the dictatorship's intelligence services. And she was a client of the bookstore. She loved buying illustrated books for her daughters, who often read them sitting on the bookstore carpet. My father and Aunt Ponnie had only seen her in person a couple of times, but what was there to lose? They agreed to call her and arranged a meeting.

Wearing so much make-up she looked someone else, the former Congresswoman received them with exquisite politeness. But they spend the entire day in their bookstore!, she said in astonishment, what can those two have done? My father and Aunt Ponnie nodded their agreement. Could they have been mixed up in something strange?, the former Congresswoman suddenly inquired. They both shook their heads. She asked questions, wanted to know certain details. She calculated out loud. Mmm. It was true my Aunt Silvia was Jewish; there was more than one socialist in the family, not to mention other things. On the other hand, she was married to a German, and that might help. After coffee and cake, without even bothering to leave the room, the solicitous former Congresswoman dialed a number from memory and asked to speak to the colonel. While waiting to be put through, she smiled reassuringly at her guests. Then she simply said:

"Uncle, it's me. Do you think you could check whether you have a certain Silvia Neuman and a Peter Schulze? With one 'n.' And no, with a 'z.' Thanks, you're a sweetheart."

Covering the mouthpiece with one hand, their hostess gave her guests one final warning look:

"You're sure they're not mixed up in anything, right?"

My father and Aunt Ponnie said goodbye politely, a taste of nausea in their mouths. The coffee was delightful. They promised to send flowers to thank her. Roses, of course, roses.

One or two nights later, Aunt Silvia and Uncle Peter turned up blindfolded in the Palermo woods.

They had been taken there in a van together with eight or nine other people. Ordered to count to five hundred before removing the blindfolds. Ten scantily clad strangers lay face down among the trees, counting under their breaths and trembling for every imaginable reason. They weren't sure they wouldn't be shot at some point during this interminable countdown. The waiting over, they slowly removed their blindfolds. They tried to refocus their eyes. Exchanged glances. And, without a word to one another, they fled in different directions.

Judging from the route the vehicles had taken on both the outward and return journeys, Silvia and Peter guessed they'd been held captive in the Regimiento de Patricios, one of the secret detention centers in the area. So my aunt and uncle had disappeared only three minutes from our own home.

While a student at the School of Architecture, Aunt Silvia had belonged briefly to the PCR (*Partido Comunista Revolucionario*), but apparently her kidnappers were more interested in something else. During her incarceration, she was repeatedly questioned about names of people with links to the Montoneros, about whom she knew nothing at all. Possibly her own name had appeared in the address book of someone who knew them.

As a person whose mind was shaped by architecture, my aunt had spent most of the time with the constant need, as well as the distressing impossibility, of establishing her bearings in a succession of cubicles that smelled of damp concrete. This had been an intangible torture, and perhaps the only one that wasn't meticulously planned. Blindfolded, feet chained together, she had been fed lumps of overcooked rice. Occasionally she could hear, or thought she heard, Peter's voice calling to her.

During the torture sessions, Silvia had discovered things about her body she would rather not have known. One of the most unexpected had been her capacity to hurt herself: the shocks from the cattle prods hadn't always been more painful than the blows to her own head and back against the surface she had been tied to. There was a moment when this seemed to her like a revelation, although she wasn't sure why.

Between her bouts of fitful sleep on the floor, one of her routines had been to continually monitor, from the tiny gap under her blindfold, the state of her underwear to check for any seepage. On one occasion, she thought she saw something, and demanded medical assistance. Without removing the chains from her feet, they guided her step by step toward a kindly voice. The voice asked her a few questions, palpated her belly, and gave her some pills. Feeling them in her palm, my aunt grew suspicious. Are you a real doctor? she said to him. Then the man clasped her free hand and pulled it downward. Silvia tried to resist, but he was stronger.

At the end of the trajectory, her fingers discovered another pair of ankles with chains just like hers. For sure, kid, the voice had sighed, I am a doctor.

While they were torturing my aunt, my uncle had been forced to watch. Time and again they had asked him how the hell a German could have a child with a Jewess. I doubt any of them knew that Coburg, in Bavaria, where my Uncle Peter came from, was the first town in Germany to have a Nazi mayor.

Before releasing them, their kidnappers advised them to go somewhere far away, not to get in touch with certain people, and many other things my aunt and uncle didn't want to talk about. Silvia and Peter never returned home. They stayed with friends. Trying to avoid too many people coming at once, they received unobtrusive visits. My grandpa Mario gave them first aid treatment. He examined Silvia and confirmed that his future grandchild was still determined to be born. He sent her to a colleague who was a gynecologist for a more thorough check-up.

The gynecologist couldn't discover any obvious problems, although he admitted he had no idea of the effect torture might have on the gestation process. This wasn't exactly what he was used to assessing. As a precaution, he gave her the option of aborting. My aunt slowly felt her own belly, attempting to read it like a braille text: what kind of messages might have got through? how much could the baby have heard? how deep could the electric shocks have penetrated?

Guided by her intuition, by a heartbeat that was now double, Aunt Silvia chose to run the risk: their chains couldn't reach that far, they weren't going to take this from her as well.

As quickly as possible, they organized passports and plane tickets. As she prepared her scant luggage, Silvia left her favorite necklace, a silver pendant, to be given to the former Congresswoman. Could this obscure act of gratitude toward her savior, her torturers' accomplice, have been a second humiliation for her, or perhaps a strange sort of liberation?

A vehicle from the German consulate took my aunt and uncle to Ezeiza airport; another seventy-two disappeared German citizens were not so fortunate. As a precaution, no one went to see Silvia and Peter off. In theory, they had return tickets. They decided to travel to the Latin American capitals where they had relatives or people they knew, to see what they could find. My aunt's belly was a calendar.

They went first to Lima, where Silvia almost got a job as an architect, and where the constant drizzle made them even more nervous. A few weeks later they arrived in Quito, where cousin Hugo lived and where they almost decided to stay. Then they moved on to Bogotá, but the good friends they had there were about to leave. After that they were for a few days in San José in Costa Rica, where Peter knew a pianist who played in a hotel in Plaza de la Democracia. They were waiting for something to happen, for some signal to make them come to a halt. They hesitated over crossing the Atlantic, suspecting people rarely returned.

Meanwhile, the pregnancy continued its course. If it was a boy, they would call him Pablo. If it was a girl, Malena. In the end, they decided to change their return tickets: maybe they had to go still further away.

There was little news of them in Buenos Aires. They didn't communicate much, just in case. Grandma Dorita, dad, and some friends sold the contents of *Jaque al Libro*. The clients reappeared for a short while. A few of them were surprised. Others could imagine what had happened.

One fine day at the end of May 1977, the family received postcards from Madrid: Silvia and Peter had just reached Spain. It was only a couple of weeks before the first elections after Franco's death. There, in the former land of my great-grandparents Juan Jacinto and Isabel, a new Constitution was being drawn up. At the same time, the Argentine Constitution was no longer read. That was why my cousin Pablo went to Madrid to be born. And why, in his own way, he is Argentine as well.

# 6

*BISHOP OF BOURGES: I demand you recant this instant. Kneel and beg for forgiveness.*

*SCULPTOR RENÉ: Considering that I don't kneel before God, Father, I'm certainly not going to kneel before a man such as yourself.*

This is how Blanca sums up the exile of my great-great-grandfather René, who left France and emigrated to Caucete in the mountains of Argentina's San Juan province. I suspect this splendid riposte is more of a legendary quote than a true anecdote. Indeed, I believe I've read about this alleged dispute between the bishop and my great-grandfather in three or four other books from very diverse sources.

The only certainty is that René had sculptures commissioned by the authorities, wasn't the clergy's favorite artist, and he and his family left Bourges in a great hurry.

The young couple knew their life would start again from zero, but never imagined to what extent this was so. Some religiously fanatic neighbor in Bourges must even have thought it was a case of divine retribution. During a stormy Atlantic crossing, two of their three children fell mortally ill. The only survivor was little Juliette, my grandmother Blanca's mother. When they finally reached the cordillera of the Andes and had just settled in Caucete, an earthquake swept away their scant possessions. Trying to save something from the catastrophe, my great-great-grandfather René suffered a bad hernia, which from that moment on prevented him from carrying out his profession normally. Dispossessed and desperate, they decided to move to Buenos Aires. That was the birthplace of their other three children, children of the new land.

René's wife's was Louise Blanche, and she was, to describe her in a few words, a very meticulous woman. Despite spending more than half her life in Argentina, never a day went by when she didn't miss her native land; or at least the imaginary paradise she created, without ever going back, under a name that was increasingly remote: *Burshe*. Pronounced with a French accent. My great-great-grandmother Louise Blanche used to call children "*m'hijit*"—combining acquired Argentine colloquialism with her outsider's roots. She stubbornly referred to *azúcar* as *asucre*, and ended up speaking perfect foreign Spanish. Her delicate skin irritated by the seams of garments, she decided to wear, right up until the day she died, all her clothes inside out.

Another habit that made the neighbors' tongues wag was her absolute refusal to touch money: like a down-at-heel heiress from the French court, she would wrap the banknotes in transparent paper and hand them to the grocer, dressed inside out, every bit a *grande dame*. According to her, what she missed most from her native gardens was the fragrance of the flowers, in particular the scent of violets, impossible to compare with the southern hemisphere's vulgar blooms.

Only in digestive matters did Louise Blanche show any disregard for delicacy. Put concisely, she dumped with true eloquence. In the eyes of someone as sensitive to volume as the sculptor René, her bowel movements were mammoth, and each time she went to the bathroom he exclaimed: *Ah, chérie! Ne me parle pas de violettes!* Faced with such a predicament, my French great-great-grandmother would give a mischievous grin and walk away humming a milonga.

Although Louise Blanche would never feel Argentine, I can't help but add that her habits fitted in perfectly with the national idiosyncrasy: a kind of tragic snobbery coupled with a tendency to the scatological.

# 7

TIME SHIFTED, STIFF on its hinges. Aged eighteen months, I could vaguely walk without falling over too often and proudly pronounce the word twafficlights.

Our country was hosting the World Cup, so naturally we had to win. "We Argentines," the military junta was to declare soon afterward, "are right and human." Maybe that explains why the young Maradona, left-footed and an extraterrestrial, was sidelined.

We had to win and we won. We did everything we could and more: the Peruvian side is testimony to that. Our goals shone in the glow of the brand-new Argentina Televisora Color. After the heroic final against the Dutch, our players ran across the turf in the Monumental Stadium amid a shower of confetti. General Videla presented the captain the trophy, congratulated the team one by one, and praised their remarkable commitment to the fatherland, while the stands echoed with applause.

My father refused to join in the celebrations.

"That's because you don't give a damn about soccer," a neighbor wearing the national team's colors reproached him.

On victory night we stayed indoors. A clamor of whistles, claxons and chants rose from the street. My father looked serious. My mother refrained from playing her violin. As for me, I only wanted to eat.

Around the Obelisk, euphoria swirled like placenta. Downtown became gridlocked: so much for *twafficlights*.

# 8

THE POLICE USED to go into cafés. Ask to see documents, question people. Customers would observe the precise gestures of these men who seemed to know what they were doing. The important thing was to have done nothing, to be doing nothing, intend to do nothing. You had to focus on that, you only had to show a sincere commitment to nothing, contemplate the hot cup, stir with self-evident calm the thick black liquid, wait for the sugar to dissolve properly, and continue to talk in a normal tone of voice, preferably hushed. Normal. And yet a lot of the customers seemed contented.

One of the officers approached my mother's table. He raised two fingers to his right temple in a swift salute, and declared perfectly politely:

"I don't know what you've got in there, señorita."

Maybe in other cafeterias in other countries, this wouldn't have sounded exactly like an order, but my mother understood. She hurriedly placed the case on her knees.

"Let's see, señorita, give it to me."

My mother knew the ritual. In a confident yet cautious tone, she asked the officer to be careful with the case. Don't touch it, please don't; in her request there was a desire to protect her instrument but also a physical revulsion: how could she bear to have this man's hands pawing the violin of her life?

The officer appeared to grow impatient, but then my mother sighed, shook her flowing jet-black locks, and began to talk, look, officer, opening the case very slowly and explaining to him the nature of her profession, where she worked, why she couldn't possibly be separated from her case, look, officer, and she described the fragility of that piece of craftsmanship, a German violin from the eighteenth century, just think, officer, and the man didn't know whether to hurry things along or sit down for a moment to listen to this young woman's speech, and my mother showed him, one by one, the replacement strings, these are a little thicker for the lower notes, and these are finer, no, no, nothing but strings, officer, look?, and in this little bag I keep a rubber and a pencil, that kind of thing, you see?, to make notes on the score, you want me to open it?, of course, of course, whatever you say, and this is a tuning fork, that's right, a tuning fork, to tune to A, to a what?, no, officer, let me explain, it's a very simple little device that always gives an A, an A natural, so we're all in tune, you know?, of course, precisely, no, please, there's nothing *inside* the violin!, officer, I beg you, it's impossible, you see, from the eighteenth century, quite right, thank you, officer, and these are the pegs, oh no, don't press them!, they just turn, look, look, like this . . .

And that's how the evening progressed. It was early September and the good weather was coming, people picked up their conversations again, preferably hushed, normal, as they did at my mother's table. The patrol car drove off, and the coffee had gone cold.

Neither in the street nor in workplaces were gatherings of more than three people allowed, at least not if they looked suspicious. The fact is, it became very difficult not to seem at least a little suspicious. As work delegates were basically prohibited, my mother was chosen as the musical representative, or some equivalent circumlocution, by her orchestra colleagues.

To be precise, work delegates were not prohibited. They simply had to refrain from holding meetings. They had a perfect right to express themselves, of course; but on their own. Clandestine meetings were dangerous, not so much because of any possible reprisals as due to infiltrators or snitches. You had to be very careful who you talked to, what you said, who was listening.

For example, the telephone in our apartment on Avenida Independencia had company. Or more exactly, two companies: one was the Empresa Nacional de Teléfonos; the other was more discreet, although one day it revealed itself. My mother was talking to a union colleague about the next meeting, when suddenly the third voice in the conversation decided to intervene. It has to be said he made his position plain in only a few words.

"If you go to that meeting we'll tear you to pieces, you filthy whore."

The meeting was due to take place the next day. There was one urgent item on the agenda: the musicians with temporary contracts had claimed the right to paid vacations, but Commodore Del Gancho, the new military administrator of the Teatro Colón, had announced his intention not to renew their contracts because of their inappropriate protests. Commodore Del Gancho didn't know much about Beethoven, but was more than interested in dance: several ballerinas had already experienced his ardent thrusts. Apart from that, discipline reigned in the theatre, step by step, note by note. No comments went beyond a whisper, while on the walls, against a black background, celebrated banners had been put up which read: "Silence. The walls have ears."

My mother couldn't make up her mind whether to go to the meeting or not. On the one hand, as a representative, it was her duty to attend. When she had decided to continue in the union, she knew perfectly well (or did she?) what she was risking. If in her twenties she didn't stand up for her convictions, when on earth was she going to do so? But on the other hand there was that third voice on the telephone. Her son. Her husband. And her husband's sister, by chance alive and in Madrid. And there was the *Jaque al Libro* bookstore. And there were those who weren't there.

That night at home until the early hours she and my father discussed whether or not she should go to the meeting. This was the pre-meeting meeting. My mother drank black coffee; my father black tea. I slept on my side at the edge of the cradle, like a fat coin about to topple over.

When she left the next morning, my mother looked round to see if she was being followed; she didn't think she was. Instead of waiting for Bus No. 29 in Calle Defensa, she took any other one to the center of the city, and then an unnecessary one to Tribunales. She glanced out of the corner of her eye to see if the other passengers were staring at her. They were. They weren't. When she had almost reached the union building on Calle Paraguay, sarcastically close to Calle Libertad, she walked around the block just in case. Stopped at a newspaper stand. Then pretended to be looking at clothes.

The union headquarters had been donated by Evita Perón. Whenever my mother thought of Evita, it was not the real person, but the Olympian effigy, her hair coiled in a bun and one arm outstretched, as she appeared in the school textbooks where her sister Diana had learned to read. *I saw Eva. Evita came to me. Evita loves me. That lady is Eva.* For no apparent reason, she thought of Grandma Blanca's piano and the tortoises a neighbor had. Making as if to light a cigarette, she shot a quick glance both ways and crossed the threshold.

The meeting dragged on. Almost everyone present spoke, but none of them seemed to finish what they wanted to say, or perhaps only said what they didn't want to say. In passing, the name of a colleague who hadn't been seen for a while was mentioned. Nervous looks sped around the table. There was a change of topic. Somebody made a joke. Tense laughter. They returned to the question of the inalienable right to paid vacations, even though the possible dismissals were also mentioned. Hours later it was agreed, among other things, that my mother should ask to see Commodore Del Gancho to convey to him, as far as was possible, what claims they had agreed on.

Leaving the meeting, my mother discovered she had run out of cigarettes. She hesitated about going to buy some. In the end she went, and nothing happened.

But in those years, it was also terrible when nothing happened. It was like an empty space pointing somewhere darker.

The next morning, my parents said goodbye with a lengthy kiss. My father had several flute pupils and was going to stay home to look after me. She was going to the Teatro Colón, still smoking.

"And I'm telling you, señorita," Commodore Del Gancho retorted, "that if they don't like the conditions, they can stop playing, and that's all there is to it."

"Those musicians, Commodore, have the same right as we do to go on vacation or to be sick occasionally. There's nothing strange about that."

"Negative. What's strange here," said Del Gancho, his gaze resting on my mother's skirt, "is that you are so concerned about the matter. You have a permanent contract. Why don't you worry about your own situation?"

"But there are colleagues who aren't so fortunate, and they are facing a lot of uncertainty."

"Not applicable. Are you speaking on behalf of others, señorita?"

"Not at all, Commodore sir, not at all. I'm simply putting myself in their place."

"Yes, yes. I see you have a frankly remarkable capacity for empathy."

"I was on a temporary contract once, I know how it is."

"So you're acting on your own behalf. Out of solidarity, as it were?"

"I don't know, Commodore sir, to me it seems like an obligation."

"You don't say. Your obligations touch me, señorita. They touch me."

My mother didn't think it over. She merely clenched her small, restless fist. What she said was almost involuntary:

"This isn't a barracks, Commodore, it's a theater!"

My mother was no longer speaking on behalf of her colleagues. Or for the vacations, the contracts, or the country. It was only for her clenched, small fist. The commodore looked at her.

As soon as she left the theater, my mother wept out of fear. She went over what she had said with a mixture of pride and remorse, and it no longer seemed so important to rebel as it had done half an hour earlier. How did you get on? My father asked when he heard the front door, dropping my dirty diapers.

At the end of that season, none of the temporary musicians were dismissed, and everyone received a month of paid vacation. It may well be that the commodore took that decision like someone conceding a gracious pardon or inflicting an inverted humiliation. As if to demonstrate that he simply had the power to do or not to do something, to give and to take. When they next found themselves sharing an elevator, Commodore Del Gancho peered at my mother's neckline with a sardonic smile.

# 9

SOMETIME AROUND 1980, my father moved into a bachelor apartment on Calle Marcelo T. de Alvear. Our place in San Telmo became much bigger, and I occasionally discovered my mother crying in secret. I was losing weight; so was the country. The things we loved were suddenly disappearing. Thankfully, on weekends my father reappeared to take me out for enormous ice creams so he could also taste them, just like *zeide* Jacobo, or to go to a park to play soccer, a sport he detested. We stood facing one another a few yards apart, and passed the ball between us. I concentrated very hard when I kicked: no way was my shot going to miss. My father seemed distracted.

One winter's afternoon, he took me to see his new home. It was awful. It was nice. I was surprised to find the kitchen was hidden inside a cupboard and opened out whenever you wanted. My father said he had a present for me. How funny, because I'd brought him a present too. Naturally, we started with his: an Argentina soccer shirt. He had also bought a number to stitch on the back.

Unable to find a 10, my father had decided to give me a 9 instead. The number was a bit crooked, as if someone had cut it out with scissors, and the fabric was red instead of black. I felt a twinge of disappointment, and at the same time, it amused me to imagine my father sewing my soccer shirt.

My present consisted of a watercolor. It's a picture for your house, I announced, solemn as a Kandinsky. He gave me a kiss and asked me where I thought we should put it. I made a slow tour of the short corridor passage and cramped dining room. I examined every wall, even the ceiling. Finally, I peered inside the bathroom.

"Here, are you sure?" my father said with surprise.

I nodded and pointed to a tile above the toilet.

"Now you have two homes," my father said, patting my head, "isn't that great?"

After my snack, I asked what game we were going to play. Anything you like, he replied, but first it's time for your bath. So I said I wanted to play tea, something we often did that year. I climbed into the bathtub and my father fetched some plastic cups he kept in his secret kitchen. He entered the bathroom looking very self-important, sat down on the toilet, and pretended we were at a bar. Hiding under the water, I waited a while before suddenly rising to my feet. Naked but formal, I asked my customer what he would care to drink. He hesitated for a few seconds before ordering tea. Sometimes it was English tea, at others green tea or an herbal infusion. With pleasure, I said, and told him I'd be right back. Then I carefully filled the plastic cups with the dirty bathwater, and held one out to him. My father thanked me. He pretended to sip the liquid. Insisted with lavish praise how delicious it was. And, when I wasn't looking, he emptied the cup and we began all over again.

After dinner, I begged my father to let me sleep next to him. For once, he agreed.

That night, the moment I lay down beside my father, the very first thing I did was wet myself in his new bed.

# 10

HER NAME WAS Franca. She had just turned sweet sixteen, and she played the recorder.

One day she didn't show up for her class or call to say she couldn't come. That's odd, thought my father. The following week there was still no sign of her. That's odd, said my father, maybe she got bored of the class, kids that age are so unreliable, aren't they? Her parents said she'd gone out with some friends and hadn't come home. Franca hadn't come home, but she had to be somewhere: people don't cease to exist from one day to the next without leaving any trace. Do they? Almost unawares, my parents started to mention her in hushed tones. Shhh. The walls had ears.

Her name was Franca and she was sweet sixteen.

# 11

IN THE MALVINAS the wind blew, the ocean roared, and so on and so forth. Patriotic planes flew across the sky on the TV screen. General Galtieri praised the Argentine people for their courage and exemplary sacrifice. I was thrilled and stuck little flags in the flower pots on our balcony. Who's winning, mom? I would ask. We don't know, sweetie, we don't know yet, she sighed. Frankly, how could we defeat the English with so little enthusiasm?

One morning, bright and early, I entered my mother's bedroom. As was my custom, I did so without knocking, ready to demand my breakfast. I found my mother awake; but not alone. Sitting up in bed was a man in a dressing gown. The mustard-colored dressing gown wasn't new. The bearded man was my father.

He beckoned me over. Taking me by the shoulders, he spoke to me at length. About us, our home, the cessation of hostilities. That year, 1982, a year of wars and truces, stumbled on confusedly. My parents were less in love, but loved each other more.

# 12

THE PLAZA DE MAYO was colored orange with joy. We jumped in the air, we sang: we were a drum. In the distance, the victorious President Alfonsín raised his clasped hands on the balcony of the Cabildo of Buenos Aires. Pregnant with my brother Diego, my mother clapped above her growing belly.

That day my new shoes pinched. They hurt so much I found it hard to remain standing. I asked my father to carry me on his shoulders. "Huphuphup!" he said, and raised me to the sky. From there I had a better view of everything. People's heads clustered together looked less alike than I had imagined. There were big banners with two capital letters. *RA*: República Argentina and Raúl Alfonsín. Perhaps it wouldn't be a lie to add that a golden sun shone.

Soon lots of other people's shoes would pinch.

# 13

THE MARIANO ACOSTA elementary school boasted it had been founded by Domingo Faustino Sarmiento, whom my textbooks affronted by calling him immortal. Before becoming Cortázar, a certain Julio had done his teacher training there. I encountered a few admirable teachers at the school. I'll avoid the worst ones, because they aren't worth mentioning.

The school was a mixture of progressive ideas and violence, French language, and stifling masculinity. Its authorities appeared open-minded, yet girls weren't allowed in their classrooms. The rules seemed fairly lax, yet after recess we would form a line in strict order of height, right arms outstretched to maintain distance. Ours was a state school without crosses or religious rituals, yet every morning we performed the liturgy of hoisting the national flag and singing the anthem that exclaimed: "High above us a warrior eagle . . . This is the flag of my fatherland, born of the sun, God-given!" All in all, this was a school for middle class Argentine kids.

Mr. Nievas would arrive in the classroom miming silent movies: he told us learning should make us laugh. Mr. Albanese would arrive making some mocking, faintly bawdy remark: he encouraged us to write stories, detested syntactic theory, helped us start a library, and succeeded in getting us to fight over borrowing books. Mr. Renis arrived bellowing like Captain Haddock: he organized math and spelling bees, about which we became as fanatical as we were about soccer. He would play the card game *truco* with us during recess, and he once hung Fatty Cesarini from a peg in the classroom for misbehaving. When we became too rowdy, he would demand silence by hurling pieces of chalk at us with a precision we all envied: his projectiles never really hit us, but would bounce off the miscreant's desk before disappearing at the rear of the classroom. It was him, Mr. Renis, who taught us that words can say things they don't seem to be saying, and that swear words are words too. When you're nine and wearing a white school coat, such small truths can seem revolutionary.

It was also Mr. Renis who first told me about Jules Verne. Once a week, if we finished our lessons without wasting time, he would reward us with a chapter of *Around the World in Eighty Days*. I can still recall the sacred music of that novel read by him. Renis's slightly hoarse voice would swell enthusiastically between dramatic pauses. Anyone doubting the hypnotic power of stories would only have needed to attend one of those sessions, to see us clutching our expectant, astonished heads in our hands, to see thirty-five ruffians begging Mr. Renis not to stop, to carry on reading from the book. Then the bell rang.

# 14

IT WAS JUNE 20, 1973, Flag Day. My mother had just gotten married and joined the Buenos Aires Philharmonic Orchestra. At the age of twenty, she had a husband and a violin. She was on a bus heading for Ezeiza airport.

Both the Philharmonic and Symphonic orchestras had been invited to take part in General Perón's homecoming; he was returning to the country after a lengthy exile and two decades of political prohibition. His plane was due to land in a little more than an hour. An official car was to pick him up from the runway and drive him two miles through open countryside, escorted by the army and mounted police, to the enormous reception platform. This was surmounted by an image of the general, with Evita on his left and his present wife, Isabel, on his right. Above the stage, scaffolding had been erected with spotlights and loudspeakers, and some huge Argentine flags separated the three images. From there, Perón and Isabel were to greet the assembled crowd, the general would make his speech, and the ceremony would end with a rendering of the national anthem.

My mother knew that the oboist Pedro di Grimaldi, who was about to retire from the symphony orchestra, had used the excuse of one of his respiratory attacks to avoid going. There was a note of tension in the air, like the closeness of a wind instrument which, silenced for too many bars, was on the point of exploding. The previous day, there had been talk of things getting out of hand, possible provocations, the risk of clashes. Over a million people had marched down Avenida General Paz, vying for a place amid the trees and tarmac. Half the country's political associations had gathered in and around Ezeiza. They included the Peronist Youth Movement, the Montoneros, militants from the ERP (the People's Revolutionary Army) and other small groups, as well as entire families, the children of followers of Perón who were going to see their parents' banished hero for the very first time. All of them were eager to welcome their leader, but each of them imagined a different leader.

Getting the musicians' bus there had been no mean feat. Almost as difficult as finding a parking space amid all the trucks, cars, and horses, and then making their way slowly forward, pushing through the mass of bodies and the police cordon, ensuring no harm came to their instruments, and climbing up one by one onto the narrow stage. It hadn't been easy to combine the two orchestras either; they hadn't even rehearsed together. Squashed together like musical mercury, hundreds of arms pulled out their scores. My mother tried to block out the noise to be able to tune up. She could smell, what could she smell? Some chord made up of macerated grass, warm wood, bow rosin, damp air, collective sweat, distant meat being roasted all day at the nearby camp sites. Some of the musicians had removed their tuxedos, hooking them onto the corners of the music stands.

The conductor raised his baton for them to start warming up as best they could. The Ezeiza countryside was throbbing like a whip cracking below a mosaic of Argentine flags, colorful clothes, and banners. From the stage, my mother managed to read among the waving slogans: "All present and correct, my General." "Evita lives." "Power to Perón." Someone tapped her shoulder and borrowed the pencil from her music stand. "Ever Loyal." "Perón or death." My mother attempted an arpeggio she could barely hear. "Your people of yesterday are your soldiers of today." Someone tapped her shoulder and returned the pencil. One group was singing: "Here we are, we are all, Perón's boys!" The flags flapped as though blown in a gale. My mother felt the need to urinate. The drums beat the light, the cymbals flattened it.

All at once, there was a sinister modulation in the sound from the crowds. Bewilderment created a vacuum, a kind of unison that faded into silence. This unexpected interlude was suddenly shattered by the chaotic rhythm of bullets and screams. Instinctively, the musicians hurled themselves to the floor and covered their heads. Face pressed against the boards, strands of hair in her mouth, my mother heard explosions, shrieks, crashes, whinnies. She felt the stage judder, and beneath it a stampede. A few bodies farther on my mother could see Ridolfi, the double bass soloist, shielding himself behind his instrument as if it were a trench. She took the opportunity to check that her violin was more or less safe, and then closed her eyes. It was only when somebody down on the ground yelled that they had to get back to the bus that the musicians opened their eyes, cautiously raised their heads, and remembered what they were doing there, sprawled on the boards, surrounded by upturned music stands and empty chairs.

It was then that their rout began, the waltz of flight. Stay together, stay together, someone cried behind my mother, no, this way, this way, my mother clasped her violin case to her chest and ran, trying to follow the disorderly trail of tuxedoed backs, bumping into other bodies crossing every which way, a sea of silhouettes, horses, trees, vehicles, while the smoke floated up, veiling their eyes and choking their throats, they had to keep running, this way, this way, and my mother collided with someone and they pushed each other out of the way, the noise of the sirens blared like tuning forks gone berserk, the bullets responded, the screams formed a vast choir out of tune, the music of terror, and on the grass they began to spot entwined bodies fighting, others wounded, others too still, and the police, tanks, trucks pulling away, overturned cars, ambulances, photographers, the smell of smoke, plastic, burning green, tear gas, the taste of acid tears. My mother recognized the orchestra's bus in the distance.

Sticks and stones were hurtling, and so was the light, making heads spin and turning up the volume, voices were hurtling too, voices that came and went. My mother clenched her teeth, her violin case, her leg muscles, and took a running leap onto the bus, which was waiting with the engine running. Her mouth was filled with a bitter taste, as if she had been drinking blood. The Argentine flags billowed, catching fire at the whim of the wind.

# 15

AT SCHOOL I had two main missions: to center the ball decently enough to enable Averame or Emsani to score headers, and to read aloud at patriotic assemblies. My grades and conduct never merited the coveted position of hoister of the Argentine flag. However, the school principal seemed to like the way I recited the texts in public. That's why he overlooked my tendency to neglect my white coat. Such sloppiness was undesirable at any time of the year, but on the eve of patriotic dates like July 9th or May 25th it bordered on the unforgivable. On those dates, any missing button was an unpatriotic button.

One morning, moments before the playing of the national anthem was due to begin, the principal came hesitantly up to me. Examining my coat and shoes, he explained that the flag hoister was unwell. I asked about my friend Paz, the reserve hoister. With a solemn expression, the principal informed me that he too was indisposed. Paz as well? Goodness: wishes weren't made to be fulfilled all at once.

Come on, Neuman, jump to it! the principal commanded. I obeyed. I walked toward the flag amid the mocking gazes of my fellow pupils. There it was, on the far side of the schoolyard: sky blue and white, with a triumphal sun in the center. I didn't think I could possibly hoist it like Paz, who was capable of reaching the top to coincide precisely with the anthem's final note. At the base of the pole, I contemplated the lowered flag. Seen up close, it looked as crumpled and sad as a plastic bag.

After the piano's solemn introduction, the anthem began to ring out: "Hear, oh mortals, the sacred cry." I felt about to throw up from fear. Suddenly my body began to itch all over. The blood drained from my head. Think of the fatherland, Neuman, the principal whispered behind me. I nodded, clutching the rope.

# 16

AS I RECALL, from a very young age I was sure what being wicked meant. Or, to put it another way, how easy it was to get away with things. It seemed so simple to go unpunished that I often felt overwhelmed by it. Added to this was another certainty I found unbearable: the certainty of death. Since there was no escape, what was the point of being good? The image I had of death was a skull in the middle of a desert, next to a cactus, like in the cartoons. The skull was mine, hollow, recognizable. Yet beyond the desert the town's lights still shone, its activities didn't cease, or the noise of its people diminish. At that point the image grew hazy, my head started to spin, air wouldn't enter my lungs and I realized, with painful clarity, that I had no words. Maybe that lack of words is the root of evil.

Every so often I would purposefully do something naughty, just to see what happened. And nothing happened. Where was the punishment? Where were the much-vaunted voices of repentance? Nearly all my schoolmates were Roman Catholic, they had interminable prayers, words to ask for forgiveness, mercy, or help. In contrast, for me to repent was an uphill struggle. And when I did manage it, I could find no higher presence to whom I could confess. It was my own shadow that listened. As my grandpa Jacinto used to say, it was simply a question of being alone with our conscience. At eight or ten, that blessed solitude felt daunting to me.

Along with my friend and neighbor Ramos, I founded the short-lived Matchbox heist gang. Returning home from school one day, I confided to him about a couple of successful raids I'd carried out, and suggested we team up. Our aim would be to collect a complete set of Matchbox cars, or as many as we possibly could. Although I had plenty of toys at home, and grandma Dorita together with a few friends had just opened an educational toyshop called *Bichito de Luz*, what kept me awake at night was the metallic gleam and perfect suspension of Matchbox cars.

So far I had snaffled a taxi, a Mercedes police vehicle, a couple of gangster cars, and a blue Chevrolet. Not one of their owners had suspected me. My strategy consisted of waiting for the moment of chaos that usually came at the end of one of the races we organized in the schoolyard, when the finish was disputed and we were all quarreling over who had won. It was best to start the argument oneself, so as to be remembered at the center of it. But in fact, after a few heated protests, we members of the heist gang would peel away from the group and steal over to the precious Matchbox cars abandoned on the track.

At this point, Ramos protested that one of our schoolmates might easily withdraw from the quarrel and catch us in the act. I'd also thought of this, I argued, because, when approaching somebody else's car, a good Matchbox thief must always make as if to pick up his own, just to be on the safe side. While performing this sleight of hand, it was essential to take a last look. If there was the slightest suspicion someone might be watching, our hand must veer away from its goal and reach for our own car. However, if things went to plan, once the other boy's Matchbox car was pocketed we must quickly conceal it in our pants, or even inside our underwear: never in the pockets of our white coat, which were too obvious. And most importantly, Ramos, I concluded in a whisper: you have to leave your car there, along with the others, get it? The last trick of the heist was to leave your own Matchbox car on the track before rejoining the others, so that when the dispute had been resolved, you could bend over and express dismay at the same time as your schoolmates over the absence of the stolen car.

Naturally, these raids weren't without danger. Being caught once would be enough to put the kibosh on the whole business. That's precisely why I needed a partner, I explained to Ramos. An accomplice would make the whole thing safer: one of us could act as cover while the other performed the theft, or fuel the quarrel at the crucial moment. Or, if the coveted Matchbox resembled either of our cars, one of us could even pretend to pick it up by mistake, enabling our accomplice to snatch the one we wanted. That way, if we were discovered, we would have a nice excuse for defending our innocence. It would all be so much easier if we became partners, and our collection would be that much better. Ramos listened with a mixture of enthusiasm and disapproval. And, to make it perfectly clear he was a good boy, he resisted a little before agreeing.

Both in school and outside it, thefts were fairly common. You had to be especially careful with money, footballs, and watches.

Whenever something was stolen from me, I made sure I got my own back with interest. But my victims weren't always the suspected thieves, or even my least favorite classmates. More than once I stole a toy from a friend. I'd go round to his place, we'd have a snack together, I would wait for his attention to wander, and my hand would dart in. Where could my poor friend have left his toy? I shrugged, angelical. My kleptomania lasted a couple of years, but my sense of shame lasted far longer. Why was I capable of being wicked to my friends? And how come they never realized, and seemed to go on liking me? Was generosity as solitary, as secret an activity as meanness?

The Matchbox heist gang didn't last long. That wimp Ramos blabbed, and glumly informed me he couldn't take part in the thefts because his mother forbade him to. When a few days later, out of revenge, I swiped one of his nicest Matchbox cars, Ramos didn't say a word.

# 17

MY MOTHER HAD come back from her tour in Germany with an object from another world. A weightless, transparent artifact that turned the simple gesture of checking the time into a joy. The straps were invisible. The dial showed the mechanism, the fantastic spinning of the seconds.

At certain times of the day, some streets in San Telmo could be dangerous. I knew them well at the hour of mists from the river and perpendicular cold. At about a quarter to seven every morning, I would walk up the deserted Avenida Independencia, cross Defensa and Bolívar, and meet Ramos outside his front door. He and I would then continue together across Chile and Mexico, and we waited for the red No. 2 bus. Alternatively we could wait for the more popular blue and white No. 86, but that meant having to put up with being crushed. One morning, or maybe even before dawn, I was on my way to meet Ramos. A fluffy scarf covered half my face. As I inhaled damp wool and contemplated my shoes taking turns on the sidewalk, I was thinking of my brand-new watch and my friends' faces when they saw it.

As I passed a shadowy doorway, two boys asked me the time. Without thinking, I uncovered my wrist, pulled down my scarf and replied. To my astonishment, instead of thanking me, the two boys started to follow me. Suspecting I'd just made a terrible mistake, I quickened my pace, gazing straight ahead. Out of the corner of my eye I saw them draw level and place themselves on either side of me. After walking on for a few seconds, I risked a pleading glance toward the boy on my right. A few seconds is a long time: maybe they too were wondering what to do next. My aim was to cross Bolívar and reach Ramos's door, where I'd be safe. The three of us were almost trotting along. Just before we reached the corner, the boy on my left said:

"Give me the watch, kid."

I found it intriguing that someone my own age should call me kid. My heart started to beat too fast. We walked on. I've always found small hoodlums terrifying. The boy on my right added, without raising his voice:

"Give us the watch, sonofabitch, or we'll shoot the crap out of you."

Ramos saw me arrive in a cold sweat. I was chewing my fluffy scarf. He seemed slightly put out by my lateness. When we were face to face, without realizing it, Ramos made the most excruciating gesture possible: he raised his forefinger to his left wrist and tapped it several times.

# 18

BAD LUCK. THAT'S what I had with my new watch. There are those who, long ago, would have declared me the jinx of the family. Inherently doomed. Born under an unlucky star. A Mr. Misfortune.

Indeed, my great-uncle Homero's life was pure bad luck. Not as studious as his sister Blanca, less handsome than his brother Leonardo, and lacking his brother Rubén's artistic sensibility, great-uncle Homero did everything he could in life to confirm his worst predictions.

"Everything I do turns out badly. Look at me, I'm a first-class *jettatore*. What can I do?"

Attracted to unlikely business ventures, Homero ran an electrical appliance store, opened a bakery, sold insurance and so on and so forth. If his three children flourished, it was less thanks to his short-lived ventures than to the modest wage his wife Lali earned as a nurse. Poor Homero, Grandma Blanca used to say, the problem is he's a pessimist. His relatives, who didn't always offer him the best advice, eventually resigned themselves to watching him fail. Homero wasn't self-confident enough to earn his luck. His bakery collapsed. He frequently overslept in the morning and would hurry to open a little late, when his customers had already gone elsewhere. In addition, a faulty oven almost burned the place to the ground. The electrical appliance store also had to close because of debts, although there's reason to suspect his brother Leonardo was the one behind the accounting problems. As an insurance salesman, Homero started out more promisingly. The contracts rolled in, and his demeanor, somewhere between affectionate and desperate, elicited the compassion of his clients. Eventually, however, Homero's success culminated in tragedy: an incredibly large number of his clients became victims of theft or all kinds of accident. Suspecting fraud, the insurance company decided to fire him.

"You see? Like I said: *jettatore*. What can I do?"

My great-uncle Homero didn't regard the achievements of others with envy so much as ominous disbelief. The day my mother was to give one of her first concerts, he sat listening to the rehearsal. When it was over and she was putting away her violin, he wished her luck in his own special way:

"Be brave, Delita! And try not to play too many wrong notes!"

My great-uncle Homero ended up the poorest member of the Casaretto family. His last dwelling was a prefab shack with an earth floor in Longchamps slum. I'm okay here, nice and warm, Homero would tell his visitors. But it wasn't hard to see the bitterness behind his deceptively easy smile. Come on, make yourselves at home, he would insist, changing the subject when asked about work. He never found a cause worth suffering as he suffered, or a steady job in which to give his bad luck a break.

The last time my mother saw him was at the opening of an exhibition of my great-uncle Rubén's work, in a small gallery in Buenos Aires province. My parents were newly-wed, and although they had to live off pasta to pay the mortgage, in Homero's eyes they were the image of triumphant youth: both were musicians, both had career ambitions, and they even owned their own apartment in the capital.

As is clear from photographs of the event, my parents were dressed with a vague air of Latin American hippies, which presumably impressed Homero even more. The three exchanged greetings. Hey, violinist, you're all skin and bone! but gorgeous as ever, oh, uncle, don't exaggerate, please, you and Victor have met, haven't you?, hi there young man, what's new, so, you stole the family jewel, how are you, señor, oh, uncle, don't be silly, where's Rubén, do you know?, I just saw him walk by, hey, niece, it's so good to see you here, give me a hug!, uncle Rubén, we were just asking after you, I think you've met my husband Victor, of course, congratulations, señor, we love your paintings, it's true, uncle, they're great, okay, okay, thanks kids, they're no big deal, but they're mine!, come with me, come on, I want to introduce you to . . .

During the opening, my mother learned that Lali had just left Homero. Two of his three children lived far away and hardly ever came to visit him, the third had died years previously in a bizarre accident which no one would talk about. My great-uncle was balder than ever, dignified in his worn clothes; at times his smile seemed to wander. That night when he said goodbye, okay, kids, try to visit again soon, won't you?, for sure, uncle, any day now, and you take good care of yourself, okay, okay, what can I do?, call whenever you want and come by, see you soon, Uncle Rubén, uncle Homero, a pleasure to meet you señor, off you go now, *chau, chau,* and congratulations once again, thanks, thanks a lot . . . That night when he said goodbye, my great-uncle pronounced the last words my mother would ever hear him say. At the exit, a mere shadow in the doorway, Homero whispered to her, with possibly ironic admiration:

"Let me touch you."

And, after squeezing her arm tight, he turned round and vanished, what can I do?, down the gallery corridor.

# 19

WHEN I TURNED ten, I decided it was high time I went to see a psychologist like everyone else in my family. This happened during the early hours one summer, in a small house we were renting near Villa Gesell beach. I still had no inkling of my Iberian future: has any Spaniard ever considered being psychoanalyzed while holidaying in Benidorm or Torremolinos? Early that morning I had a good cry, tossed and turned in bed, complained as best I could, and my parents, each with years of therapy behind them, finally agreed.

The consulting room was a perfect cube. I remember wondering, as I walked in, if the room was as high as it was long. Much to my disappointment, I didn't see any couch. There was a wide table, a black leather armchair on either side and, to the left of the door, a chalkboard. I thought Doctor Freidemberg was nice and not as clever as my mother. I was very surprised she didn't ask me anything about my family, my sorrows, my lies. She only asked me general questions. That must have been the trick: those questions were too easy and that lady listened too much. Doctor Freidemberg avoided mentioning what she really wanted to know, she circled around, waiting for me to drop my guard.

During one of these sessions, she appeared to change tactics and asked me to draw something on the chalkboard. It occurred to me to imitate one of my classmate Aguirrebengoa's caricatures— he was left-handed and good at drawing. I worked at it for several minutes; aware that Doctor Freidemberg was scrutinizing me, I tried not to let it show that I was copying from memory. She asked me what the drawing was. I explained, and she made a remark that gave me the awkward impression it had little to do with the caricature. I became slightly irritated: if Doctor Freidemberg didn't concentrate, we would never get anywhere.

She asked me to do another drawing. What of? I said. Nothing in particular, whatever you wish, she replied, something you like, or something imaginary. Not easy at all; those were two very different things. Then, as my mind remained a complete blank, I started to do sums on the chalkboard. In my neatest possible writing, so that Doctor Freidemberg could follow my calculations, I multiplied three-figure numbers by three-figure numbers; then I divided the result by one of the multipliers, and obtained a number identical to the other multiplier. When I asked Doctor Freidemberg if I could check it on her calculator, she told me with a sigh that we'd run out of time.

"How did it go, darling?" my mother greeted me in the waiting room, closing the pages of a magazine.

"Worse than at school," I said, "I don't think I'll pass."

# 20

THE YEAR MY parents took me to see the psychotherapist, we had a maid called Silvina. Inscribed on the calendar of my childhood are the names of countless young women from Monday to Friday. To all of them, my mother was *la señora*, even though it made her feel awkward and she tried her best to adopt a teacher-like face for them. My father was *el señor*. He addressed them formally, and avoided too much familiarity, maybe because he still remembered Gladys, the young woman from Chaco province who one summer, returning home earlier than expected, he had discovered with two men in the marital bed of *los señores*.

Gladys has been naughty, my parents announced the following morning. And it made me sad to see her so forlorn, trying her best to smile at me through her false teeth. I didn't like the thought of us having to say goodbye, because I was very fond of Gladys and thanks to her I had learned to read a few words, which, in turn, my mother had taught her to write. Gladys has been naughty, my father said, and it struck me as odd, because that's what she used to say about me. She had dry, dark skin, and she left giving me one last big hug, weeping muddy tears.

They came from the north of Argentina or from Paraguay. They drank sweet *mate*. With a few exceptions, they couldn't read. Wasn't I also a complete ignoramus about their world and their language? I didn't even know where Chaco, Formosa, Misiones, or Asunción were exactly. Nor did I understand why no girl from Buenos Aires ever worked for us. Until I received a dose of education. Classes about class.

"Mom, why did María come from so far away?"

"Because this is where she found work, my love, and she wanted to work."

"Yes, but why didn't she look for work close to where she lives?"

"Oh, sweetie, I don't know, maybe she thought she'd be better off here."

"So far from her family?"

"Yes."

"I don't get it."

"Well, María has a family here too, doesn't she? While she takes care of you, your dad and I take care of her. Do you understand?"

"No."

"Why not, my love?"

"Oh, mom!"

"Listen to me. Where María and her family live, people are very poor. So she came to Buenos Aires because she could be better off here. That's why we're happy she's living with us, and María's also happy she came, despite having to travel a long way. She wants to work a lot here so she can send money to her parents, that way everybody's better off. Now do you understand?"

"So María has to work hard in Buenos Aires because her family's poor?"

"Yes, my sweet."

"And are we poor as well?"

"Oh, son, how can you say such a thing!"

"I mean, you and dad work hard too. You work all day! You leave in the morning and come back at night."

"That's because your father and I are very lucky. We're lucky to have plenty of work."

"So, María's lucky too?"

"*Chau*, son, give me a kiss. I'm late for rehearsal."

We only had one maid who came from Buenos Aires province. She lived in the La Salada shanty town and made the journey to San Telmo every morning. Sofía was tall as a tree, strong as a tower, and had curls like wire. She wore thongs when she worked, her huge feet covered in callouses. She always sounded slightly hoarse. I remember her being efficient and kind. One day she arrived with a black eye, bruises on her neck and even hoarser than usual. She said she'd had an accident. Nothing serious. That weekend, my parents went to La Salada. We're going to visit Sofía's house, they told me, we'll be home this evening. Much as I protested, they wouldn't let me go with them. To compensate, they allowed me to stay two nights at my friend The Raven's place. The following Monday, Sofía's husband called to say she was quitting.

Benita's native language was Guaraní. During her first few days with us, she taught me how to pronounce what sounded to me roughly like *rojaujú etereí*. In Guaraní that meant I love you very much. Up until then, I'd never loved, or hated, any of our maids the way I did Benita. She usually dressed in pink jeans and T-shirts that showed her belly button and, just beneath, a furtive trace of down. The possibility that a girl had hair growing there felt to me like a mind-blowing discovery. Together we would watch Venezuelan soap operas (with tragic tendencies), Colombian ones (with a hint of humor) and Argentine ones (with vaguely philosophical pretensions). We played games of checkers which she frequently won.

We chatted, we fought, we hurled accusations at one another in front of my parents. I insulted her shockingly and she abused me without laying a finger on me. A paid big sister, an unprotected protectress. I liked to watch her when she had an afternoon nap, lying on her back on top of the bedspread. Contemplating her while she was asleep, I sometimes felt an urgent need for her to breastfeed me. Luckily Doctor Freidemberg never knew this.

Although she ignored my questions about evil or death, Benita instantly memorized the rules governing Spanish accents and stresses which I explained to her one morning over breakfast. I gave her the same exercises I remembered doing at school, and Benita would work them out as easily as she beat me at checkers. She didn't rely on pure instinct, natural intuition, or anything of the sort; on the contrary, she clung desperately to the power of reason. I know I treated her unfairly: she was the rest of the household's absence.

Unlike her predecessors, our next maid Lili had been to school: overcoming all manner of difficulties, she had achieved good grades in a Santiago del Estero high school. She spoke fluently and accurately. My parents had a special fondness for her, as well as a kind of political gratitude: she momentarily renewed their faith in a non-existent meritocracy. Lili's eyes shone from all she observed. She had a big nose and a tuneful voice.

Of course, Lili wasn't willing to remain trapped in domestic servitude. She wanted to improve her position as rapidly as possible. Hence the reason why she rifled, with perfect precision, every wardrobe, cupboard, and drawer in our apartment. She carried out her intelligent pillaging while my brother and I were at school. In winter she stole our summer clothes, and vice versa. She knew which day my parents brought home their pay packets, and where they hid them. She calculated her spoils carefully, making sure she restrained herself if the amounts she found were too exact or too small. Lili managed to collect a tidy sum before they found her out. My parents didn't report her to the police, less out of compassion than political embarrassment. As far as I can recall, she was the last maid who worked at our home.

# 21

DURING THE SUMMERS, in Miramar, my father played at being a little boy. Were you a little boy once, dad? The things you say.

In Miramar childhood came and went, came, and went. The same way as words. Like someone doubting what they recall.

The air was salty and the days burning hot. *Zeide* Jacobo smoked on the sly. Her brow furrowed, *Baba* Lidia made jam. My grandparents Dorita and Mario let their hair down a little and visited other families. Among them, the Timermans, and the Roths.

Señor Timerman was a journalist and would go on to be editor of *La Opinión,* a newspaper the dictatorship made it their business to silence, the way they did everything that spoke out. Señora Roth was a singer and mother of two children, Cecilia, and Ariel. Cecilia had the face of an actress. Her brother, the hands of a musician. But let's not get ahead of ourselves. Because back then Ariel could barely reach his bicycle saddle, and his sister laughed. Blonde, light, Cecilia laughed.

When the Roths went out to dinner, they asked my father to babysit Cecilia. She still didn't know who she was. My father stroked her little blonde head, and she was dazzled. How lucky you are, daddy boy, with your first beard.

Ariel had fallen asleep, composing lullabies to the future. The Roths were still not back. And so my impatient father whispered:

"Come on, pretty one, grow."

But barefoot Cecilia didn't grow.

Of course, those things needed rehearsing. Some scenes take years to perfect. Every so often, my father would repeat in her ear:

"Come on, grow quickly, please."

But Cecilia, determined to ask her Prince Charming for seconds of flan, was having none of it. And the door opened, and the Roths came back.

# 22

GABRIELA WAS THE daughter of our second-floor neighbors. Our families vacationed together in the summer. Gabriela, ballerina. I remember you as being tall, although I know you weren't. Your nipples absorbed the light of Villa Gesell. What mean bikinis. Would I be as old as you if you stayed still? But you twirled around me, in perpetual motion.

I know your ears stuck out a bit. Because they were asking to be nibbled. And I haven't forgotten your beakish nose. Because that nose was also seduced by your perfume, Gabriela. You had muscular thighs, you dreamed of dancing at the Teatro Colón. You walked with feet turned out, the tips of your toes bruised, each foot pointing to its own path.

I was right eager to grow, Gabriela, but I was so sluggish. That's why, accustomed to being satisfied with hints, I thought I was hallucinating when one evening in Villa Gesell, you rang the bell and found me alone, Hi, come in, and you kissed me a bit less as a child. You'd brought a towel and a canvas bag. You'd come to take a shower, you told me. There was no more hot water at your place. My parents and brother were out. I don't know if you realized, Gabriela, that this was too much for me. You slid your feet, swinging east and west, toward the bathroom. Thanks, I won't be long, you yelled, undressing on the other side of the door. Your heels scraped the tiles and the shower ran like a nuanced silence, I translated every movement suggested by the flow of water. There the keyhole, your feet making noise, here my heart, with its keyhole, and you splashing the melody of urgency.

Shall I say I spied on you? That, turning off the water, you called me? Or did I, almost imploringly, knock on the door? Shall I say you opened it, or weren't surprised when I did, and that you didn't reach instantly for the towel, Gabriela, allowing me to memorize you? Shall I confess your pubis looked wider and darker than I'd imagined? Shall I say that in a way you took pity on me, that maybe you were moved by the last thread of my childhood? That, boldly compassionate, you closed the door and stared at me? That with a smile promising another world, you came closer to me so that the water, like a returning silence, flowed again?

Did it happen? Is it true? Is it a lie?

Those aren't the right questions.

# 23

MYSTERIOUS UTOPIA, THAT of our white school coats. I never understood why it should be precisely that color which accompanied our tumbles in the schoolyard, shared our ice creams or Fantas, shielded us when it came to defending our alleged honor (you motherfucker!, call me any name you like, but leave my mother out of it . . . !), or which we used as a cloak, whip, or a goal post. Maybe that was why we had to wear a white coat: to keep us quiet.

I found myself buttoning up my utopia, a task especially delicate that morning as I'd lost two buttons. When one at the bottom was missing, you could get away with it. You just had to walk carefully. But if one of the top buttons went AWOL, you were in for it. The worst possible mishap when the principal was there to take register, give us our yearly reading exam, and stamp our books. Paz, the reserve flag hoister, looked at me scornfully. His coat was spotless.

What a sight we were. Thirty-odd warriors with swords always at the ready, shoes scuffed from countless battles with a football, thirty-something riders of proven pluckiness, all suddenly cowed: quivering steeds and paper shields. Each of us frantically straightening our pencils, vainly checking our exercise books, or tugging those two sleeves that were never the same length.

We didn't even feel tempted to pass each other notes under our desks: Mellino desperately combed his hair, which panic had turned a darker shade of blond; Alonso couldn't decide where to put his glasses, from nose to pocket, pocket to desk, desk to nose; speaking of noses, there was Ramos's, struggling with a handkerchief in one of his famous sneezing bouts; Yepes sweating as he tried to line his textbook to hide the lewd pictures he'd been drawing all year; red-faced Botana apparently unable to tie his shoelaces properly; Tagliabue discovering to his horror that he'd spelled his surname with a "v" rather than a "b" on every page of his exercise book; Iribarne regretting not having washed his hands after the last recess; Guerrero considering the option of ripping up the principal's report and running away to become a homeless soccer forward; Cedrola completing the previous day's equations with the furtive aid of a calculator, and just to make doubly sure checking his answers with the hateful brainiac, Ríos, who was suddenly the object of rare courtesies; only Emsani, cool as a cucumber, joked with Mizrahi as he waited his turn.

It wasn't any of them, however, who managed to catch my attention. Someone tragically different amazed me.

Santos was a chubby-faced boy with a precociously fuzzy upper lip. We all considered him the laughing stock of the class. He seemed unaware of this situation, or he meekly accepted it, or he didn't give a damn. He was the fixed target of our frustrations, which is why I admired him. You needed to be exceptionally tough or exceptionally wise to ignore our classmates the way he did. I myself never had the courage, so simply played along with them, and defended my territory. It was rumored that Santos's mother was in the habit of beating him. His father was a ghost: we knew he existed but we'd never seen him. And yet what fascinated me weren't the unknowns about his home life, but rather the mystery of his language. Because Santos didn't speak. Not a single word.

Despite not saying a word, Santos wasn't mute. His vocal cords were just fine. He simply abstained from speaking. Without quite knowing why, I sensed some connection between my nervous talkativeness and his unbreakable silence. When Santos smiled, two holes appeared in his chubby cheeks, which on any other face would have seemed like charming dimples. But, on his sorrowful countenance, they looked more like the scars of joy. His head was jet black, almost shaven; his skin milky white, as if it had only seen winter. I imagined that, in the blurry distance, my short-sighted classmates must see his face as all gray.

The alphabet had already devoured my surname and I received the usual, "good progress excellent reading skills room for improvement in handwriting and behavior." Victors or vanquished, most of us had fought the good fight, although Yañez and Zavadivcker were still frantically trying to memorize the text to avoid any slip-ups when reading. Then the moment I'd most been waiting for finally arrived. And the same letter that summons the silent, solitary, stolid, suffering, submissive, or smart dragged Santos toward the principal's desk. He shuffled forward. His white coat, utterly utopian. The entire troop fell silent, less out of respect than mockery.

Santos stopped in front of the principal. He opened his book and stared straight at him. Every year we witnessed an extraordinary moment, when Santos overcame his fears and dared to speak. Go for it, chicken!, came a voice from the back. Santos puckered his downy lip. Although now I suspect maybe he didn't. He gave a little cough. I wonder where Santos is today?, who is he silent with? He clasped the book and raised his arms. Maybe that was the only time Santos felt obliged to give in. He held his breath. The humiliating retreat from his repudiation of his stubborn silence. He breathed out slowly, looking at us askance.

# 24

THE CORPORAL LOOKED askance at them, slowly puffing out the smoke. He kept an eye on the future conscripts as if they could possibly escape from the room, half-naked as they were, sitting on those uncomfortable wooden benches.

The stocky corporal was smoking at his desk, glancing in a bored fashion at their draft orders. He marked the number 1 beneath the collarbone of the ones still to be examined by the barracks' doctor, and sent them out. Those like my father who had already been examined were rewarded with a number 2, and kept in the room with him in their undershirts and shorts. They had been ordered not to get dressed again, in case the medical had to be repeated. Some were forced to wait the whole day without their clothes or having anything to eat.

A cold breeze was blowing through the room, and my father began to be afraid that his obviously flat feet might not be enough to save him from military service. At least not in 1969, in the midst of a dictatorship.

Seated next to him he saw a flabby young man smiling at him in alarm. He soon forgot his first name, but remembered the last one forever: Cesarini. My father, who at that moment didn't even imagine he was to be my father, would have been even more surprised to learn that, fifteen years later, his own son would meet Cesarini's son. The two of them got on and whispered confidences in each other's ear.

The cold was becoming more intense by the minute, the wooden bench cut into his buttocks, and my father could see that many of his companions emerged from the medical room with a terrified grimace on their faces. Every so often, the corporal reluctantly uttered a name, and someone stood up from the bench, walked head bowed to the desk, and received the documents allowing him to go home. A timid voice asked if he could have a cigarette. The corporal looked up, blew out a mouthful of smoke and replied, pointing to the wall:

"Obviously not, conscript. Can't you see the sign? Or can't you read?"

All the future soldiers were hungry. Progress was still fitful, and seemed to depend more on the whim of the doctors or the corporal than on any pre-established system. Almost all those who had left were the ones whose enrollment papers had been stamped with the dreaded *Fit for service*. My father was drowsy, his back hurt, and he had a hole in his stomach. Cesarini muttered that he was about to pass out. Somebody had a fit of coughing.

All of a sudden, the corporal stared intently at one of the booklets. His eyes opened wide and he shouted:

"Let's see! Neuman, Víctor! On your feet and come over here . . ."

Startled, my father obeyed. Cesarini pressed his lips together as if to say "Good luck," or "I'm sorry for you." As my father approached the desk, it seemed to him the corporal was staring at him too intently for it to be good news. So skinny, in his shorts, much younger than I am now, my father began to quake. He was completely surprised by what the corporal asked him:

"You wouldn't by any chance be related to *Tank* Neuman, the forward who plays for Chacarita, would you?"

Confused, my father smiled silently, trying to gain a few seconds to think.

"Are you going to answer or not, dammit? Do you know him at all, *Tank* Neuman?"

My father felt an icy Siberian wind run down his back, as if the breeze was rushing in from the distant past, and then felt the push of an idea that made the time suspended in that room start to race along. With all the aplomb he could muster, my father told the corporal:

"Well, as far as knowing him goes, I should think I do know my own brother, yes."

The corporal raised his eyebrows. He half-opened his lips in a crooked smile that made the cigarette roll round.

"Come closer, for fuck's sake, or aren't you and I going to be able to talk man to man? That's better. So he's your brother, you say? Really and truly?"

"Oh, if you only knew, Corporal sir, how often people ask me that very same question!"

"Yes, of course, I can imagine. No less than the *Tank* himself! And do you know how often I've been to the ground to see him play? Because you must be a Chacarita fan too, aren't you?"

"Of course, Corporal sir," replied my father, who had never in his life been interested in soccer.

"That's my boy! What a coincidence! I can't believe it! Shit, what a goal your brother scored the other day, eh? Well, please let your brother know that here in the barracks we all think highly of him, and consider him to be an example for the youth of Argentina. Be sure you pass that message on, Neuman."

"Yes sir, I surely will, Corporal sir."

"As I was saying, three of us here in the barracks are Chacarita fans."

"Excuse me for correcting you, Corporal sir. But right now, there are precisely four of us."

"That's my boy! That's how everyone should be! Upright men of Chacarita! So what's your brother doing now?"

"He's training, Corporal sir, like he does every day."

"But hang on, wasn't he injured last Sunday?"

"No, yes, you're right. The poor guy's got an ice pack on him all day at home."

"What crappy luck! So in the end he isn't going to play against River? They didn't mention anything on the radio."

"Well, in fact I, look, er . . . Can you keep a secret for me, Corporal sir? Bah, not for me, for my brother."

"Tell me, tell me," replied the corporal, straightening up and bringing his shaven head close to the desk edge.

"It's like this, Corporal sir. They don't say anything on the radio, nobody says anything, because in the club they don't want the people at River to know, you see? So that if at the last minute my brother can play, then our enemies will be forced to change their plans, right?"

"That's my boy!" the corporal whooped, dropping back into his chair. "Don't you worry, Neuman, a Chacarita fan knows how to keep a secret. Not a word to a soul, I swear!"

"My brother and the club are very grateful to you, Corporal sir."

"Ah, and here are your papers, Víctor. You can go without a worry."

"Many thanks, Corporal sir."

"And give my warmest greetings to your brother," added the corporal, stamping the document *Unfit for Service*.

"It'll be a pleasure, Corporal sir," my father said, receiving his booklet and turning to go and get dressed.

"Ah, one other small thing!" said the corporal.

My father stopped in his tracks and turned slowly back to face him.

"Yes . . . ?" he asked, terrified, in the faintest of voices.

"Nothing, kid, except it's a good thing your brother wasn't born with your flat feet, isn't it?"

Guffawing, his head enveloped in smoke, the corporal lowered his eyes and carried on flicking through the other documents, as bored as before.

# 25

A GRAVEL SCHOOLYARD. Yells from all sides. Gusts of wind. A bell about to sound. Shoelaces undone. And something else. What? A ball. Orange plastic or leather with frayed seams.

Soccer saved me from lots of things. From being the weirdo, a more or less aspiring poet, bullied in the schoolyard every day. From being unable to exchange more than three or four vaguely grammatical grunts with my classmates, whose roughness intimidated me. From the risk of ignoring my body, prone as I was to living in an imaginary world. Soccer taught me that, if you're running, it's best to do it forward. That to fight alone is a bad idea. That beauty always gets a kicking. And that our opponents are very similar to us.

I didn't inherit Boca Juniors; my grandfather Mario supported Racing and, during the brief time we shared in this soccer-playing world, he never gave up trying to persuade me to follow his example. When I told him I was a fan of Boca, my grandpa replied laughing: "But they're a bunch of klutzes!" This description seems to enclose a triple foreignness. Identification with a different team than the family; the gulf between the language of successive generations; and the transfer to another country where nobody says *klutz*.

In accordance with his iron-clad Marxism, my grandfather Jacinto was inclined to regard soccer as an opiate. Occasionally he would indulge me and we'd go out to kick a ball together. But it was more a workout than a passion for him and, as far as I can recall, he never showed a preference for any team. Nor did my father have any great interest in the matter. If asked who he supported, he'd declare himself vaguely a Racing fan out of deference to his own father. Even my best friend The Raven was a huge River Plate fan. So for me it wasn't a family thing. I don't know why I became a Boca fan, just because, because how could anyone not become a fan of Boca.

The club I was destined to adore was the one that suffered a decade of disasters. Four trainers in one season. The post-Maradona depression. The interminable seven-year drought: half the time I lived in Buenos Aires. I saw River win and I couldn't understand why we never did. I saw "Prince" Francescoli dance, Beto Alonso score, Pumpido save clumsily, and I wondered what had become of the team that I was told had won the Copa Libertadores and the Copa Intercontinental the year I was born. Hearing of those past exploits, I felt like a late arrival to a party everyone said they'd been at. Even so, I have no regrets about growing up with Boca: their defeats were another school.

One of the things I most disliked about the passion for soccer was the arsenal of alluding to the players' manhood: that misconception which confuses talent with the groin area. Half my childhood I had to listen to the criticisms of my favorite player, "Chino" Tapia, whenever he lost the ball. A left-footed mid-fielder, "Chino" had that electric speed some playmakers have, able to think and make a decision while they're being pressed. Chino was intrepid driving forward, visionary at spotting gaps, and unexpectedly generous in his final pass. I was enchanted by his stooped, rhythmic dribbling. And yet, Sunday after Sunday, if some subtle move came to nothing, the groin brigade would scream: For fuck's sake, Tapia, you look like a ballerina! Don't be a faggot, Chino!

The memorable World Cup in Mexico taught me another uncomfortable lesson: generous players are usually substitutes. "Chino" Tapia had to sit out every game on the bench. He parleyed briefly with the ball against South Korea and played the English for fifteen minutes. After a brief exchange with Maradona, for once Chino decided not to yield center stage to anyone and shot from a long way out. The ball hit the post; meandered along the goal line as if unsure what to do; then rolled a few inches away. At that very instant, the delicate Tapia pulled a groin muscle.

# 26

I WAS READING the newspaper at my grandmother Dorita's apartment. The center pages celebrated the Argentine team's triumph in Mexico. By all accounts, a divine hand had won us our second World Cup and, this time without the military, got revenge for the Malvinas. Maradona smiled from the Aztec Stadium, raising the gold cup like a solar toast.

While searching for a mention of "Chino" Tapia, I suddenly came across the photograph of an elderly gentleman with half-closed eyes. I was astonished that some old fogey should take space from soccer. It was June 1986. The remains of this fellow Borges had been laid to rest in Geneva.

On the very same page they recalled the death of Cortázar, who had also been buried abroad. The book he was working on just before he died was entitled: *Argentina, años de alambradas culturales* (Argentina: Years of Cultural Barbed Wire). I still have the copy I was to find many years later in my grandmother Dorita's house. Inside it I saw, underlined in thick pencil, the phrase: "The Argentine military junta stands out when it comes to costumes: some are as huge as the World Cup. Writing and reading is a form of action."

A year after Cortázar's death, and a year before that of Borges, the Argentine military was put on trial. Borges, who had had lunch once or twice with General Videla, attended one of the hearings. Horrified by the depositions, he wrote what was possibly his only political article: "I felt I was in prison. The most terrible thing about a prison is that those who have entered there can actually never leave. It is curious to note that the military, who preferred kidnapping, torture, and secret executions to the public exercise of the law, now wish to benefit from this relic of the past."

A journalist reproached him: Why didn't you speak out before? And you?, Borges retorted, where were you that you didn't ask me?

I skimmed through some of those things in the newspaper that day, without understanding them. As I discovered subsequently, the press had once asked Borges what he thought of Maradona. Forgive my ignorance, was his reply. They had also asked Maradona if he knew Borges. The number 10 had said: What team does he play for? I'm not sure which of the two was more mistaken.

# 27

MY GREAT-GRANDFATHER Jonás Kovensky, grandma Dorita's father, came to Argentina with his family as a boy. His father Itzkjok had been a blacksmith. His mother Beile, a washerwoman. They had endured a life of privation in Grodno, a town in Belarus then under Russian occupation, and whose inhabitants, due to their past, tended to consider themselves Polish-Lithuanians. Repeatedly invaded by armies of different origin, the natives of that small frontier town must have been brought up with a mixture of nationalism and fear, or fear of the nation. Let's attribute to a trick of fate that the name of the town's river, the Neman, is nearly my surname.

My great-grandfather Jonás's family made up part of the contingent that, fleeing pogroms in Russia and Eastern Europe, was to repopulate the Argentine countryside under the auspices of Baron Hirsch, a German Jew and founder of the Jewish Colonization Association. Provinces such as Santa Fe and Entre Ríos received a larger influx of immigrants, more investment, and were furnished with railways, cars, telephones. However, Jonás, his brothers and his parents, were sent to Bernasconi, on the edge of the dry Pampa, where they rebuilt their lives in a hostile climate. They got used to coexisting with the foolish, fearsome thistles that, due to the incessant winds, scratched their faces and burrowed into their clothes.

When he wasn't working the land, my great-great-grandfather Itzkjok would study the Talmud next to a window with shutters that banged and let in sand. "He lived in profile": that was how my grandmother Dorita remembered him. "He could spend hours mounted on his cane," she would say, "without speaking to anybody." Meanwhile, his wife Beile took care of the house, looked after their six children, and showed a growing inclination to sigh. "She was a smart woman," my grandmother described or defended her. "It was a forced marriage," if that's not redundant. "She was one of those who wore a headscarf, but she was no fanatic." A cane and a headscarf: stumbling and sweating, walking, and remembering. "At my age, I'm more a historical era than a person."

My great-grandfather Jonás had been born in January 1900: his life is that of the twentieth century. Learning Spanish at the age of eight produced in him a sense of strangeness and extreme care for the language. It was and wasn't his own tongue. He felt it belonged to him, yet he mistrusted it. At home, he and his family spoke colloquial Yiddish; at school he thought in Spanish. Rather than creating an inner obstacle, or precisely because it was an inner obstacle, this double shore turned him into a speaker of monstrous precision, according to those who had the opportunity to hear him. After going to school on the Pampa, Jonás moved to Buenos Aires province, where he attended a high school in Bahía Blanca. When he looked up, Jonás didn't know whether to direct his gaze toward the beguiling north leading to the capital, or to look much further east. It was no coincidence that whenever he pointed at the horizon his destiny split in two: a large scar ran down his right hand's forefinger from nail to knuckle, as a result of slicing it as a young boy on a piece of farm equipment.

Despite his flair for mathematics and his love of theater, my grandfather Jonás chose to study dentistry at the University of Buenos Aires in order to earn a living as quickly as possible. He attended lectures at the university in the mornings, studied at night, and in the afternoons gave Spanish classes to immigrants fresh off the boat, or taught Yiddish to his children. In summer, when he visited the family home, he would help with the harvest. The hyperactive Jonás still found time to take on an occasional role in amateur productions, and to keep abreast of what was playing in the stages on weekends, a passion he would pass down to my theatrical grandmother Dorita. At that time he joined Poale Zion movement, of which he was a life-long member and on whose central committee he also sat.

His first contact with Poale Zion was through León Jazanovich, activist, and editor of the magazine *Broit un ehre* (*Bread and Honor*). Jazanovich had dared denounce the terms imposed by the Jewish Colonization Association on its communities, describing them as "philanthropic feudalism." Contracts containing numerous obligations but few rights, often signed by people unaware exactly of what they entailed and without any corresponding translation into Yiddish; a minimum twenty-year period working the land before they obtained any right of ownership; restrictions on hiring laborers; a monopoly on loans and no option of making advance payments to reduce interest rates; and a paradoxical etcetera, the alleged aim of which was to prevent one person from accumulating too much land or individual wealth. As much a thorn in the side of the Jewish community's ruling elite as they were politically awkward for the government, Jazanovich and some fellow militants ended up being deported in accordance with the Residency Laws, aided and abetted by the Jewish Colonization Association itself, which accused them of fomenting unrest among their workers and stirring up anti-Semitism among rightwing nationalists.

The militant members of the Argentine branch of Poale Zion were to the left of the socialists led by Alfredo Palacios, with whom Jonás had dealings. Typically, at Poale Zion's second Congress, the movement split into two new factions: there is no unanimous utopia in its own ranks. Jonás chose the dissenting faction. He was in charge of publishing the newspaper *Palabra Obrera* (Worker's Word) and, as a representative for La Pampa, participated in the union of Jewish farming cooperatives. Jonás's speeches, as persuasive as they were calm, made him much in demand among youth movements. Doctor Kovensky's eloquence entered his comrades' ears with the same precision that he would later probe his patients' mouths. I assume that his penchant for debate also earned him the mistrust of many of his comrades.

What opinions would my great-grandfather Jonás have held about the future military campaigns of the state whose creation he had so often dreamed of? How would he have felt about the policies of Likud? Would he have seen them as traitors to his ideals, or perhaps defended them on the grounds of national security? And what would his esteemed Ber Borochov have thought about it all, the man who inspired socialist Zionism and believed in the common interests of the Arab and Jewish working classes? The same year Jonás joined the party, Borochov had publicly predicted: "Some people accuse us of the heinous crime of planning to oppress and expel the Arabs from Palestine. Yet when the barren land is ready to be cultivated, when modern technology is introduced and other obstacles are overcome, there will be plenty of land to accommodate both Jews and Arabs. Normal relations between the two peoples must and shall prevail."

Sara Resnik, my grandmother Dorita's mother, was born in the town of Terespol, on Poland's eastern border. By a curious coincidence, Sara was also one of six children, although her parents were slightly more comfortably off than those of her future husband and (yet again!) first-cousin Jonás. The two kept up a loyal, flirtatious, and incestuous correspondence between Poland and Argentina. She arrived in the country when she had, as the saying goes, seen seventeen springs. As well as a good few other harsh seasons.

Great-grandma Sara's life had been spent on the banks of the river Bug, a strategic location on the border of present-day Belarus and the scene of never-ending conflicts. Throughout history, Terespol had been invaded, plundered, burned down; it had changed hands (the town was successively Lithuanian, Swedish, Austrian, Polish, Russian . . .) and even moved several kilometers west, with the consequent destruction of all its buildings for military reasons. Between the two world wars, the town's population was largely made up of Polish Jews, nearly all of whom were to perish in the Holocaust.

During bombings in the Great War, Great-grandma Sara and her family had become accustomed to living in their basement. Always slightly detached from her surroundings, and with a remarkable ability to go without blinking for a long time, Sara fixed her gaze on the wall while the explosions were going on. The family had plans to emigrate to the United States, but they never came to fruition. Finally they crossed the Atlantic and settled in the tiny promised land of Moisés Ville on the Santa Fe plain, where a relative of theirs called Asa, along with a group of Jewish gauchos, had recently established a farming cooperative.

Great-grandma Sara had blossomed into a young woman with large, deep-set eyes. For some reason people tended to find her presence intimidating. She was one of those people whose authority rests upon the unswerving manner in which they remain silent, and whose greatest mystery resides in nobody quite knowing if they have some mystery about them. However that may be, Sara's dreams of the New World did not involve working on the land. Since her father Abraham had no intention either of spending the rest of his days living in a commune, as soon as he was able to he and a business partner opened a boarding house in Buenos Aires.

The establishment opened its doors in the heart of El Once neighborhood, an authentic Jewish quarter back then. Among the clientele were people newly arrived from the provinces, traveling salesmen, and a handful of pensioners with no other home. Abraham, my grandmother Dorita recalled, "declared himself orthodox, but he was a bit of a rogue. A crafty devil who was orthodox only when it suited him." Apparently my great-great-grandfather possessed certain traits making him the perfect candidate for being Argentine: a good talker, funny but authoritarian, apt to break his own rules, not entirely Jewish, an émigré and a host to immigrants.

With her mother Lea's consent or silence, Sara worked seven days a week at the boarding house in El Once. She did so with the apathy of an exiled princess, turning her large, deep-set eyes to the wall. Until Jonás (who as his own daughter Dorita liked to point out, "was no Don Juan") fell in love with her. Angered at the way Sara was being exploited, Great-grandpa Jonás resolved to move into the boarding house for a while. Amid the stirrings he felt over these injustices and other stirrings his cousin produced in him, it's hardly surprising Jonás begged her to marry him. My great-grandmother accepted without any great joy, with a wintry resignation. Jonás advised her against telling her parents, doubled the number of classes he gave, and a few months later they went to the registry office together. Before eloping, Great-grandma Sara remembered to leave a tray of freshly baked *barenikes* on the table, so as not to disrupt the day's menu. As she walked off carrying her luggage, my great-great-grandparents Abraham and Lea stood in the boarding house doorway and hurled insults at her by way of goodbye: as well as a daughter, they were losing an obedient employee.

The young couple moved into a room in a tenement block on Calle Lavalle. Having not yet graduated in dentistry, my great-grandfather continued to give Yiddish and Spanish classes, as well as receiving the occasional patient behind a curtain he had installed to partition off his surgery from the bed. According to my grandmother Dorita, who had a memory for figures that would astonish any accountant, Jonás brought home less than eighty pesos a month. Although I couldn't begin to work out how much that was, I assume it was a pittance.

With only a couple of pending exams to complete his degree, Great-grandpa Jonás ran into Bernardo Houssay, the future Nobel Prize winner. Not exactly adored by his students, Professor Houssay took pleasure in browbeating them with his knowledge.

A world authority on the human metabolism, Dr. Houssay fostered a kind of anti-Semitism which, given his specialty, could be described as visceral. On five consecutive occasions Houssay refused to pass Jonás, whose prior work had been impeccable. My great-grandfather repeated the same exam over and over, stubbornly believing his professor would eventually recognize his efforts. There came a point when Sara, who had helped him prepare so many times, could have passed the exam herself. The solution, however, came through rather more expeditious means. One morning several students marched into Houssay's office, dragged him to the Faculty entrance, took him by the shoulders and, without any great scientific protocol, threw him down the steps. I've never been able to ascertain whether my great-grandfather took part in that thuggish solution. The fact is, that year he finally passed the subject, thanks to a sudden access of benevolence on the part of Dr. Houssay, who today graces the square outside the Faculty of Medicine with his name.

Sara and Jonás's eldest daughter, my grandmother Dorita, was born in 1924, when my great-grandfather was just about to graduate. The couple decided to leave Buenos Aires as soon as he got his degree, since there was a greater demand for dentists outside the capital. Jonás took out a small loan to set himself up (alarmingly precise, my grandmother Dorita reckoned it was five hundred pesos) and for a while ceased his activities in the party.

My great-grandfather clearly recalled the Tragic Week in Argentina and the pogrom during Yrigoyen's first government. The president had won the election courtesy of a suffrage as universal as it was symptomatic: made up of only native-born or naturalized males. Even though the electoral laws excluded the majority of workers and immigrants, this rise of the middle class to power worried the elites, who rehearsed with Yrigoyen the putschist tendency they later perfected against Perón. Metalworkers had begun to demand improved conditions: following the First World War the sector was in a terrible state, salaries had collapsed, the working day was eleven hours, Sundays weren't always a rest day, and everyone was talking about the Russian Revolution. Strikes broke out amongst dock workers and at Talleres Vasena, where they manufactured mailboxes. Ports and mailboxes: the entire history of migrations is encapsulated there.

Jonás had watched the marching workers from behind his round spectacles, just as he watched the police respond to one death with another five. The demonstrators stormed through the city in homage to the victims. Vacillating, the government refrained from suppressing them, and let the army intervene; they soon silenced the streets. In some neighborhoods, the self-styled Liga Patriótica Argentina (Argentine Patriotic League) set up private militias, especially in the Jewish quarters of El Once and Villa Crespo, with the avowed intention of eliminating "foreign agitators." Armed with rifles, nightsticks, and all-powerful national blue and white armbands, the militias arrested every man with a beard they could lay their hands on to interrogate and teach a lesson. The clean-shaven Jonás escaped this educative experience.

Poale Zion's headquarters also suffered an opportune fire. Men with rifles surrounded the Hotel de Inmigrantes, decorating it with a concise slogan: "Jews to Russia." My great-grandfather told himself he already knew that part of the world. The patriotic patrols feared that a Bolshevik revolution would follow the strikes: you had to be especially careful with Russians and Jews. Those were the exact words one of my great-grandfather's neighbors came out with, as he opened his mouth in Jonás's old dentist's chair. Smiling grimly as he approached him with his drill, Jonás asked him if he hadn't realized that the man he was in front of was pretty much both those things. Sure, and my grandma's a streetcar, the neighbor retorted, clenching his jaw all of a sudden.

So my still very young great-grandparents embarked on a third exodus. They stayed in Moisés Ville just over a year. From there they moved to neighboring Sunchales, at that time a small community of Italian immigrants without a single dentist among them. There Sara, Jonás and their baby girl lived in a house with a well and magnificent peach trees, "giant Royals, big, white and juicy, a variety that doesn't exist anymore," Dorita used to say, "like so many things nowadays!"

As the only person with any medical knowledge in Sunchales, Jonás enjoyed a certain reputation. As a result, the family could afford to buy a second-hand car, "one like the Chicago gangsters had." Jonás would go around the region visiting patients in neighboring towns. Sometimes they paid him in money, at others in hens. On one occasion, his vehicle overturned on the road. Jonás emerged unscathed, but had to watch the frantic hens escape out of the windows of his gangster automobile and scatter across the endless plains. During those months my great-uncle Cacho, Dorita's brother, came into the world. They say Cacho weighed eleven pounds when he was born, making him more of a meteorite than a baby.

In 1931, not long after the fascist coup led by General Uriburu, my great-grandfather confirmed that his head was irrevocably in Buenos Aires, and so the family returned to the capital. With the money they'd put aside, Jonás was able to pay off their debts. Yet, as grandma Dorita would reproach him with a hint of admiration, he never managed to make his fortune: he was in the habit of treating his regular patients for free, and spent much of his working day reading. In a bizarre coincidence of genealogies, the family's new home was on Calle Uriburu, named for the putschist general's uncle. Jonás never went back to acting, but he kept up the custom of taking Dorita to every premiere of Lorca's, his great platonic love. Jonás devoted his energies to founding the Central Organization of Jewish Secular Schools. He saw the first center open on Calle Sarmiento, followed soon after by a second on Calle Gurruchaga. Both received the name of the Yiddish author and humorist Scholem Aleichem. There are few living witnesses to those days, which is why each one of their recollections is something of a miniature resurrection.

Moshé Korin, educator, and cultural director of the AMIA (Asociación Mutual Israelita Argentina), attended one of Jonás's talks when he was still at elementary school. I am appropriating Mr. Korin's childhood memory so that for an instant in the text he wrote I can hear my great-grandfather, whom I never knew: "Sporting his impeccable bow tie, Dr. Kovensky addressed his audience with characteristic vigor and conviction in the Spanish language. It was unusual for a guest speaker to talk in Spanish to a gathering at the Scholem Aleichem centers. Most speakers used Yiddish, because over ninety percent of the audience were Eastern European immigrants. And for us, their children, even though we were born in Argentina, Yiddish was our real mother tongue." And so, by mixing his native language with Spanish, my great-grandfather became who he was. Combining his allegiances to forge his own identity. In this new phase, Jonás took part in drafting the new statute for the AMIA, which democratized its internal election process, as well as coordinating assistance for Jewish victims of the Second World War. He became as sought after by his social milieu as he was missed by his family: his commitments were often in other homes, on other streets, other fronts.

Meanwhile, in their apartment on Calle Uriburu, grandma Dorita and great-uncle Cacho wasted no opportunity to quarrel. Sara could hear their adolescent squabbles from the kitchen. She would sigh, count to three, four, ten, before going to see what the fuss was about. She would glare at her daughter, and without raising her voice declare: Leave your brother alone, can't you see he suffers from his nerves? My great-uncle Cacho's nerves would become a family obsession. It would seem only natural for him to do everything he could not to disappoint them, and aged eighteen he was diagnosed with a peptic ulcer.

The year after that, Dorita met her future husband. The year after that, Perón won his first election. And the year after that Perón's wife made her first official trip abroad. Franco gave her a warm welcome and was glad to see the back of her when he discovered that Señora Perón was more than willing to air her opinions, and wasn't as sympathetic toward the armed forces as her husband was. Aggrandized by her diminutive, Evita was cheered by crowds in Madrid's Plaza de Oriente. The whole of Argentina watched the scene in black and white. In the meantime, Great-grandpa Jonás ramped up his political activities. Great-grandma Sara continued to accompany him, but was already starting to resemble the portrait on a black background that I knew.

Whenever my father visited him as a boy, Jonás made an effort to compensate his absences through dentistry: my father would literally end every visit with his mouth open. "Brush your teeth, kid," was Jonás's most consistent advice, as if it encoded some legislative kind of cleanliness, a sort of moral mouthwash. In-depth check-ups were also common. If my father cried out in pain during these procedures, Jonás would snap: "No, no, that's impossible." It seemed that, in matters of odontology, my great-grandfather also employed utopian thinking.

Many years later, in her apartment on Calle Libertad, facing Sara's stern portrait, I would drink *mate* with grandma Dorita and listen to her arguing with aunt Ponnie. The *idishe mame* and her youngest daughter disagreed about Israel. As they spoke, I imagined Jonás's distant voice underneath, overlaid by other voices that had arrived on these shores; it was like a chorus of echoes. Dorita made *barenikes* and chocolate mousse, served me tremendous helpings, and told me about the first attacks by those who would later make up the PLO and Al-Fatah, "followers of Arafat, who pretends to be nice as pie now, you see?, but I haven't forgotten how as a youth he took part in the massacres at the *kibbutzim*, their prime objective was the destruction of Israel, that's exactly what it says in the political agenda of Hamas, or Iran for example, and they expect Israel to disarm?" I don't know, grandma, I said doubtfully. "Yes, yes, they carried out bloodthirsty massacres, sadly that became the norm on both sides, and now it's our daily bread." Our daily bread: that's what my grandmother said, and I was struck by the way she spoke about dead people and then moved on to food, hunger, as she filled my plate once more. "But, mom," my aunt Ponnie grew impatient, "stop forcing this stuff on the boy. We can't go through life believing we're always right because there was a genocide or because we were persecuted. How long are we going to avoid talking about all the atrocities for fear of whipping up antisemitism? Why don't you tell him about the settlements, or, I don't know, the massacre at Deir Yassin, or what's going on in Gaza?" "The boy needs to know both versions," insisted Dorita, "what you're saying is what he'll hear out there." I don't know, I said.

"Under Stalin," my grandmother insisted, "in Russia there were anti-Semitic purges, and the communists abandoned the Jewish communists." "How is that relevant?" Ponnie cut in. "It's very relevant, because back then the State of Israel was in its infancy, and had to throw itself into the arms of the Americans. They're the ones who make all the rules." Dorita was fired up, waving her arms about. "That's precisely my point," said my aunt. "What kind of rules are we talking about here? About a country with a Jewish majority, or a country only for Jews? The problem is, both sides have turned what was essentially a territorial dispute into a sacred mission, a global religious conflict. Which is a lot harder to resolve." "Of course, my dear. But aren't extremists like Hamas also questioning, and I'm talking about terrorists here, not Arabs, our way of interpreting culture, freedom of the press, secular education, women's rights, all those things, which go way beyond any territorial dispute?" "Okay, Mom, but Israel today isn't the greatest defender of secular values either, is it? Besides, terrorism doesn't simply begin when a crazy person straps a bomb to himself in the middle of the street, and of course there you have to take action. The question is, what are we doing wrong that makes a five-year-old kid think about becoming a terrorist in twenty years time, don't you see? Otherwise, we'll never get anywhere." "Look, my girl, listen to me, I don't know if you remember when . . ."

My head rocked from side to side and I didn't know what to say. Although I was incapable of expressing it at the time, it seemed to me that in some sense there were parallels. Israel had been created after a war, when nobody would have wanted to take in all those survivors and displaced people. They needed to be given a piece of land, a gilded cage, or at least so I'd heard my schoolmate Mizrahi's father say. But then as a result the Palestinians became exiles, due to the actions of another people who had always been just that. Which is why I thought Jews and Palestinians had more reasons to identify with each other than to hate one another. If Scholem Aleichem was the Yiddish author grandma Dorita had translated when she was young, *Scholem Aleichem* also meant "peace be with you," and on television I had seen Arabs greet each other with the words *Salam Aleikum*. A greeting so sonorous, so similar, Scholem Aleichem, Aleikum Salam, peace be with both of you.

Outside the window of the Calle Libertad apartment, afternoon faded and slid down the far side of the dividing wall. My great-grandmother Sara's portrait, hanging next to the cat painted by Alonso, appeared to slip sideways into night. Aren't you still hungry, sweetie?, asked grandma.

# 28

AT SCHOOL I had two Jewish classmates. By that I mean two who knew for sure they were Jewish. These were Emsani and Mizrahi. Mizrahi was a River fan, endlessly on the move; despite having a quick temper, he knew how to appreciate a joke. Emsani was a Boca fan, immensely studious, and under no circumstance would he tolerate anyone touching his hair. His mane was unlike any other. Soft, springy, with frothy curls. Golden and impossible to comb. Anyone who touched Emsani's hair (and a fair number of us succumbed to that temptation) instantaneously received, without a word, a violent slap. Just one, and no more: he would swing round, deliver the slap, and calmly return to his seat. As the school year progressed, Emsani's untouchable crown acquired a mythical status that led us to venerate it like the holy relic of a saint or a prophet.

The thing I most envied about them was that they followed a different calendar. Emsani and Mizrahi seemed to live in two worlds at once, in ours and in a separate, older, or more convincing one. They observed feast days which we others didn't, they knew stories we'd never heard of. They were amphibious. Or they had two heads. Did I say we? Not quite. Mizrahi and Emsani observed the *sabbath*, frequently attended *bar mitzvahs* and their diet seemed mysterious. At the same time, my other classmates had confirmations, went to catechism classes and on Sundays they munched on wafers. They knew how to repent, and on top of that they were always forgiven. I wasn't even baptized, I had a hard time feeling guilty, and on Sundays I didn't even make a pilgrimage to La Bombonera stadium. My calendar was that of a castaway: I wasn't them, nor was I us.

I went through a phase of crossing myself whenever I passed a church. I delighted in the warm approval on the old ladies' faces when they saw me do this. But I nearly always got distracted or touched the wrong shoulder when making the sign of the cross. That made me feel doubly an impostor. As for my fantasy of trying to be Jewish like my two classmates, I was forced to rule that out and accept defeat after Mizrahi explained to me the secret of his foreskin.

One morning, while Mr. Renis was taking register, I noticed Emsani eyeing me inquisitively. What are you staring at, moron? Nothing, nothing. So why the hell are you still staring? It's nothing, it's nothing, it's just, you aren't a Jew are you, Neuman? Geez, no, Emsani, for real: I tried but I couldn't. Yeah, but your surname. What about my surname, sad-ass? My mom told me if it's written like that, with one "n," you are for sure. For sure what? A Jew, you dummy! My parents never told me that. Really? I swear! Well, ask your dad, you'll see.

I didn't manage to see myself as Jewish (let alone Catholic), and if I ever was, I had no idea. Regarding that, Mizrahi confirmed one day that I was a lost cause. We were walking in El Once, for all I know close to where my great-grandparents Jonás and Sara lived during the early years of their marriage. Koreans lived in the neighborhood now, many of them selling sneakers like those worn by Emsani and Mizrahi, only less expensive. We were leaving from school, and Mizrahi was coming back to my place for a snack. I confided to him about my conversation with Emsani concerning my surname. Then Mizrahi, who understood about these things, enlightened me. He asked me what my mother was, and I told him a violinist. He said yes, he knew that, and not to be such a moron, but apart from that was my mom a Jew or not. I had to admit no one had ever asked me that before. I hesitated briefly and then tentatively said no, I didn't think so. He shook his head sorrowfully and told me in that case I should forget it, as I could never be one. And then we started to talk about soccer.

# 29

WHO WOULD HAVE thought that when my grandmother Dorita was twenty she was "cripplingly shy." Or so she told us breezily when we asked about her younger years. She was very tied to her parents and the social circles they moved in. Jonás and Sara's acquaintances included many interesting people, but few youngsters her age. In addition, Dorita would go beet red whenever a boy came over to say hello.

In the hope it might take her mind off things a little, her parents enrolled her at La Hebraica, a Jewish social club and athletic center. She didn't learn to swim there, or indulge in any other activity that required moving one leg after the other. "What do you expect, at home the only thing we exercised was our noddle," Dorita explained as she served herself *mates* and rubbed her ankles with little grimaces of pain. My grandmother didn't win any medals or acquire any special knowledge at La Hebraica; but there, at least, she had a curious romance.

Grandma Dorita met Grandpa Mario through a notice board. Or, more precisely, she saw an article he'd written posted on the club wall. The subject of the article was atomic energy. The year was 1945: the issue was still barely publicized although, alas, totally topical. Another kind of energy, of a more endogenous nature, must have stirred inside the inquisitive Dorita. She instantly wanted to know who had written the article. Somebody told her its author had been locked up in Devoto jail for taking part in a student protest. Dorita asked if the young man was a student of physics and was told no, he was doing medicine. My grandmother was surprised, and maybe she blushed as well. Like a beet.

Together with a group of girl friends, Dorita went to visit the jailed La Hebraica students, who were expecting to be released at any moment. They took them cakes, cigarettes, and news. Among them was Mario, who spent all day reading anthropology textbooks in his cell, enveloped in a long grey overcoat, and didn't participate in his friends' passionate debates. He whispered sheepishly that he'd been arrested by mistake, this was the first time he'd been on a protest, and he didn't give two hoots about either Farrell or Perón. My grandmother became more and more intrigued by this young man who seemed to be the antithesis of a hero. Meanwhile, my grandfather, in that deliberately passive way of his, let her be curious about him.

As soon as he was released, Mario returned home with his grey overcoat infested with lice. My great-grandmother Lidia greeted him with a frown. She gave him an avalanche of homemade food and an insult it took him ages to forgive: rather than dispatch to the cleaners that flowing garment, companion, and witness to his captivity, she threw it straight into the garbage. So my grandfather's brief adventure as a protestor, like so many other things that embarrass families, ended up in the trash can of oblivion.

Soon Mario and Dorita started to meet alone. "The truth is we got on," that's how my grandmother summed it up elliptically, and all of a sudden I could indeed picture her as a young girl blushing in male company. And so, getting on remarkably well, they decided to write an article together. Their chosen subject proved quite unexpected: ambidextrous children. That's how they seduced each other, swapping hands. Mario promised to tackle the medical aspect of the question, while Dorita dealt with the educational part. A few years later, Mario would himself learn to be ambidextrous. A surgeon with a rock-steady hand, he was the only person I ever saw light a match one-handed. As for the article, it never got written. My young grandparents soon devoted themselves to other manual dexterities and cared for other children.

Aunt Silvia was the first. My father, the second. In 1955, year of the so-called *Revolución Libertadora*, President Perón had to leave the country and Grandma Sara, this world. She did so without complaint, turning her face to the wall. At the time, Dorita was pregnant with her third and last child. Since it was to be a girl, she decided to follow tradition and name her after her deceased mother. However, Dorita's youngest daughter rejected that funereal legacy. As soon as she could think for herself, the little girl, who had inherited Sara's disconcerting eyes, felt an intense dislike for her given name. I hate it, I hate it, she would declare angrily when she came home from school. So she decided to change her name. On account of her long hair, which she wore in a pony tail, she chose *Ponnie*. That was exactly how she spelled it out one day and that's what she came to be called.

My aunt, weaver of tapestries and fan of Brazil, my indomitable, galloping aunt Ponnie.

After his wife died, grandpa Jonás remarried. Anita seemed like the antithesis, not to say the antidote, to my great-grandmother Sara: cheerful, funny, and raunchy. Like a good Marxist, Jonás embraced the dialectic. His new wife wore pants and, even more outrageous, drove her own car. Grandma Anita, younger than anyone.

# 30

I REMEMBER YOU well, Mario. I recollect your warm voice, your handlebar mustache, your generous forehead. That cautious smile of yours. You drank a lot of *mate*. You were never a late riser, grandpa, apart from the odd Sunday. I guess grandma Dorita and I must have brought you quite a few breakfasts in bed, but I recall just one. Let's settle for that. Let's prepare it slowly.

Dorita and I are in the kitchen. She's giving me instructions. There's an old, rather cumbersome tray, green I think. Are there *Criollitas* crackers? Maybe not, these ones are darker, whole-grain. Some cream cheese. *Mendicrim* comes to mind, I'm not sure. And *mate*, that's for sure. Grandma and I creep down the corridor, unnecessarily since we're going to wake you up anyway. The new day dawns overcast, but it dawns, the light struggles in, and when finally it makes up its mind, it's a white torrent that floods the apartment and washes away all fears. I clamber onto your bed, and find you awake, and you smile, pretending to be surprised and I believe you, you can't believe it, breakfast! How wonderful, my boy. And I give you a kiss, or you give me one, like sandpaper. You didn't shave much on weekends.

I remember you well, grandpa. I didn't know you properly. Might I know what team you support? You asked me once, driving your orange Dodge. Boca! I shouted. But they're a bunch of klutzes! you said, peering at me in the rear-view mirror. You're the ones who are klutzes! I protested. And that, precisely that, is the laugh of yours I remember. The one spilling out of you then, when you were so pleased to know that, even if I didn't support your team, your grandson at least liked soccer. A frank laugh, with mouth wide open, not over-exaggerated, a nice laugh, grandpa, congrats.

I also have a night, any night. We were watching a game on TV. I know Vélez Sarsfield was playing. I can't remember the other team: Ferro Carril Oeste perhaps? We were sitting on the bed in what had been Aunt Ponnie and Aunt Silvia's room. You were explaining the players' movements like somebody wielding a piece of chalk or a surgeon's knife, telling me that real soccer is played without the ball. Aged six, that seemed a really strange idea to me. And you were such a doctor, or such a pain in the ass, that at half time you made me turn my back on the TV because it was bad for my eyes. I did as I was told, and covered my face with a pillow. You meanwhile carried on watching the adverts. Grandpa, aren't you worried about your sight? Forget it, it's already ruined.

The very last thing I saw you do was plant a tree. Damn it, you really knew how to die symbolically. It was a weeping willow. On the little plot of land you and Dorita and my parents bought. Near Monte Grande, on the way to the airport. We planted the willow together. Well, I couldn't even lift the spade; you sweated too much. Lean, almost hairless, your pectorals sagging slightly, you plunged the spade deeper and deeper, as though you already wanted to enter the earth.

You who were usually so easy-going got irritated over nothing, you were grumpy. And you knew why. Better than anyone, of course, wily old doctor. It was your heart. The roots weren't properly watered. Nobody worried much about your health, least of all you: just like Great-grandpa Jacobo (are our self-destructive habits inherited, too?) you smoked secretly in the bathroom; like an aged child, you took suspiciously long walks and came back sucking mentholated sweets. You continued to overwork. You never wanted to be your own patient.

I'm jotting things down in your notebook now: I got hold of one of those pads you had in your office a long, long time ago. At first I considered preserving it intact, blank, like a relic. But then I thought you'd have preferred me to use it. And, when it was full, you'd have let me have another. And so, slowly, carefully, I use up your pad. Small, narrow pages. I read your letterhead once more.

Dr. Mario Neuman, yes. Mat. 9433, I don't understand that number. Assistant Professor of Anatomy at the Buenos Aires Faculty of Medicine, a teacher, of course, my father and my brother Diego had to get it from somewhere. Head of Surgery at the Policlínico Ferroviario Central, they say you were an extremely dedicated doctor, that you went to the public hospital on Sundays to change light bulbs and visit patients, that you took care of their affairs, you were their grandfather too. General Surgery: apparently you excelled as a thoracic surgeon; I remember you at mealtimes using the knife to strip the chicken bones.

And then, in the bottom left-hand corner of the page, your private consulting hours: Mondays, Wednesdays and Fridays. Hey, today is Wednesday; though quite late. Would you see me anyway? Could I get an appointment with you just by calling 983 5112, a number that no longer exists? What would happen if I dialed it? I know you took out of hours calls. Also on your home number 784 6122.

What if somebody suddenly picks up at the other end? Maybe I'd hear a frank, open, not over-exaggerated laugh. I'm not sure, in emergency cases like today's, I'd prefer to see you in person at your office: Calle Medrano 237, ground floor, Apartment A. No stairs to climb. I simply enter the building and bump into your shadow.

I scarcely knew you, Mario. I remember you well. Increasingly, as time goes by. I recall the future, the years we didn't spend together. I see how they would have been, look how they are.

I know you weren't a hero, Mario. Heroes are portraits seen from too far away. I'm also getting to learn about your lies, your silences, your evasions, but so what? We all need a grandfather, and so I insist on writing to you. Since you aren't there, let me invent you. Mario, grandpa. Words can sometimes leave us so lonely, and yet it's a good thing they exist.

# 31

MY BROTHER DIEGO began to like soccer the moment I convinced him everyone wanted the ball because it was full of gold nuggets. After that my little brother played with more enthusiasm, although for a while he absolutely insisted on being the goalie.

Diego had a black tooth, a rotten milk tooth which he was on the point of losing because of my soccer lessons and my tackles. It pained me to look at this rotten tooth, while he dreamed of it falling out so that a certain fairy he'd heard about would come to reward him, possibly with gold nuggets. My brother liked soccer more and more. I vowed to myself I'd never tell him that to play well you had to be a tough guy.

One day I bought him a blue and gold Boca Juniors shirt, and so my brother was a Boca fan throughout his short time as a child in the country of his ancestors. Some of them, in their own way, had also come in search of nuggets of gold. My brother met hardly any of them. He never managed to lose his blackened tooth there.

He scarcely had time for his memory to be filled with tales from the other shore. Doubtless though, he still remembers them. My brother, who also dreamed of being a player one day. My Spanish brother Diego, who is left-handed and in spite of everything, Argentine.

# 32

MANLINESS: WASN'T THAT a tautology? Did we really need to prove we were something we already supposedly were?

Learning manliness from men, the highest praise I ever received from my classmates happened on the day when, during our recess, I accidentally vanquished Fatty Cesarini, who was in fact my friend. Without being the strongest boy in our class (that honor belonged unquestionably to the brutish Averame, followed by Nardi with his huge bearlike body), Fatty Cesarini was scary when he lost his temper. As for me, prior to that day I'd been in very few fights. I tried to wound my opponents with words, to weaken them with insults rather than fists. Not that I was by any means a pacifist: I was simply terrified. Terrified others would break my bones, make me bleed or smash my face in. Terrified too, and I this recall with utter clarity, of throwing a punch. I felt perfectly at ease exchanging slaps, and I loved to shove someone, that classic prelude to male confrontation when man and ape are on the point of once more converging. And yet, beyond that threshold of controlled violence something held me back: to my frustration I felt incapable of sinking my fist into somebody else's face. Perhaps that's why I imagined it so often, every time I closed my eyes.

I found it intriguing the way we all tacitly understood and respected physical hierarchies and their distribution of power. It was obvious who the strongest were, and nobody ever openly challenged them. Nor do I recall any fights between them, or even among those in the second strongest group. As if somehow they all considered themselves representatives of the same privilege which they had to protect.

In this second group were Fernández, due to his silent force, Alonso due to his karate skills, Emsani due to his legendary short fuse, and maybe Paz, slow on his feet but devastating. Immediately after, and to some extent overlapping with them, vying for the final positions of honor, were the wiry Guerrero, the snakelike Ríos, the frantic Yepes, my neighbor Ramos, Mizrahi (who was short but very feisty), possibly also Tagliabue, and of course Fatty Cesarini. Then came the middle-class fighters, a populous group where you did your best to assert your own violence, in order not to sink to the bottom rung, the small inferno of the schoolyard: the weaklings.

Their members wavered between impotence and surrender, obliged as they were on a daily basis to suffer all manner of threats, intimidations, and cruelties. If you were one of the weaklings, you damn well better find a protector in one of the higher groups, or else try to hand out candy, share your sandwiches, lend your toys, have the best-ever birthday parties. Failing that, you were lost. Weaklings seldom put up a struggle: knowing escape was impossible, they would instantly submit to humiliation.

If my liking for sports, and perhaps my verbal aggression, allowed me not to be wholly identified as one of them, it wasn't enough. And so, in the interest of securing my precarious status, I needed to be involved in an occasional scuffle. And the problem was that it was a while since I'd last demonstrated my supposed manliness. As we advanced through school, fights became more conclusive, more precise: in sixth or seventh grade, any boy who still hadn't punched someone in the face was suspected of belonging to the inferior group. This was the danger I confronted, and I felt unable to avoid it.

In schoolyard bouts, the onlookers behaved according to the category of the two adversaries. If a couple of weaklings clashed, we would give it our perfunctory attention before stepping in to separate them, as if such a pathetic spectacle didn't merit the spilling of blood. If the combatants belonged in one of the higher groups, we would form a tight circle round them. We'd chorus their names, egg on one, then the other, enjoying the thrill of the uncertain outcome and, when the contest or recess was over, the winner would be decided by separate judges conferring with one another. That's why the highest praise I ever received from my classmates was when, without knowing quite how, I managed to throw a dazed punch for the very first time in my life, and almost by accident hit Fatty Cesarini's angry face.

He had been on top in the fight. He grunted. He roared. He pounced on me, scarlet with rage. My panic had chosen to show itself as speed, and so far I had dodged his blows. During one lunge, however, my right hand had gone up to block his punch and had landed fortuitously on my opponent's mouth. That's all it was, a blind strike, a misunderstanding. But the luck of apes would have it that Fatty Cesarini's fleshy lower lip began to bleed. And blood was always the clincher. Astonished and with no visible wounds on my own face, throughout the next class I received all manner of claps on the back: it was true, I wasn't one of the weaklings, so I could continue to claim my petty privileges. Fatty Cesarini on the other hand needed a couple of quick skirmishes to regain his rightful place. He and I didn't stop being friends.

As time went by, at school we adopted the habit of sneaking up behind our classmates, grabbing them by the waist, and feigning the act of sodomy with a pelvic thrust. It was our prank, our war cry, our smoldering manhood. And, why deny it, it titillated us. Things went further at the YMCA, an athletic club where, as well as competing until we dropped, going camping like good explorers, traveling to fight to the death with other swimming clubs, yelling and jostling each other in the gyms, there were the changing rooms. And in the changing rooms, manly as ever, some of my naked companions would offer one another their erect members, or brace their arms against the lockers and arch their backs, awaiting the onslaught. Laughter and yells and communal showers followed.

I remember one day Iribarne, at our apartment on Avenida Independencia, hesitating for a moment. We were eleven or twelve. We shared a sweet friendship, one of the few real ones I enjoyed at school. I admired his sense of humor and the fact he almost never needed to fight. We were drinking milky coffee. We did our homework together and occasionally, we'd entertain ourselves with the game of clasping each other from behind. Uneasy all of a sudden, Iribarne asked:

"Hey, Neuman, isn't what we're doing gay?"

"But we're not gay, you idiot!"

"Yeah, you're right, what a jerk," he said and nodded thoughtfully.

# 33

HAVING MORE THAN one shore isn't something to feel sorry over. Having origins in two places can duplicate time. As a child, my great-grandfather Jonás exchanged Grodno for the Pampa. As he approached old age, he also learned to transfer his affections.

Great-grandma Sara had passed away in the spring of 1955, when in Buenos Aires memories of the smoke from the bombings of Plaza de Mayo were still fresh. A few years later, Jonás got remarried to Ana María Naidich, whom we inevitably had to call Anita.

Also a widow, cheerful, infectious, and brazen, Anita was—in a few words—a great-grandma in jeans. Her hunger for youth puzzled the youngest members of the family: her risqué conversation captivated everyone. Anita beguiled without being a beauty. Her face wasn't what you'd call attractive. Or her eyes exotic. Nor were her lips a cupid's bow. She cleverly arranged her sparse hair over her brow. Mind you, her legs were still shapely, and she never ceased to display them. Stretching back over generations, the family's sexual repression seemed to unravel with Great-grandma Anita. The relationship between affection and body were transformed. You might say the family began to touch one another when she came on the scene. No one can recall her now without chuckling.

Persuaded that our fate is always the one we're living in the moment, Anita loved to fool around with Grandpa Jonás, who doubtless discovered the obvious at the age of sixty. I wonder whether he also started paying more attention to his clothes, to the way his hair looked before he gave a talk. Probably my great-grandmother learned her philosophical flirtatiousness from her own mother, Doña Genia. Somebody once asked Doña Genia why she never wore black. She was over eighty at the time, and replied that she'd wear black when she was old.

Anita drove her own car, too fast it has to be said. She smoked with cinematic archness. And she had the habit of playing poker with her mother; both of them delighting in betting. My great-grandma complained that Doña Genia cheated, but that was neither here nor there, because after the last game they'd both get tipsy on the winner's takings. Two of my father's favorite childhood toys were in fact a card shuffling machine and the colored chips mother and daughter used for placing bets. Aged two or three, I myself played with those raffish toys. I've even been told that Great-grandma Anita tried to teach me the basic rules of poker before I was properly out of diapers.

Like a good hedonist, she had a flair for cooking wisely, that's to say: she could make a feast out of leftovers. Among her specialties were pastry *knisches* stuffed with potato or cheese, and *barenikes* seasoned with unbelievable sauces. Occasionally, when there was a family dinner, Anita's guests would come in smacking their lips to find her slumped on the sofa, claiming she had a terrible headache and apologizing for not having prepared any food. Only when she saw the look of dismay on her grandchildren's faces did she leap to her feet and run laughing into the kitchen to turn off the oven. Anita would never dream of complaining. I wonder if, as often happens with compulsively cheerful people, she cried at night when nobody could see her.

As if happiness were controlled by a pair of scales, Jonás was denied most of the pleasure he could have enjoyed. In 1967, he suffered a hemiplegic stroke and one of his shores no longer responded. The Six Day War had just broken out, and my great-grandfather failed to pronounce a single word on the subject. He lost the ability to speak, and would regain it only partially after prolonged efforts. My father was about to graduate from the Colegio Nacional de Buenos Aires, and would stop by to visit him and speak in hushed tones with Anita. Jonás strained every muscle to make himself understood. She, protecting herself with smiles, did her best to translate her husband.

Doña Genia had left Russia to get married in Junín, a town forever associated with Eva Perón. And so whenever Doña Genia told stories about Junín, she would begin humorously: "Evita and me . . ." Later she moved to Cruz del Eje, in Córdoba province, where a certain Doctor Illia practiced medicine. In this tiny town, Doctor Illia had half-jokingly promised Doña Genia that if ever he became president, she would be the first citizen invited to the Casa Rosada presidential palace. To her astonishment, shortly after he won the election, President Illia summoned her to a meeting in his office. The good doctor may be slow, but he's a man of his word, Doña Genia would often declare. Illia's opponents did indeed accuse him of being slow, as well as a bit dumb. He became the object of public ridicule; the press portrayed him as a tortoise. After the coup led by Onganía, whom the tortoise valiantly resisted until the army had to eject him from his shell in the presidential palace, Doña Genia saw Doctor Illia return to his tiny town, where he continued to live in the same modest circumstances as before.

My great-grandfather Jonás, progressively imprisoned in a silence that seemed littered with opinions, died in October 1973, the same week Perón reclaimed the presidency after twenty years in exile. The irony of fate would have it that my most anti-Peronist ancestors ended up seeing their anniversaries coinciding with the Peronist calendar. After Jonás's funeral, Doña Genia moved to Buenos Aires to live with her daughter until the end of her days, which by the way were many and generously soused in vodka. Twice widowed, Great-grandma Anita declared she was no longer interested in marriage. At her age, she insisted, she'd settle for men who were aroused by a good sense of humor.

"At this stage in life, you let sex take a back seat. The problem is men my age are so dull! Oh well, it's their loss."

Anita concealed her illness from the family until somebody became aware of her frequent hemorrhages. Grandpa Mario intervened and diagnosed bowel cancer, which, if caught in time, could perhaps have been treatable. What pains did you keep to yourself, Great-grandma? While undergoing some tests, Anita escaped, took herself to the hairdresser, and picked up a rug from the dry cleaner in passing. Once they'd examined all the results, they decided to operate on her, and for a few days she needed a catheter for her calls to nature. This gave rise to a series of scatological jokes which had the nurses who changed her bag in stitches. Hey, girls, she used to say to them, I'm the one who should be pissing myself, not you!

Hours before she entered the operating room, never to emerge, Anita received a visit from my father. When he asked how she was, my great-grandmother replied:

"Longing for a fuck, just in case. What do you want me to say, son, you're not a kid anymore. Pass me my mirror would you? It's over there, on the table."

# 34

IT WAS A box with a five-hundred-piece jigsaw puzzle inside. The puzzle showed a biker, poised in mid-air as he jumped through a ring of fire. I don't remember if I ever managed to finish it. And yet it was my favorite puzzle: in the box, besides the tiny pieces and their muffled rattle, I hid my stash of pornography.

Namely, a *Penthouse* magazine picturing a bikini-clad girl with disproportionate breasts, cradling a not very subtle watermelon in her arms. An anniversary issue of *Playboy* with no text, hallelujah, and more than a hundred pages of photos, which I'd got from Tagliabue in exchange for writing the essays Mr. Albanese set for us. A third magazine called *The Parrot* or *The Parakeet* or some similar bird, terribly printed but with a powerful effect on my senses. And a couple of issues of *Sex Humor*, also produced in Argentina, whose content was much more inventive.

Over time, new additions were incorporated into this repetitive repertoire (perhaps the most accurate epithet to describe these stirrings). I can remember, for example, a Brazilian issue of *Play-*

*boy*, whose Portuguese captions I found particularly conducive to fantasizing, as well as one of those magazines with explicit content that captivated me instantly only to gradually disappoint, as it didn't lend itself to reimaginings.

I kept all these together with the jigsaw puzzle of the kamikaze biker. My subterfuge was far from discreet: I'd take advantage of any quiet in the corridor to climb onto a stool, take down the box and head straight for the bathroom, with an exaggeratedly nonchalant air. As for my lengthy confinements, I imagine they were more or less understandable. I'm not sure if the maid thought the same when she walked in on me one day, magazines open wide, on my knees or something similar. Not particularly deductive, Silvina asked me what I was doing.

# 35

UP TO A certain point in my childhood, I refused to accept books. I refused to read them because I found it unbearable that my parents, grandparents, teachers, absolutely everyone insisted I did. And if grown-ups were unbearable and grown-ups read books, why follow their example? Given my early penchant for telling lies in all sincerity, it's quite possible that already back then I wanted to be a writer. I just didn't know yet that I liked to read.

If I began by rejecting books because I found older people unbearable, I started to need them when I realized I couldn't bear myself. I was desperate for advice. Asking grown-ups was clearly out of the question: even we desperate people have our pride.

One dull afternoon, on a weekend like any other, a friend of mine told me about a writer who was so frightening he robbed you of your fears. His name fascinated me: three concise, resolute words: Edgar. Allan. Poe. This guy had written short stories and poems. My friend liked his poems best. There's one poem, "The Raven," he said, that's even better than the movies we watch. Partly to annoy him, I chose the short stories, translated by another guy called Julio Cortázar. I took one of Poe's volumes, thanked him, and we said goodbye. Ever since that day I've called this friend The Raven.

The title of the opening story was "William Wilson." I began reading it warily; continued in amazement; finished it in shock. It was about somebody who meets his double. Somebody whom another person, identical to him, persecutes to the point of ruining his life. The story left me perplexed. I felt as though the character's tragic end struck a match in the room: there were also two "me"s in my life, and they were constantly quarrelling with one another. One was what everybody else saw, or wanted me to be. The other hid himself, secretly despised that impostor and wanted to take revenge on him. Most people only knew the first me. And, because I never managed to introduce them to the second me, I found myself unbearable.

The Raven called me to ask what I thought of the book. I played it down, replying: Humph, not bad. After we hung up, I rushed back to finish reading it.

A few days later, I was still thinking about Poe's story: perhaps there had never been two William Wilsons. William Wilson had always been one and the same person, but, like me, he found himself unbearable. Unless I wanted to end up like him, I reasoned, I mustn't fight my other me, but befriend him instead.

I went over to The Raven's place to return his book. I was grateful to him for not laughing at me when I asked to borrow some of Poe's poetry. Since The Raven also lived in San Telmo, in an old rambling house on Calle Perú, I became a regular visitor to his bookshelves.

The second author he recommended was quite odd. For starters, he was the same person who had translated Poe's stories. This discovery so amazed me that for some time I was convinced that all writers had translated one another. Basically, that was true. When I read Cortázar's *Cronopios and Famas,* I almost went crazy. The book was a list of useless instructions: it described with insane precision how to cry, how to blow your nose, or how to climb a staircase. I tried to follow the instructions about how to cry, and only ended up dying of laughter. I tried using a handkerchief the way the book prescribed, and nearly tied my fingers in a knot. I did all I could to climb the staircase in our building following those instructions, and was paralyzed on the first step. And yet, without really knowing why, it seemed to me there was some kind of truth in that absurd book. I read it twice. I had fun. I didn't get a thing.

One night, while I was thinking of the instructions for winding up a watch, I was called to dinner and arrived late. At the table, my father kept on scolding me. You're always late! And don't pull that face! Watch how you answer me back! Did you do your homework at least? It reminded me of school, where the whole day we were told how and when we should learn this or that, but were never asked if we were interested in learning those things.

Just a moment! There was something there. That was it, exactly: Cortázar's orders were written to be disobeyed.

It was a time of brutal discoveries, as everything obvious is. It turned out Jules Verne had written a stack of novels besides *Around the World in Eighty Days*; that Kafka had wanted to burn his own books; that Ray Bradbury was the author of those famous Martian chronicles; that Oliverio Girondo had written poems with non-existent words; that Frankenstein was the idea of a woman no one had told me about before; that Tom Sawyer was an invented character; that Borges wasn't born blind.

After reading almost all The Raven's books (actually, there weren't that many), I finally resolved to check out the ones my parents had, which they had so often offered me.

I waited until they both left for work. I went into their room. I climbed on a chair. I tilted my head to one side and began deciphering the spines. Among a host of unfamiliar names, I was surprised to come across books by Poe and Cortázar. I found several other volumes The Raven had lent me, including some by Silvina Ocampo. How was it possible that these treasures had been there all this time? It occurred to me then that grown-ups also felt double and alone.

# 36

WHEN MY MOTHER turned fourteen, Grandpa Jacinto took her to the Collegium Musicum. They caught the subway from Florida to Retiro, and from there took the number 101 bus to Calle Libertad. The same street where, a little further on, stood her future workplace: the Teatro Colón. The same street my grandmother Dorita moved to when she was widowed. Libertad, where dreams and fears resided.

The director of the Collegium Musicum youth orchestra was the celebrated maestro Evzen Radick. Of Czech origin, born in Croatia and educated in Paris, Maestro Radick had come to Argentina during the Second World War on a tour from which he never returned. Everyone knew him as *the old man*, Old Radick, although he wasn't so elderly and moved among the music stands with a nervous agility.

Legend had it that when he was young, if he ever was, Old Radick had been fortunate enough to play with virtuosos like Jacques Thibaud, Alfred Cortot, and Zino Francescatti. His precocious solo career seemed destined to be brilliant. But, during an ill-fated horseback ride, he had been thrown and broken his wrist. The injury didn't stop him from playing the violin, but it prevented him pursuing a top-level international career. Since then, Old Radick had dedicated himself to teaching, imparting the secrets of the instrument to his pupils and making them suffer in every key. The fact is, despite his eccentric methods, Argentina's finest musicians had passed through Radick's hands, through the wrathful memory of his broken wrist.

Pupils of Old Radick soon became familiar with the rigors of professional discipline: anyone leaving their pencil, eraser, or mute at home was instantly ordered to leave the rehearsal. Old Radick was a maestro of the old school: you shed blood to learn the notes. Your fingertips bled, but above all your pride.

On the eve of her audition at Collegium Musicum, my mother learned that one of the maestro's pupils had, to coin a phrase, been percussively praised at the prior rehearsal. Abruptly interrupting the orchestra, Old Radick had fixed the young girl with his gaze and told her that her sound was truly accomplished: never, declared Radick, had he heard anybody imitate a braying donkey so well. A perfect imitation, bravo, bravo!, the maestro applauded, inviting her fellow musicians to do the same. The poor young student had fled the hall in tears, while Old Radick bid her farewell shaking his head. If you can't survive me, he'd shouted after her, how will you survive the stage?

My teenage mother now walked through the front door of the Collegium Musicum and nervously extended her hand to the maestro, shaking the wrist of wrath.

In the audition Old Radick had granted her, my mother had to play a *concerto grosso* by Handel and a piece by Pergolesi. She must do so without stopping under any circumstances. My anxious grandfather Jacinto waited on the far side of the door. Galán? complained the maestro, Galán? Difficult to have any talent for the violin with a surname like that, Old Radick told my mother, surprised he hadn't taught her to play that way himself. Nearly all his pupils were descendants of German or eastern European Jews. At best, descendants of Italians. But Spaniards, how was that possible? Galán-Casaretto, maestro, my mother added as if by way of apology. Ah, well, that's a bit better, isn't it?, but not much, so, tell me, Señorita Galán, who is your teacher? My mother's teacher, aside from her own father, was Eduardo Acedo: his family was from Andalusia, my future land. Ah well, Acedo, Radick conceded, one of the few Argentine violinists who at least plays in tune, don't you agree?, but heavens, what an unfortunate surname you have, Galán, honestly, never mind, let's continue, child. Maestro Radick called all his female pupils *child*, and continued to do many years after he stopped teaching them, hey child, how are things, good to see you, but don't have too many kids, you need to keep studying, girl, don't you agree?

My mother was accepted, and joined the circle of youngsters who suffered voluntarily for the sake of their instrument. Old Radick would plug his ears and grimace whenever one of them played a slightly wrong note. Don't do what I tell you, he would say to his favorites, do something better! As for those who are no good, he would argue, best they find out now so they don't waste their time! His pupils ended up developing an early resilience to frustration, although many would secretly weep after leaving rehearsals at the Collegium or his private lessons. My mother would go round the block several times before ringing his bell, weighed down by her violin and her fear of failure, wondering whether to run away, thinking of the bar of music she couldn't quite get right, that damn bar at which Old Radick would undoubtedly interrupt her, arms akimbo, but child, what are you doing!

Maestro Radick had two sons, Prudencio and Pascual. Pascual, an oboist like my father, would in due course play with my mother at the Academia Bach: the music world is small and full of unisons. During her early rehearsals at the Collegium, Old Radick placed my mother at the back of the second violins. Gradually she moved through the music stands, until she was nominated assistant concertmaster and secured a place at the front, next to Prudencio. You have a strong back, child, he used to tell her, and that helps you bear the weight of the row. My mother, who'd always been slightly embarrassed about being broad-shouldered, smiled and bowed her head.

It was at the Collegium Musicum, in the midst of old Radick's calculated reprimands and insults, that my mother realized for sure she wouldn't be a schoolteacher or a psychologist, that she wanted to try to live by her instrument, for which in any case she already lived. Maestro Radick impressed upon her that to truly understand an instrument, she needed to appreciate all forms of art, that when a musician played they revealed the entirety of their culture. Either we make a whole world sound through our fingers, or we're merely typewriting, child, you understand?

My mother got to know other young people who shared the same perfectionism and the same desires. She would go out to the movies with them on Saturday afternoons after rehearsals, and they would have coffee in a splendidly luminous café on Calle Corrientes, a world away from high school and non-musical teachers. But, more than anything, in that orchestra she discovered what it felt like to share in raising an edifice of sounds on the surface of silence. Old Radick never refused to lend a piece of sheet music to any of his pupils. And it was rumored he had them all. In the maestro's legendary cupboard, crammed with manila files and annotations, you could find any piece of music ever written for violin. My mother turned to him on more than one occasion. Like many violinists, Old Radick was despotically organized, methodical to the point of obsession. He classified all of his papers according to genre, composer, opus number and so on. He would always lend originals, never copies. A responsible musician, child, should know how to care for sheet music as she would her own health, do you understand?

I like to picture you, mom, in a train to Retiro, a couple of plastic bags at your feet, your violin case on your lap and on the case some book or other, to see you like that, impossible, younger than me now, taking advantage of the journey to revise your fingering with your raven hair, groomed with the perfectionism of a violin player, mom, quick to respond to the wink of another young musician sitting opposite you, without a thought for time. Perhaps with Old Radick you cried less than you learned, the stage never forgives, child! I suppose that's why the stage was your home.

# 37

HE WOULD ARRIVE, small and upright, say hello to his daughter, chiding her briefly for the signs of fatigue on her face. Place his beret on the piano and ask where I was. At that very instant I was hurrying to lock myself in the bathroom, my fortress. Sitting on the toilet lid, I enjoyed a few moments of rebellion as I heard my mother's four-stringed voice, announcing it was time for Grandpa's lesson.

At the time, aside from biographies of composers, my grandfather Jacinto read only Borges and Balzac; authors who somehow between them embrace half the world's library. He adored Casal's cello playing, and continued to venerate the legacy of Sarmiento as if he'd known him in person. Despite having once declared he would never waste his time on grandchildren he hadn't asked for, every Thursday my grandfather Jacinto would quit his home in Florida suburb, cross the entire city on a train, then a bus, and an hour and a quarter later ring our bell. Always punctual, always upright. He greeted me sternly. He never asked how I was. And yet hidden in his pocket was a sweet.

Patiently, year after year, Thursday after Thursday, without ever catching a cold, my grandfather Jacinto would witness my extremely slow progress. "Little by little," he would repeat calmly. Then I grew. I lost interest in learning sheet music. Finally, when I turned twelve, I abandoned my violin lessons. My grandfather wasn't surprised.

I began to see him about once a month, when we went to Florida to visit him and my grandma Blanca. Jacinto continued playing every morning, taking his midday walks and rereading in the afternoon. When he felt he was done with Borges, he burned all his books. He did the same with the rest of his favorite authors. As if, having reached a conclusion about them, he wished to have the last word.

Extremely frail in his final years, he could no longer play his violin. It was then my grandfather felt the time had come for him to do what he must. Something grandma Blanca chose not to mention in her letter.

I still have imaginary exchanges with Jacinto. Sometimes he wins me over, sometimes I win him over. I still regret not practicing my scales more.

# 38

MY FATHER ALSO got to play under director Evzen Radick. This was at the Conservatorio Juan José Castro orchestra, and later in the Radio Nacional youth orchestra. In both places, and who knows where else, Old Radick was always present, ever more feared, ever more celebrated, increasingly tireless with age. Not having a car of his own, he used public transportation to travel between orchestras, moving from music to music, unfailingly punctual, as if he were also directing the concert of traffic on Buenos Aires's unpredictable streets. However, my father's experience of playing under the maestro's baton didn't inspire him much. He complained that Old Radick paid less attention to the wind section: the tough, caressable strings were his passion.

But my father had had his own maestro. For some time, he had been devotedly attending concerts by the Sinfónica Nacional and the Mozarteum Argentino wind quintet. He would always try to sit where nobody could block his view of oboist Pedro di Grimaldi's face and hands. Thanks to Di Grimaldi, my father succumbed to the sound of what was soon to be his instrument.

It was almost too late for him. My father had sung in choirs, studied musical appreciation, had mastered the recorder, and played a little piano. He had been in a percussion group at Collegium Musicum, where he'd studied under Antonio Yepes, father of my schoolmate Yepes. The music world is indeed small and full of unisons. My father wasn't lacking in musical experience, but he'd never had an oboe between his lips. It was almost too late. When he resolved to go to the maestro and ask if he'd give him lessons, Di Grimaldi received him with a solemn expression. My father declared how much he admired the maestro's sound, adored the oboe, and so on. Di Grimaldi, with what remained of his pomaded hair, his gestures as measured as a metronome, listened to him, and kept saying *aha*. He peered from behind his spectacles and pulled at his mustache. The whole of his pointed face seemed to direct itself toward one sole excess: his nose.

When my father had finished his speech, Di Grimaldi simply asked him how old he was. My father confessed to being seventeen, and maestro Di Grimaldi declared, pulling at his moustache:

"That's old. But we can try."

Things went quickly after that. My father began to practice with the urgency of someone who needs to run to reach his destiny. As the lessons progressed, a semblance of a smile appeared behind Di Grimaldi's mustache. Maestro Di Grimaldi used to listen to his pupils in the most peculiar posture, undoubtedly suited to his skinny body: he would swiftly cross his legs and tuck one ankle behind the other calf. His entwined limbs seemed about to form a treble clef. Di Grimaldi didn't look at his pupils once as they played. Head bowed, he shielded his brow with the edge of his hand, blinded perhaps by some emerging radiance.

My father was never taken to task by his teacher. Implicit in every one of his objections was an encouragement: a step back was a preparation for a bigger leap forward; a lack of progress, a mere hiatus prior to an evolution. Restrained in his judgments, Di Grimaldi seemed to possess a fiendish patience. If a pupil hadn't practiced enough, he would calmly repeat the previous lesson step by step. If someone didn't interpret a passage adequately, he would resort to his most famous remark. Slowly removing his hand from his brow, Di Grimaldi would raise his eyes and breathe out softly before saying:

"Ye-esss; but not yet."

Di Grimaldi always had an array of freshly sharpened pencils in front of him. He liked to spend his leisure on all kinds of handicrafts. His nimble, precise fingers were like a surgeon's: my father always looked for safe hands that would treat him well. Di Grimaldi taught him to prepare his oboe reeds. First you fastened them to the mouthpiece. Then you scraped them with a knife, which it was essential to sharpen regularly on a razor strop. He also insisted on the need to carry on scraping for several days, until you achieved the optimum sound. This type of manual skill was peculiar to Di Grimaldi and only suitable for obsessive personalities. I suspect I was born of two obsessions and a single ear.

Di Grimaldi's black bag: exaggerated harmony. Pages neatly ranged like an untouched pack of cards. Music sheathed in transparent plastic. Pencils like spikes. Impeccable reeds, of course. And yet a stray element poked out amid his bag's surgical realm: the glorious ham and cheese sandwich his wife Ester furtively slipped into it every day. Di Grimaldi would open his bag in front of his students, pick up the wrapper containing the sandwich between forefinger and thumb, click his tongue in loving annoyance, and smile despite himself. If the pupil was playing well, Di Grimaldi would offer the sandwich to them. He seldom had any appetite. And during class he played less and less.

Di Grimaldi always said he had smoked too much in his youth. He began cancelling classes. Soon he had to drop out of his quintet. And later the orchestra as well. In the mid-seventies, my father was to hear Di Grimaldi's last solo: the *allegretto* in Brahms's second symphony. A wonderful solo, a parting breath. In retirement, Di Grimaldi devoted himself entirely to teaching, although he wasn't always well enough to attend to his pupils. He continued to huddle on his chair, swiftly folding his legs and searching for the sound behind the visor of his hand; but he no longer blew his instrument. My father strove to perfect his playing, to breathe all he could. In a sense, he was trying to blow air into his teacher, too.

I remember Di Grimaldi, the first person in the world who succeeded in keeping me quiet for several hours: he taught me to play chess. I was very young and he became a sort of ephemeral uncle. Whenever we went to his apartment on Calle Rio de Janeiro, I knew an electronic chessboard with the pieces set up would be waiting for me on the coffee table next to the sofa. Di Grimaldi told me not to be impatient. And, most of all, not to talk: you had to think, think long and hard. We were playing against the machine and the machine was very, very smart. Every so often he would glance at the game and move a piece. He explained to me briefly, but with absolute precision, what was happening. Fascinated, I observed the board, the flashing lights. If I grew restless, Di Grimaldi would place his hand on my head, tugged at his mustache as he looked at me. Then I would concentrate again.

A year after Grandpa Mario died, Di Grimaldi followed in his footsteps. In fact, when my father found out about it, he was at the old office on Calle Medrano, which had just been put up for sale. Medrano 237, Mondays, Wednesdays, and Fridays. That afternoon, emptying his father's office, my dad realized he was left with only his own hands.

# 39

I LOVED A redhead who had no idea I loved her. Ariadna. Admittedly, with a name like that, I ought to have suspected. But at that age no one has the patience for mythology.

Every January I would meet up with Ariadna again and yet I never caught up with her. We met at a summer camp in Almirante Brown. That wide, urgent sky. That lawn at our disposal. Those shimmering swimming pools. Those dressing rooms, oh, so close together. In Almirante Brown I was driven to despair by the bronze Ariadna and her infinite smile. When she narrowed her eyes, I thought they'd never open again. Her skin was a constellation. The down that shone on her thighs, those muscular thighs of hers. A poison of joy, I contemplated Ariadna and could find no words.

I dreamed about riding up on a charger to her apartment on Calle Juncal, no, on a motorbike, or screech to a halt in my convertible, like a Matchbox car on a gigantic scale. Spying me from her balcony, she would descend in her cotton nightdress, and our car would speed off, Ariadna's hair leaving a trail of reddish particles, and we'd escape together until we reached my bedroom at home where, thrilled, and anxious, I lay on my back inventing the scene.

When I imagined her from afar like this, I was continually concocting every kind of bold adventure. But when she was right in front of me, all I could muster were innocent gestures like brushing her hand, combing her hair on the grass, or presenting her with a daisy. I only had to see her to feel my head spin. A blissful fear. We talked, we walked, we played together. Anything but attempt to do what I rehearsed alone every night, kissing a mirror.

The only caresses I exchanged with Ariadna were pretend ones. This was possible thanks to a game of random kisses called traffic lights. Although by now I could pronounce *twafficlights* effortlessly, I was no less clumsy when it came to articulating the two or three words that would have sufficed.

My redhead was a girl who wore designer trainers and attended private school. She lived in the posh Barrio Norte neighborhood, in an apartment with endless passageways and rooms where her friendly parents offered their guests imported tea. That's why I believed that, if I were to have any chance at all with Ariadna, it would have to be preceded by a high-flown, princely speech, as flaming as her tresses. What a fool.

The summers passed, together with their silences. Every year, as if we'd made a pact, Ariadna and I would stop seeing each other completely until the next camp season. In the summer of '88, or was it '89, I arrived in Almirante Brown a little heavier, with the veiled traces of a mustache, resolved to declare myself without preamble or rehearsals. On the first day of camp, I trotted aboard the bus ready for anything, and cast a panoramic glance round the seats; but I couldn't see Ariadna. Soon some of my friends told me her parents had taken her to the States to perfect her English.

I instantly lost all interest in summer camps. I also lost all trace of Ariadna. We didn't exchange letters, although I did write her a few poems that would have made her weep. With dismay.

# 40

MY FATHER'S HEART literally skipped a beat the first evening he saw my mother play. And, since life has a sense of humor, this happened at a bachelor party.

My mother had been hired as part of a quartet to play Mozart's *A Little Night Music*, which was the bride-to-be's favorite piece. She asked the musicians to play it several times in succession. Divine! Divine!, cried the bride-to-be, unaware she would soon be divorced. Meanwhile, my father had become smitten with Mozart's summery skirt.

The encores over, my father went up to the quartet and congratulated each of them, although reserving his greatest enthusiasm for the young violinist. My mother was accompanied by her boyfriend, who was none other than the quartet's second violinist. The three of them chatted for a while, drank a glass of something, exchanged points of view on different recordings. And, even though my father continued to behave impeccably toward the other violinist, the fellow had begun to notice a worrying intensity about his way of addressing his partner, and so attempted a more forceful intervention, reminding my mother how tired they both were, or suggesting he and she move on somewhere else.

Dignifiedly jealous, the second violinist announced that he was going home and, when he realized she didn't seem keen to leave so soon, he had the good taste to leave them on their own. So it was that my mother and father stayed together at the party. And, although nobody performed any more Mozart, all through the night, for those with ears to hear, a little music kept playing.

All well and good, but had they exchanged phone numbers? My mother wondered about this when, a few days later, the telephone rang at her home and grandma Blanca told her someone called Víctor was calling. Did they get as far as exchanging numbers or not? In any event, his voice was pleasant. After a chat that went on longer than anticipated, my mother hung up contented: she had just recovered her music stand. She'd been searching for it for days, until finally she had given it up for lost. Yet lo and behold my father, such a nice boy, had found it. He explained that she'd left it behind at the ballroom, that he discovered it just after they had said goodbye, and that he'd be more than happy to return it. In passing, he invited her out for a coffee or perhaps to a movie. While they were about it. No strings attached, of course. She said all right. Why not. Just to thank him for her music stand. Those things were so expensive. And she was so relieved. Exactly. See you Saturday, then. A kiss back.

Only much later on, my father confessed he had hidden her music stand that night without anyone noticing. Smiling, my mother confessed she'd always hoped he had.

# 41

A NEW FIGURE, in a nightgown, advances along the corridor in my grandparent's apartment. A barefoot figure with long dark hair, like a remnant of the night. Day has just broken. A foot in each pool of light, half-asleep, my mother has just come out of my father's bedroom. It's the first time she has walked along that corridor, looked for that bathroom, examined those doors and paintings. So it's no surprise she takes a wrong turn. Or changes her mind and decides to see what the kitchen is like. Or maybe she's thirsty: love leaves the mouth dry.

However, to reach the kitchen she first has to pass through the living room. And in the living room, Mario, a habitual early-riser, is already there. My grandfather Mario in, for example, his red and black robe. His tranquil mustache. Ensconced in his armchair. A *mate* gourd in his hands, about to lift the metal straw to his lips. Lips that form a distracted *O* that all of a sudden turns to *Oh!* Mario has just glimpsed a strange woman in a nightgown at the far end of the living room. My mother's eyes are now fully awake. Her cold feet come to an abrupt halt. Let's add a little awkward cough. Instinctively, her hands make to pull the nightshirt down to her knees. Which of the two is more taken aback?

Mario breaks the silence. He smiles at my mother. Raises his eyebrows. Extends a hand.

"Would you like a *mate*?" he asks.

# 42

TO SHOW MY feet embarrassed me. The footsteps of insecurity led me to hide them from other people's gaze. Other people's? Maybe I was hiding them from myself.

It was hard to get changed in the Young Men's Christian Association locker room, where the non-religious and not particularly sociable boy I was learned to swim. My parents had never talked to me about religion, except when I asked questions that had been upsetting me. Despite this, they decided the best club for me was the YMCA. In theory, I hadn't grown up in a terribly patriarchal home. However, the school they chose to send me to had no girls. Let's call it an education.

And so I bared my fearful feet in the club locker rooms. Later, safe beneath the water, they swam rapidly. Just as at school, at the club we competed incessantly. Everyone counted the medals they won. From time to time I got one as well. I kept them all together above my bed, hanging from a ribbon with Argentina's national colors. Until one night while I was sleeping they fell on my head.

Our coaches explained that, to reach perfection in the breast stroke, we needed to hold our heads like amphibians, neither completely submerged nor raised very high: the water line should be at the level of our eyebrows. And we had to learn to breathe after every two strokes, to lessen the delays that occurred when we took in air. Our arms had to be thrust forward together, the hands meeting at chest level as if we were praying. To advance through the water, until our bodies were completely stretched. Then the hands were pulled back and folded against our sides, before curving round and coming together once more. As though the arms were drawing a heart, our coaches explained.

I'm not sure if I tried too hard to complete this picture, or whether I was suddenly fed up with competitions, but from one day to the next I began losing against not only the rapid swimmers but also much worse ones. My feet were increasingly slow in the water, and didn't want to show themselves in the training sessions. Can one fall asleep swimming? In the YMCA pool I used to close my eyes and be tempted to take a deep breath through my nose, to see what would happen in my lungs. The sharp chemical taste of the chlorine soon woke me from this fleeting daydream, and forced me to aim for the surface almost without realizing it.

And yet I was never worried about showing my feet to Gabriela. I would bare them in front of her in Villa Gesell, facing the gnarled Atlantic. That was the beach where I learned to compete against nobody, against time, to catch up with the unbearable Gabriela, the ballerina with bumpy toes and the admirable callouses of someone who treads the ground with conviction. She taught me a better way to swim: to plunge in for pleasure, accepting the twisted dignity of feet.

The beach is a place of desire, but is also a stage for all that doesn't happen: fantasy romances, inaccessible bodies, other people's feet. Sand has something about it of the blank page where everything is yet to be told. One afternoon, Gabriela entered the water and I followed her. I started copying her movements. If she raised an arm, I raised mine. A turn there, another here. Like choreography at a distance.

We swam along, accidentally together, until a yellow blotch came zigzagging through the waves. It was something far more alive than a fish: the top half of a bikini. I saw Gabriela spinning around in a distressed manner. She hadn't even noticed I was there.

Without a moment's hesitation, I stuffed the flimsy cloth into my swimming trunks. It was me who hid it, Gabriela, while you were swimming about—just as my father had once stolen a certain music stand. I came back quickly to the shore and covered myself with my towel. A short while later she emerged concealing her breasts, smiling at someone who was never me.

That yellow fetish, which I slept with all that summer, still gives me goose bumps in a way that only what is called fiction does. As time strode on, my feet's embarrassment diminished in the distance. I'm writing this barefoot.

# 43

IS THERE ANY more tragic loyalty than that of eternal promises? My great-uncle Leonardo never betrayed his own character. Ever faithful to Leonardo Casaretto, the dandy of working-class Lanús. Dangerously lovable, guiltily affectionate, this suburban seducer usually wore pink shirts and had a pencil mustache trimmed to the millimeter. His movements were like those of somebody on the run: partly gentle, with a rehearsed calm, yet at the same time there was something disturbing, vaguely vulnerable about them. He lived making promises and survived apologizing.

My great-uncle Leonardo's natural vivacity was at odds with the slowness of perseverance. In the neighborhood, from an early age people commented on his brilliant future. What possibilities that boy has, and just look how handsome he is. He didn't finish his Law studies. That Leo is going to be someone, just you wait and see. Nobody in the family could avoid falling out with him on some occasion or other. Yet no one failed to succumb to his triumphal smile and to forgive him. His dimples made them forget.

No one, apart from my grandfather Jacinto. Forever implacable in his judgment of Leonardo, maybe also a bit jealous, from the outset he had predicted that his brother-in-law would come a cropper. That guy's going to end up badly, was his mumbling verdict every time they met. The Lanús dandy would breeze in, bestowing kisses on all his nieces. My mother and my Aunt Diana would sigh, intoxicated by the cologne he wore. My grandmother Blanca would glance at her husband out of the corner of her eye and skip, somewhat hesitantly, to embrace her brother. You're so pretty, Blanquita, such a shame you're married! Laughter all round. Jacinto would shake his head. How are you, brother-in-law, you look a bit out of sorts. Jacinto extended a cement hand.

In west Lanús, where my great-uncle lived, the houses were low and the sun set on beaten earth streets. In the east, by contrast, trams heralded the day on cobblestones. My mother lived in the east, at the center of the margins. Every so often she and a cousin would go to hunt frogs in the western part, near Leonardo and his wife's small house. On the nights when he didn't come home, Normita would chew her nails and weep buckets. She would embrace her children and tell them not to worry, while she made plans to leave him. She would open the closet, stare at the shelves lined with cellophane, and tell herself she had had enough. The next morning, Leonardo would reappear with his beaming smile, apologetic and full of ideas. Together with her fingernails, Normita swallowed her pride.

An untested polyglot, a music lover *ma non troppo*, my great-uncle Leonardo adored the French cinema fashionable in those days. One Sunday, over family lunch, Jacinto and he were arguing about it. They had both just seen Agnès Varda's *Le Bonheur*, although they didn't appear to have watched the same movie. They began politely, their faces somewhat stiff, pretending to be willing to admit their opponent might be right. Little by little the argument grew heated. To a sublime soundtrack of Mozart's clarinet quintet, the movie began with adultery and ended with accepted bigamy. Leonardo recalled the scenes with delight. Indignant, Jacinto kept shaking his head.

"But don't you see what that film leads to?"

"To a revolution, Jacinto! To life beyond bourgeois conventions!"

"To indecency, that's where it leads. And leave the proletariat out of this, if you don't mind."

"Forgive me, Jacinto, but you see as indecent anything that escapes the boredom all around us."

"And I also see as indecent the lies of capitalism! You reckon you're so smart, but can't you see that movie sells sexual freedom in return for class silence?"

"The movie isn't selling anything! What it does is refuse to buy. To question the model of the conventional family. What I see in it is an admirable lesson, what more can I say? It's something else if we're such hypocrites that we're scandalized by it."

"Didn't you ever stop to think—it's something very simple— what that playboy is living on when suddenly he finds happiness? At the beginning he's a carpenter, and then what? What about his hours at work? Is it that simple to be free, is it enough just to decide it? So those of us who get up every day at six in the morning to feed our only family, what are we, indecisive? Come on, stop talking nonsense!"

"You're a good man, Jacinto. What you lack is a touch of daring."

"That's possible, Leonardo. And what you lack are principles."

"We're talking about movies, not principles! You're so obsessed with morality!"

"I'm talking about movies as well. And this one is garbage from start to finish."

"I don't believe you! Don't you even like the music? You're always playing the violin, yet you won't admit how marvelous the soundtrack is?"

"Let's change subjects, Leonardo."

"I don't follow you, Jacinto. That quintet!"

"You let the music lead you astray."

"Such a beautiful quintet, and someone like you . . . It's so strange."

"Be quiet, dammit! In this house Mozart is mentioned for much better reasons. They used him, the poor thing!"

My great-uncle Leonardo was always just about to conclude the deal of his life. It was a matter of a few hours, days, weeks. He often asked for short-term loans. He handed out IOUs like Christmas cards. Every time he got into debt, Leonardo would put on his most dazzling smile, polish his dimples, and arrive at my grandparents' house with a bunch of flowers for Blanca and a toy for the princesses. On one occasion my grandmother pleaded on her brother's behalf and despite all his reservations, Jacinto agreed to be his guarantor. Leonardo promised him immediate dividends. It was such an incredible deal. He wouldn't be sorry.

When that venture failed like all the others, my grandfather's patience was exhausted, and for the next eight years Leonardo no longer set foot in their house. Not even Blanca, whose love was based on obedience, was allowed to be in touch with him. Little by little, my great-uncle lost contact with the rest of the family: no doubt many more of them had been guarantors. It was said that at times the blinds on his house in west Lanús suddenly came down and the lights went off, or that Leonardo would disappear, and sometimes strangers would knock at his door or ask after him in a very unpleasant manner. Grandma Blanca would be very anxious, but didn't dare say anything to Jacinto. When she was on her own at home, waiting for a pot to boil or for the floors to dry, she would dial Normita's number and the two of them would converse in whispers.

Before Leonardo reappeared at last, disheveled and with a twisted grin on his face, every neighbor had their own theory. Some suggested he had run away because of gambling debts. Others mentioned being arrested by the police. The most alarmist spoke of suicide. The mythomaniacs on the other hand preferred to imagine him anonymous in a foreign city, carefree and surrounded by several señoritas, with his perfect mustache, impeccable pink shirt, and a sublime Mozart quintet in the background. And I say this is going to end badly, Jacinto repeated, looking up from his newspaper.

When my mother was an adolescent, Blanca and Leonardo met up again. Their reencounter took place in west Lanús. My grandfather Jacinto, who had finally given in and lent his approval, preferred not to be present. It was agreed that from time to time they would again organize the family meals they used to enjoy, and in the end Jacinto himself joined in. There are even those who remember yet another seductive promise, yet another loan.

One cold spring morning in the mid 1970s, not long before I was born, my great-uncle Leonardo's body was found in the trunk of an abandoned car. Normita had not had any news of him in a while: she no longer had any fingernails. When he heard the news, Grandpa Jacinto said nothing. He simply kept a thoughtful silence, and took away a smiling photo that Blanca had on one of their bookshelves.

Normita shed bitter tears over her husband, but not as long as she had imagined. Nobody in my family was able to give me precise details of his ending. After all, they seemed to think, the police details would add little to the misfortune of the story. Who knows whether, moments before he ended curled up in the trunk of that abandoned car trunk, Leonardo had not finally kept his promises.

No one could or would supply me with any more information, until many years later my aunt Diana mentioned something in passing that I had never heard before. Leonardo had been active all his life in socialist circles, and in his final years his political position had become more radical, closer to Trotskyism. For some reason, this was never mentioned when we talked of my great-uncle Leonardo: in the family imaginary he was a dandy, not a militant. A man who, when it came down to it, would have more easily been forgiven his swindles or even his mafioso friends than any revolutionary activity.

Toward the end of that conversation with Aunt Diana, when I kept on insisting, she added in a whisper: "Well, someone once said it had been the Triple A." The paramilitary group that carried out state terrorism and killed more than a thousand people between 1973 and 1976.

This made me revise my views about Leonardo's life. Every characteristic and habit he had. His continual loans and debts. The mysterious expenditure, always attributed to some failed business scheme, to his love of clothes, alcohol, his unproven addiction to gambling. Those sudden nocturnal disappearances, when he spent days away from home without any news, and which in the end everyone preferred to imagine were blatant infidelities. Those occasions when the blinds were drawn in his house, and the lights suddenly went off. The strangers knocking on the door asking after him. And I thought that, beyond whatever the truth about my great-uncle, this lack of questions pointed not so much to the uncertain destiny of one person as to the sordidness of collective silences.

# 44

ON AVENIDA INDEPENDENCIA midway between Calles Defensa and Bolívar, there was a small ice-cream parlor called *Pazzo Telmo*. Some of the neighbors from our building used to go there. Whenever I met them, they would send greetings to my parents and I would feel a pang of shame, because I was there thanks to stealing some of the money for our household purchases.

The owner of the parlor, José Luis, taught me to serve cornets and to improve my chess. We talked for hours in the basement where he prepared the mixtures. As he was in the habit of generously refilling the portion I had eaten, my ice creams there had the enviable property of being infinite. My star combination was grapefruit and chocolate of the house; very occasionally I varied this with zabaglione. I see myself going into the parlor in T-shirt and shorts. While the other customers eyed me suspiciously, I would triumphantly cross the line and slip under the counter. At the rear, down a few steps, I would find José Luis stirring the containers with the ingredients, immersed in one of his books on chess or drinking *mate*. I don't think I ever caught him doing anything other than those three things: ice cream, chess, or *mate*.

From José Luis I learned that, once you had grasped the basics and practiced some openings, a game of chess is won—excluding a serious mistake—by the modest, hard-working pawns. At first, this lesson in patience met with some resistance on my part. As youngsters we wanted to win with the queen's furious ubiquity, with the straight storm of the rooks, or at the very least, the bishops' swift arrow. It was José Luis who made me see my mistake: he was the second person, after Di Grimaldi, who managed to keep me silent for hours. Every so often, José Luis would look up from the board, smile mischievously and say: Unlucky. This brief challenge would give me a mixture of a shudder and delight, grapefruit, and chocolate of the house.

José Luis could speak broken English and Italian, was excellent at accounts, and above all seemed to know a lot about life. He had run away from home and been forced to abandon his studies. He had been working since the age of twelve, which was how old I was then. He was still relatively young, although care-worn by a kind of premature melancholy. He had thin, wavy hair that tended to fall out. Very sharp features. A slender nose I always envied. Dark lines beneath his eyes that appeared painted on, and slightly diabolical eyebrows. A smile that was too fleeting to hide his spoonful of bitterness or irony, mocha, or lemon. Apart from his brother, who worked with him and did weightlifting, I never heard him mention any other relative.

It is a handful of casual beings who complete our family picture. People who appear and disappear from the story, including some we only meet for an instant. Would the ice cream man even have suspected how much I was going to miss him?

I'll never forget your face, José Luis Martínez. I still owe you a hug between adults.

# 45

LEONARDO WASN'T MY only great-uncle who tried to be a dandy. There was also Cacho, grandma Dorita's brother. Cacho, an awkward phantom. Present in our silence. After his death, the family tended to omit him or simply lament: Poor, poor Cacho. So young, so nervous. A mixture of protective compassion and implacable distance. The same in his childhood: so irritable, the poor thing, best not upset him, leave him alone, they all insisted. That's how Cachito, surrounded by the nervousness his nerves produced, never belonged entirely to this world.

My great-uncle was someone in a gaseous state. "Cacho didn't die. He evaporated." somebody told me one day. "There are people who leave no real trace, no material, tangible memory, but the feeling of a fictional character." His imprint is definitely obscure, and has more to do with the chain of posthumous reactions that his name produces in other people than with memories he himself played the lead in. "But at the same time you feel guilty for that void, as though you were unintentionally collaborating with oblivion." Which is the reason for these words now: to search for the bodily substance of my great-uncle Cacho. So that his elusive, elegant silhouette can recover density, as he strolls whistling through the center of Buenos Aires.

The youngest child of my great-grandparents Sara and Jonás, his real name was Oscar Kovensky. Rather than Cacho, he preferred his friends to call him *Okay,* those were after all his odd initials. Married to my great-aunt Delia, they had two children, Hugo, and Martín. Always on the verge of a panic attack, argumentative, vehement, somehow stronger the sicker he became, Cacho's bright eyes would suddenly gleam. He had a deep, resounding voice, which lent him a subtle authority as soon as he opened his mouth. He overwhelmed anyone he was shouting at with a strange sense of style. As if in growing angry he never entirely forgot someone was watching him. To split himself in two when in full flow, to become detached from oneself: wasn't that rehearsing to become a phantom?

My great-uncle Cacho combined his frequent angry outbursts with an extraordinary ability to tell jokes or make witty remarks. His mental agility and his ever-changing moods perhaps concealed a fear of being overlooked. Despite studying industrial engineering, Cacho fancied himself an entrepreneur. He became co-director of a small aluminum-making company, but his partner swindled him, or he sold his share when he needed money, or perhaps both of these. Yet the great project was always close at hand. My great-uncle was one of those who bury their fear beneath more or less unrealizable plans. It is only in this way, thanks to this paradox, that they feel safe from failure.

Despite often availing himself of his medical services, Cacho didn't have a high opinion of his brother-in-law. Just like my great-uncle Leonardo was in the habit of arguing with Jacinto, accusing him of being a conformist, Cacho looked down on Mario's hard-working dedication, reproaching him for his docility. As *Okay* would pretentiously say, Grandpa Mario lacked *swing*. He and his sister Dorita continued with the interminable dispute that had begun in their childhood. Even though they didn't really see eye to eye, he got on more readily with my father: they had music in common. An enthusiastic music-lover, Cacho collected records. He had once sung in a choir, and although he never learned to read music, he was able to reproduce the whole of any tune he heard. Taking advantage of this gift, he had even appeared on one of those TV competitions where the participants have to recognize the music from the first bar. No one remembers if he won.

My great-uncle Cacho would regularly announce that he'd run out of money. He would say this almost as a boast, like a prince fallen on hard times who thought it noble to squander the remains of his fortune. In spite of this, his record collection continued to grow until it was unbelievably extensive. There are some things, my dears, he would say, smoothing down his shirt, that one should never give up.

It cannot be said that, as a father, Cacho was blessed with the mother of all virtues: patience. My cousins Hugo and Martín grew up with the crushing demand that they be child prodigies. Cacho often rudely interrupted his children whenever they insisted on a particular topic. If they did not accept his initial explanations, he grew irritated and fell silent, shutting himself away to listen to music. When my great-aunt Delia remarried, her children soon accepted Mauricio as another father, or as a more sympathetic version of their own father. When asked where he was going, my cousin Hugo often replied: I've come from my parents', and I'm going to my father's.

Cacho was and was not the father of his children, just as he was and was not the man he dreamed of being. In that sense, my great-uncle *Okay* lived like the herald of the phantom he was to become. The memory he left in his children confirms that disembodied presence. "My father visits me in dreams," my cousin Martín once told me. And even though such oneiric encounters are quite common, in Cacho's case they acquire a strange retrospective validity, as if that kind of visit had taken place even when he was alive. Or as if that had been the secret of his power of suggestion, his ability to seduce without getting too close. "My father visits me in dreams," my cousin Martín would say, and with that the dandy Cacho came in through any window, as he had done with his first wife until someone, or perhaps he himself, closed all the windows of his house.

His first marriage lasted a little more than a decade. It was not hard to suppose that sooner or later the break would come, and this happened in the same period as when the spectral President Guido appointed General Onganía as head of the Argentine army, the future King Juan Carlos of Spain began his unreal marriage to Sofía of Greece, and Marilyn Monroe was overdosing on barbiturates or the Kennedys. It's likely that his children often heard shouts, fights, tears. Or perhaps not: maybe all their ills were silent like an ulcer. When great-aunt Delia married her second husband Mauricio, a documentary director of tango movies, Cacho took advantage to vanish from Buenos Aires for a while.

On his return, my great-uncle worked for a while as a publicist for some Mendoza wine merchants. He designed labels and posters. As ever, this was a provisional measure until he was offered an opportunity commensurate with his aspirations. Cacho never liked talking about the job he had, but about the one he would soon secure. The same day Aunt Silvia had her fifteenth birthday and in Dallas the Kennedy car was riddled, Cacho had an accident as he was driving to Mendoza. Grandpa Mario sorted out an ambulance, brought him home, and installed a bed for him in my father's room. Cacho stayed there a whole year. Sharing with him wasn't easy: *Okay* was more appealing when he was slightly absent. My father tried to protest at this invasion. Poor Cacho, leave him be, grandma Dorita would insist.

Once he had recovered from the accident, Cacho rented a small apartment near Plaza Italia. He had had too many arguments with his sister Dorita, had clashed more than ever with his brother-in-law Mario, and as if that weren't enough, everyone in the family seemed to be in love with Mauricio, the man who had supplanted him.

Cacho had to get away, to find a change of scene. And that was something my great-uncle had a talent for. Little by little contact with his family became more sporadic, until he was a shadow only cautiously named. His influence could be felt above all in the care everyone took to avoid saying his name.

The next time the family heard of him he was going out with an heiress who called herself Chiquita, and who divorced a wealthy businessman. A determined blonde, Chiquita always walked very upright and worked as a gym instructor. Although her relations with the family were in the main rather distant, she allowed my father to play the splendid grand piano she had at home. In addition, since Chiquita was an expert masseuse, she offered to walk barefoot on him.

It didn't take Cacho long to move to her splendid apartment on Calle Pampa, alongside her three daughters. He started wearing designer suits, silk neckties, and exotic leather shoes. His manners became almost choreographed. Anyone who met my great-uncle in that period might well have thought he had spent all his life among business executives and fashion designers. For several years, the couple lived together without problems. Cacho meanwhile expanded his record collection and opened a consultancy. He became accustomed to frequenting restaurants where he always had a table reserved. He got to know businessmen similar to what he had once wanted to be. He bought imported presents for my cousins Hugo and Martín. He smiled more than ever, he livened up reunions, was devastatingly funny. His quips seemed to reach new heights, although a careful observer might have noticed that he struggled to come out with them with a nervous anxiety close to panic, like someone rushing off stage tap-dancing. And while he was dancing, my great-uncle *Okay* seemed to be telling himself that everything was fine, that he had a nice apartment, that his children were growing up healthy, that his wife was rich and in love with him. A second life. A parallel world.

It's not clear what brought on his final depression. Maybe some mistake in the consultancy robbed him of all credibility, perhaps some marital problems arose, or perhaps simply it was due to his own nature. He decided late in life to learn to read music with my father, but his patience (of which of them?) didn't last more than a few classes. His voice became more opaque, and his tendency to dominate conversations was replaced by a disgruntled silence. Then there was the famous ulcer. The attacks came increasingly often. What sort of pain did they produce? I imagine it as a burning urgency. Then there was a sign: Cacho renewed his visits to his sister Dorita's apartment. There were still arguments, but now there was something softer about them. After that, more attacks, and medical tests. After that, the operating room. Despite not having grown old, Cacho's weakened organism did not survive the anesthetic.

On the morning of his father's funeral, my cousin Martín had to go for the medical examination for military service. He had to take a taxi ride from the army barracks to the cemetery. This was only a few months before the 1976 coup.

I realize, unknown great-uncle *Okay*, that it's been difficult trying to imagine you. Not because of your phantom quality or the ellipses of those who knew you. More because I suspect it is more legitimate, perhaps more real, to narrate out of love. Described from very close up, everyone drowns. But from very far away, they hollow out.

For example: when you brusquely crushed your son Martín's anger each time as a boy he persisted in an argument, could it be you were trying to protect him from that same pain, that burning urgency you had passed on to him, and which you recognized?

The portrait of someone depends less on the viewpoint than on the point of arrival. That's why, great-uncle Cacho, I can no longer avoid loving you a little. Because somehow narrating leads us to love for what we are narrating. And I would go so far as to add that, when this transformation doesn't take place, what's written is a lie. The true lie.

# 46

BACK THEN THE San Telmo neighborhood was not so much on display. Of course there were tourists, but they were limited to tango on Calle Balcarce, the market on Plaza Dorrego, and the antique shops on Calle Defensa. They would never have ventured along Calles Peru or Chacabuco, on the Avenida Belgrano side, camera slung round their neck. The neighborhood was not yet being gentrified, and its bohemian character was tough. I learned to walk through it watching my back, to love it accepting its uncertainties. San Telmo was full of crossroads where night suddenly fell (be careful, son) and of boys my age who seemed older. I can remember one evening with my friend The Raven, in that square just before Avenida 9 de Julio, crossing Calle Tacuarí. And I remember those boys who, before stealing our football, were strangely polite enough to ask if we'd play a game with them.

From our balcony above Number 331 on Avenida Independencia, we could see buses stop, open their doors, and spit out tourists, who scattered like lizards. They looked happy and slightly bewildered. They herded together then headed off toward the famous El Viejo Almacén. To us, that place was not a mythical doorway, a temple to the bandoneon, or an illustrious survivor from the days of hair oil: it was the bothersome dive where the noise of our sleep came and went, our building's street corner. We witnessed its moments of splendor and decadence. It was closed. Reopened. The stickers on its windows remained the same. Diners Club, MasterCard, Visa, Cabal. Later on it had to close again. It's a problem with dollars, my father explained.

But round the corner from El Viejo Almacén, on the opposite side to my house, a police station never stopped functioning perfectly well. In the entrance was a cabin with bullet-proof glass and a metal crest. Next to it, while all of us were asleep, the garbage collectors moved silently, furtively taking the black bags with them.

On some early mornings, I managed to slip out of my bedroom and go out onto the balcony, with a jersey on top of my pajamas. From there I spent a long time contemplating the veiled stars, the sky's gray wall, the tilted street lights. And I could see how, beneath my feet, the weary refuse men worked. Fluorescent, they descended from their truck to take away everything we didn't want, what was foul-smelling in our homes. I wondered where they could go, where they would hide all that, how the city wasn't filling up with waste yet, how the crap didn't spill out.

Every morning by the time I left for school, everything looked clean and tidy. Not a trace was left. That was why, the day I caught one of our neighbors rummaging through the black sacks, I thought the garbage collectors must have been asking for reinforcements.

# 47

THE APPOINTMENT WAS in Avenida de Mayo. My great-grand-father Jonás didn't like to go into that kind of place. If he had to go into a café run by Spaniards, he must have thought as he put the book and the newspaper on the table and unbuttoned his coat, at least they could have met on the other side of the avenue, where Republican exiles and some of his friends often went. But he'd been asked to go on the opposite side of the street, and he didn't want to appear rude. He sat down and looked uneasily at the press clippings and photographs framed on the walls.

A short, burly waiter came striding toward him. Despite his appearance, he was extremely polite. Jonás returned his greeting and asked for a black coffee. The waiter noted this, then stood there peering at the newspaper headlines. Those were anxious times for my great-grandfather: as well as Hitler's unstoppable advance, first through Jonás's native Poland, then Holland, Belgium, and France, and now threatening to overrun Great Britain itself, a few days earlier, Trotsky had been assassinated in Mexico.

"Did you see this?" the waiter asked in an unmistakably Spanish accent, pointing to the photograph of President Ortiz, whose resignation the Argentine Congress had just rejected. "What do you reckon? Now it looks as if we're all going to have to go down on our knees so that this sonofabitch doesn't leave! And pardon me for intruding, sir, but there are things that make my blood boil."

My great-grandfather Jonás weighed the possibility of making no reply, or of giving an evasive answer. And yet he couldn't hide his annoyed grimace or an ironic comment:

"I'm surprised you're so against someone who when it comes down to it is a compatriot of yours."

"My compatriot? What do you mean?"

"President Ortiz has Basque forebears, if I'm not mistaken."

"That's where you're wrong, sir, I'm from León, the true heart of Spain! But that's no matter, this fellow has sold out to the English."

"That's what the nationalists say."

"Good for them, sir. This is my country as well."

"No doubt about that."

"There you are then. Let him go, and amen to that."

"I see you have strong opinions."

"Yes sir, that's right. When it comes to important matters, strong opinions. And it gets up my nose that blessed fool will soon be completely blind. Serves him right for not wanting to see anything."

"I understand. Because doubtless you prefer Vice President Castillo."

"They're all the same to me! Listen, if I had to choose, the one I prefer is Fresco. What's needed here is more order and less chaos, if you follow me? I'm talking from experience, sir. You only have to see how this avenue has become full of Reds."

Jonás adjusted his round eyeglasses, peered at the clock—he had arrived too early—and then the entrance.

"I'm sorry, but I have a meeting soon," he said, unscrewing his fountain pen.

The waiter apologized fulsomely. Jonás sighed as he watched him move off. When the waiter returned with the coffee on a tray, he continued in an aggrieved tone:

"You may say that kind of thing is none of my business. A lot of people here think that way. But I always say that, wherever you may come from and whatever your job may be, you still have your opinion, and . . ."

"Just a moment, just a moment," Jonás, who was no stranger to uprootings, felt obliged to clarify. "I totally agree you have every right in the world to your opinion. The thing is, sometimes it's good to think, how shall I put it?, very carefully about these matters."

"But sir, I do think about things! That's why I'm so concerned we could end up in anarchy, if you follow me. What we need here is a real leader, like they have elsewhere."

Jonás was thoughtful for a moment. Then, sipping his coffee, he ventured:

"You won't be offended if I ask you a question?"

"Of course not. Ask away."

"Well, I just wonder, now that the Spanish Civil War is over, wouldn't you feel more at ease in Spain?"

"I'm not sure, you know. It's been almost ten years here, if you follow me. Ever since Primo de Rivera was forced to step down.

And yours truly has a life here, a family. And two more children. Plus affection for this country. Of course, there's also homesickness. I'm not saying it's impossible, but going back now would be complicated."

"I understand," said my great-grandfather, this time without the least irony.

Jonás looked at the clock again, rested his chin on his hand, and his gaze strayed beyond the café. Then suddenly, as if waking from a dream, he sat upright again.

"I'm sorry, did you say Primo de Rivera? It's a shame then."

"Why a shame, sir?"

"Because this country of yours," said Jonás with a smile, "also turned out to be a republic."

"Huh," grunted the waiter. "Excuse me. More customers have arrived."

"Off you go."

My great-grandfather Jonás finished his coffee. He decided to read for a while until it was time for his meeting. He opened the book a friend had recommended he buy, published by Losada. Its brief title was *Poesía 1924–1939*. The author, who had recently arrived in exile to Buenos Aires, was Rafael Alberti. Jonás chose a poem at random. If he liked it, he'd give it to his daughter Dorita to read.

# 48

MY MOTHER APPEARED alarmed: I couldn't understand why. I had given her a short story to read that had taken hours of work, a story written painstakingly in a lined notebook, and later transcribed, letter by letter, on our typewriter. The plot was simple. A young man devoted himself to cutting up a series of girlfriends, fitting them together like the pieces of a jigsaw puzzle until they formed the image of his dead mother.

Terrified and confused, my mother told her friends that lately her little boy seemed a lot happier, but that he was the author of horrors such as "Help!" (a man is pursued by his neighbors, who have suddenly turned into pyromaniacs, until he finds protection and solace from his grandmother, who after listening to her grandson strikes a match with an evil smile on her lips); "The Little Fish" (obsessed by the gaze of animals, a man revenges himself on his goldfish by flushing it down the lavatory, but finds his house is rapidly being flooded by a sticky, dirty water); "That Word" (a famous poet suffers a creative crisis when she finds it impossible to write the word *death*, and later on her family discovers strange blanks in several parts of her will); "Him" (a schizophrenic writes a desperately Maupassian letter to his best friend, asking for his help because his other self is constantly torturing him, and when he finishes it his other self destroys it for the seventh time, just before the character for an instant regains control over himself and descends to the cellar to sharpen an axe); "Multiplied Murderers" (mirrors as the ones in Borges, but much less subtle, endlessly reflect the protagonist, who tries to flee from them after discovering that his reflections have taken on a life of their own and go around committing crimes, until one day he realizes he takes great pleasure in wounding his neighbors and turns into one of his own reflections); and many other awful stories, each one bloodier than the previous one.

There was only one adult who, against all expectations, enjoyed such tales: my grandmother Dorita. It was to some extent understandable that these horror stories should attract the attention of a few of my classmates, or that despite his best efforts not to seem impressed, my friend The Raven's breathing should speed up a little when I read them to him over the telephone. Yet I found it frankly astonishing that grandma Dorita should walk over slowly and wearily, settle on the sofa and, adjusting her glasses, carefully pore over every page I handed her.

Grandma, you who wanted to be a respectable lady and who read the classics, how could you have spared the time to read such nonsense? You would underline dubious phrases, cross out adjectives, question endings, tell me what you thought about the characters. Dorita, novel-loving, chatty, nosy grandma of mine, I'll never be able to thank you enough.

What I can do is recollect something that we all helped be forgotten. That, in a youth your fingers cannot reach, you translated Scholem Aleichem and Isaac Leib Peretz into Spanish. That I keep a copy of the latter's *The Inheritance and Other Stories*, printed in Buenos Aires in 1947. That back then you were younger than I am as I write these words. That the story I like best, called "The Return of the Scaffold" begins: "In a country there were, as is common, common people, not completely good and religious, and not completely bad; one a little worse, another a little better, depending on the person and the time." And that those lines sound like a demographic assessment of every country.

I was surprised to find one day, in a remote corner of your bookshelves, the three or four books you had translated into Yiddish. I asked why you had never shown them to me. You went toward them very slowly, your body slowed by inertia. And you told me you had forgotten they existed. On that abandoned shelf, grandma, are stacked the merits of whole generations of grandmothers who thought that what they were doing was unimportant.

Following a worried consultation by my mother, Doctor Freidemberg spoke to her about drives, catharsis, channeling. And expressed the opinion that those imaginary atrocities were the guarantee that in all likelihood her son wouldn't so much as swat a fly in his life. Besides, I protested, my mother tended to mention only the most gruesome ones. What about my little spy novel, *A Secret Agent Searches for the Plans*, or that other more bucolic one, *Unintended Adventure in the Wood?* I kept all my absurdities and palimpsests in a folder divided into sections. Of course there were slots for terror and science-fiction. But there was also a much more solemn one marked "Drama." Another entitled "Satire" (a word

I had just discovered) containing grotesque anecdotes and complicated word games stolen from the poet Oliverio Girondo. Plus another with unforgettably forgettable poems.

Almost all these poems were from the years '88 and '89. In addition to an extravagant ode to a pizza, I recall one that was pretty much an Argentine imitation of *Lucy in the Sky with Diamonds*. Scribbled during the months of the collapse of Alfonsín's government—that my family had hung their hopes on—it began by inviting an improbable reader to take themselves, if they were fed up, to a land of dreams. That realm was supposed to be filled with "smiling stars," "mischievous clouds," and a boundless list of clichés. The walls, roofs and floors were made of glass. There were also "leaders made of wax / that can melt / if they don't keep their promises." Apparently not even a child could dream far from the street.

# 49

AMONG THE CHILDREN my French great-great-grandparents brought up in their new land, I think with curiosity (that wishful curiosity with which we recall those we've never known) of Juliette. My great-grandmother Juliette Pinault reached Argentina at the age of two or three, and all her life refused to speak in French, the language she babbled her first words in. I wonder for how long her early memory secretly translated from one language to the other, when was the first time that instead of *soleil* the day dawned with a Spanish *sol.*

Whereas Juliette succeeded in freeing herself from her mother tongue, she never managed to do the same with her widowed mother. Despite the fact that Louise Blanche tried by all means possible to oppose her daughter's marriage, Juliette gave her the best bedroom in the marital home. That was where my great-great-grandmother spent her final years, glancing through magazines and hostile to her son-in-law. "But her maternal instinct wasn't wrong," grandma Blanca writes, "and Juliette did in fact suffer from an unfortunate marriage." With her usual restraint, Blanca doesn't add anything further about her parents' life together.

It's not easy to paint a portrait of Juliette's husband, my great-grandfather Martín Casaretto. The chiaroscuro is so great that there's a risk his face remains partly invisible. Unsociable and community minded. With lofty visions and despicable emotions. A guitar lover with a tendency to pretend not to hear.

Martín undertook countless cooperative ventures, founded a library, organized literacy classes and neighborhood workshops, wrote manifestos, and tirelessly defended the workers' cause. Constantly praised by his colleagues, my great-grandfather Martín was faithful to the tradition of the great man who neglects to bring justice home. His wife belonged to the same class he was fighting for: Juliette had worked from the age of five scrubbing stairs and mending. And yet every night my great-grandmother had to wash her socialist husband's feet. She was forbidden to disturb him when he lay in the garden hammock. She cooked for him, their four children, her elderly mother, as well as for a female relative Martín had rescued from poverty. Juliette served her food whilst under the table he stroked the thigh of this supposed young cousin.

Almost illiterate, my great-grandmother Juliette bequeathed to Grandma Blanca a love of the piano, a disdain for self-pity, and a tendency to confront misfortunes as if they were nothing more than weather inconveniences. Despite continual economic hardship, she wanted to give Blanca the education of a proper young lady, which she herself had never been able to be, or which she tried to be in the person of her daughter. An exquisite embroiderer, she used to make her daughter light hats so that the sun would not burn her skin. She never let her scrub a floor tile. Blanca adored

Juliette, as years later my aunt Diana did: she had great fun smearing my great-grandmother's face with talcum powder. The two of them would dress up together, examine themselves in the mirror, and burst out laughing. The more her husband's profile darkened, the more Juliette's face was powdered white.

In addition to working as a stenographer in Congress, where he became friends with the congressman Alfredo Palacios and endured the privileged torture of having to transcribe, word for word, some of the most absurd speeches in Argentine history, my great-grandfather Martín wrote an *Historia del movimiento obrero en Argentina* (*History of the Workers' Movement in Argentina*). Apparently this was the first systematic study of the worker and trade union struggles in our country. I saw the two volumes, printed in 1947, in Grandma Blanca's apartment; I don't think they were ever republished. A rather blurred photograph between the covers and the prologue gives some idea of Martín's look. Very dark hair fiercely swept back off the face, as if he had to fight it or insist with the comb. A low, broad forehead, oppressed by his lofty concerns. Eyebrows almost meeting in the middle. Emphatic cheekbones. His upper lip absorbed by the speech of the lower one. Somewhat indigenous features.

Indigenous? A Casaretto? As soon as I came across that portrait of my great-grandfather Martín, I did some biographical research. Among the scant information I could gather, I found nothing that would clear up my doubts. Blanca had scarcely known Martín's mother, and didn't seem to know much about his father. Born shortly after Martín's death, my mother had not inherited any memory of him either. Finally, when I consulted Aunt Diana, who as the first born had some slight recollections of my great-grandfather (and a second photograph where he looked even more indigenous), I got a surprising reply.

Some time earlier, Diana had explored her family tree. No one appeared to have paid too much attention to her findings, or perhaps they had done so sufficiently for them not to want to spread them more widely. My great-grandfather Martín's blood line was not Casaretto, but Passicot. His father, a wealthy gentleman of French stock, had made pregnant a humble young woman by the name of Chazarreta. I deduce that she was a mixed-race girl with indigenous and Basque forebears. For reasons of status (and we could add ethnic reasons as well) my great-great-grandfather's family was in no way willing to contemplate a marriage with someone like my great-great-grandmother Chazarreta. And so the child was recognized, but Monsieur Passicot swiftly married another woman of his own social position. This was why Martín always rejected his family name and as soon as he reached adulthood, invented a different one, echoing his mother's family name in an Italian style: Casaretto. This was the second invented name in my family; perhaps this custom illustrates the fictional vocation of some of its characters.

So my great-grandfather Martín's roots were French, Basque, and indigenous from the pampas. As well as some entirely apocryphal Italian ones. Who knows whether his militancy and his contradictions didn't both originate in the impossible encounter between my great-great-grandparents Passicot and Chazarreta? His activist passion and his desire for social respectability. His determination to marry a poor French woman, as well as his disdain for her family. His fight for workers' rights and his domestic despotism. My great-grandfather never seemed too concerned about Juliette's diabetes; her thrifty diet consisted mainly of bread, butter, and lots of milk jam. Martín destined part of his salary to the Socialist Party and another to his ample wardrobe. Not only did he turn up well-dressed to the sessions of Congress, but he also enjoyed night-time dances and fiestas.

During Perón's first mandate, my great-grandfather Martín was offered a small official post, at a time coinciding with the publication of his study of the proletarian movements. He rejected the proposal, aligning himself with those who maintained that Peronism did not encourage class consciousness or the emancipation of the people, but instead their dependence on the government and electoral clientelism. This conclusion was unanimously adopted by the succeeding generations, who seemed as little inclined to question their ideas as to investigate their mixed-race origins.

Until she drew closer to him toward the end of his life, grandma Blanca always mistrusted the figure of her father, quietly reproaching him for everything that perhaps her mother lamented in silence. Juliette spent her last few months helpless in my grandparents' house. Diana, then still a child, had to share her bed with her. Every morning when she woke up she could see my great-grandmother's huge varicose veins that slowly mapped out her path. Just before her passing, Juliette allowed herself one of her life's few luxuries: to send packing the priest who came to persuade her to accept extreme unction. I wonder whether, at that anti-clerical moment, she somehow felt she was bringing her father, the sculptor from Bourges, back to life. After her death my great-grandfather moved to another house with his lover. He survived his wife less than a year.

Great-grandfather Martín, how many people were you? Which should I remember best? Knowing the stories about you, I can't really admire you: I keep thinking of Juliette's anonymous embroidering. Or I think of your friend Alfredo Palacios, who respected Evita Perón much more than her husband, and who was the first Socialist member of Congress (didn't you transcribe that part, Great-grandfather?) to put forward legislation on discrimination against women and their right to vote. Everything fought for by Alicia Moreau, Carolina Muzzilli, and other female colleagues with family names quite similar to yours.

You know that in our family there's been a few musicians or painters. Music with images, that's what our memory is like. But nobody in words. I thought I was the only one of us to do that, Great-grandfather Martín, until I discovered the secret of your juvenile verses. I have read at least one poem with your name printed underneath. I'm not sure whether your book of poems, which you innocently called *Fuegos juveniles* (*Youthful Fires*), was ever published beyond the mention of its title at the bottom of those verses. But the mere possibility is part of the narrative.

There is quite a lot of padding, Great-grandfather, in your civic poem in honor of Sarmiento. Your rhyme schemes are movingly laborious. There are too many moralizing adjectives for my taste, and to tell you the truth, I find it a bit long. But there are also nice discoveries, metaphors that I can identify with you. In one of the stanzas, you seem to playfully quote the national anthem: nowadays that's known as intertextuality, who would have thought it? And in another, you cleverly rewrite a tango. There are amusing rhymes (¡*peñasco* and *Damasco*!), and your impeccable hendecasyllabic verses betray an avid reader (had you just immersed yourself in Rubén Darío?) who dreamed of becoming a poet. Forgive me for being so frank. After all, we're family.

# 50

IT WAS MY last year at elementary school: the one Sarmiento had founded. The masters of finance were playing dice with the country. Alfonsín was still clasping his hands in the air during public appearances, but now it was more in front of his face, as if he couldn't bear what lay in store for him. My mother still sent me to buy things at San Telmo market, but now there was a new urgency.

Rather than enter the market by Calle Defensa, I used to go in by the Carlos Calvo entrance, because that's where the second-hand magazine stalls were. My favorites were the Chilean *Condorito*, the Spanish *Mortadelo y Filemón*, and the Argentine *Sex Humor, Isidoro*, and *Patoruzú*, as well as the fabulous *International Chess Review*. The first two were magazines for boredom, the ones you read when you had nothing better to do. *Sex Humor* was destined for the box with the motorbike rider jigsaw puzzle, and therefore was put to a different use. At school Fatty Cesarini and I exchanged copies. I kept the reading of the indomitable Patagonian indigenous Patoruzú (a mixture of essentialism à la

Rousseau and telluric moralism), and the tireless playboy Isidoro Cañones (an archetype of the worst Buenos Aires upper classes, nephew of a military man, as hilarious as outrageous) for the ice creams I bought from José Luis. With my friend the ice cream man we commented on the games in the chess magazine, where the bad-tempered Kasparov would face the polite Timman and crush him ruthlessly when playing white, or where the patient Karpov playing black defended a weak position, or where our veteran maestro Oscar Panno came honorably close to gaining a draw against the fearsome Ivanchuk.

But the dice went on rolling, and the dealer took all. A short while earlier I had been with my parents and hundreds of thousands more in Plaza de Mayo to hear President Alfonsín announce that the rebellious military under Colonel Rico had been brought under control, and that the house was in order, the presidential palace pinker than ever, and off you go to celebrate Easter, Argentines. On that occasion, my father hadn't lifted me on to his shoulders, and I was beginning to understand the words of the songs we were all singing.

Not long before there had been the Ley de Obediencia Debida (Due Obedience Law): those who had violated the Constitution out of military discipline had done nothing. There had been also the Ley de Punto Final (Full Stop Law): all those who had violated human rights out of pure patriotism had done so too long ago. Although not long before all that, Colonel Seineldín had just led a mutiny: the comprehensive Pardon Law was still to come. The government had put down this latest insurrection, but a checkmate seemed possible. What the barracks didn't destroy, the markets would demolish.

We couldn't make ends meet, and a new nervousness was obvious whenever we went shopping. There were also fewer coins left for my ice creams, and we didn't really know if they were australes, pesos, or what new currency. On the hundred denomination notes Sarmiento's bald pate was turning red. There were long lines at the market stalls. If I was a bit slow getting the cart for the shopping, whether out of laziness or because I was choosing which magazines to swap, I would immediately hear my mother's weary voice from the far end of the corridor:

"Get a move on, before the prices go up."

# 51

AT SCHOOL ALMOST all of us admired Fernández. He was strong and silent, which made him seem invincible. Since no one bothered him, he had never needed to defend himself. One of the things that most impressed me about him was that, even though he spent the recesses chasing a football or taking part in the toy car races, at the end of the morning his uniform would still be spotless. Perhaps that was the secret of Fernández's elegance: to always emerge stain-free from things, to take part in everything at a certain distance.

I liked going to his house on the outskirts of Buenos Aires near Luján, where he had a yard with trees, black dogs, and a shed where we hid to smoke (well, I pretended to) or exchange magazines that weren't exactly cultural. Fernández often climbed onto the shed's tin roof to jump down into the neighbors' garden and steal oranges. I never had the nerve to climb so high, and from the top of the wall between the two gardens he would laugh and shout: Chicken! Then he would reappear with fruit for us both.

When we went out for a ride on his bike, one would sit on the saddle and the other perch on top, trying to keep the balance. On the way back it was always Fernández who pedaled, because he seemed completely immune to fatigue. I can't recall a single occasion when he said he was scared or unable to do something he wanted to.

Fernández's story ended one afternoon when the tin roof of the shed suddenly gave way and his head smashed against the concrete paving. The same roof his parents' had forbidden him to climb on, the same one I'd never dared reach, from where Fernández, high above, unattainable, had shouted at me. His was the first death of a friend. And a strange lesson about the survival of the weaker.

At the vigil attended by most of the school, I couldn't stop looking at his face, which was and yet was not Fernández's. I was puzzled to find it so similar to when he was alive, his hair in fact better combed than usual. Although I had never seen a dead body in person (was a dead body still a person?) I had taken it for granted that death would produce some kind of drastic alteration to the victim's features. But Fernández looked virtually identical, sleeping a kind of pale sleep. What do we do if he suddenly wakes up? I heard Fatty Cesarini whisper. Tell him what we've been doing these last few days, replied Iribarne.

# 52

MY GREAT-GRANDMOTHER Lidia outlived her husband by more than a decade. Although I didn't arrive in time to know my *zeide* (that's why I write), I did get to see my *baba's* sapphire eyes. She retained her sprightly attentiveness behind the wrinkles, the increasingly thick glasses, and her ever demure sadness. "A woman has to stand on her own two feet": that was the code that, once she became a widow, Lidia continued to strictly follow. She refused to change her habits or for anyone to look after her. She no longer bought paintings: she had lost her capital as rapidly as the country had. And yet, whenever anyone was critical, she went on retorting:

"*Tsch, tsch,* don't do Argentina down!"

I remember her last den on Calle San Luis. A dark, small apartment. A few paintings still on the walls, not very visible in the gloom. At all times of the day, a gap in the balcony let in the same milky, hesitant light. In the living-room was a sofa covered in a plastic sheet: for a long while I identified old age with the particular smell of that sofa.

On the evenings we went to visit her, my great-grandmother used to receive us with a restrained joy that was the height of dignity. She didn't want us to know that she was longing to have visitors. She made us tea from herbs she kept in a small bag inside a tin canister that was itself inside another bigger bag. I got on with her from the start; it's possible that in the gloom she didn't see me so much as my dad in his childhood. I never dared tug at her flaps.

It was only once the consequences of arteriosclerosis became obvious that Lidia agreed to live in an old people's home. She did so without fuss, as if she were joining the end of a line. At first she remained reasonably in control of her faculties. She was still able to defend Argentina or make ironic comments. Very occasionally I would go to visit her with my parents and my brother Diego. As the home was out in Buenos Aires province and wasn't very far from my grandparents Jacinto and Blanca's house, we used to stop off there on our way home.

I could see that old age became an increasingly uncomfortable sight for anybody witnessing it, a contagious future it was best not to get too close to. And yet I wasn't bored at all in Lidia's old people's home. I chatted for a while with my *baba* about the weather, my school, and the nurses. Afterward I would roam round the tree-filled patio, where I sometimes met another child in the same situation as me.

I'm not sure how many months it was from the day she first went there until for the first time, my great-grandmother Lidia did not recognize me. Grimacing, my father suggested I go outside to play. He stayed talking to the *baba,* and everything else seemed to go smoothly. On our next visit, or possibly the one after that, her sapphire eyes were clouded. She barely replied to the nurses' questions. Now we used to travel to the home in a taxi, and the price went up insanely each time. Everything was increasing out of control. Also losing control, Lidia's head began to droop.

From then on, apart from a couple of interludes of confused memory, she didn't recognize anybody anymore. She stared blankly into the distance. She didn't stop talking, but what she said was no longer intelligible. And yet she still got up every morning, allowed herself to be dressed and descended meekly to the yard to get some fresh air, like someone doing their duty. She babbled constantly in a strange way. The nurses no longer paid any attention to her muttering. It occurs to me now that perhaps my great-grandmother Lidia had gone back to being a foreigner and was saying goodbye in Lithuanian, without anyone understanding her.

# 53

CHILDHOOD IS SOMEWHERE where we all sing the same songs and learn the same TV advertisements. I'm not too sure where my childhood was.

Averame, Tagliabue, and Fatty Cesarini howled triumphantly: "I'm surrounded by old sourpusses, all around me!" and I agreed, we were surrounded by adults, they made our lives a misery and all that, but the group Sumo's music wasn't mine. Others like Iribarne or Paz preferred "Switch it off, switch it on, I can't go on like this!" This song by Soda Stereo about TV addiction made me laugh (in fact, my father always said the same), and I actually liked their music more, but that still didn't do it for me. Later on, I began to appreciate Charly García and the Redonditos de Ricota when my friends had almost given up listening to them. To my dismay, I was never cool. I never really followed what in Argentina we called *rock nacional.* Funnily enough, rather than our common *vos,* on those national songs they used the peninsular Spanish pronoun *tú,* which sounded completely foreign to me, even though shortly afterward I would end up using it myself every day.

Apart from the classical music that filled our home all day long, I listened the timeless, spaceless songs of The Beatles. A bit of Pink Floyd, another of King Crimson. Some of my schoolmates mocked my outdated tastes. But it was thanks to those groups that I began to learn English, and to painfully work out, song by song, its irregular verbs. Because what we were taught at school was not English, *pas du tout!* On our first day a lady wearing what looked like a wig strode into the classroom and declared:

"*Bonjour les enfants, faites attention! Si c'est la, c'est elle. Si c'est le, c'est il. Vous avez compris? Répétez maintenant!*"

"Who's this dimwit?" Iribarne whispered in my ear.

Our first reading book was called *Le Ballon Rouge*. On the cover, a boy looking like a simpleton was holding a balloon. We came to know the book by heart. Every day, an hour of French. Every year, a different woman teacher, all of them much better than we believed back then. *Aujourd'hui, c'est lundi. Aujourd'hui, c'est mardi.* We wrote down the date, day after day, for seven years. We learned to pronounce passably, and to understand spoken French. And to dream of Madame Nené. We never found out what her true name was.

In our French lessons I finally managed to sing a song that was all the rage: the addictive "Voyage Voyage" by Desireless. The most important thing was not to pronounce the "s" between the words *les hauteurs*; there was no way the two words could be joined up like with *des idées*. Anyone not remembering that was bound to fail. Madame Nené taught us the words to sing at the end of year celebrations. She would grow delightfully furious whenever we pronounced that forbidden "s," followed by a warning smile, then with the same elongated lips would say a very, very open "e," pointing to her mouth.

In our Argentine childhoods we got used to repeating a lot of foreign things we didn't fully understand. Not just in our French classes. We read the subtitles in movies. To phonetics' misfortune, we learned to speak like Stallone; we even twisted our mouths the way he did. Iribarne, Mizrahi, Emsani, Paz and I went to see a movie together one day. It was Stallone breaking people's arms or Stallone killing Vietnamese or Stallone back into the ring for the umpteenth time, I'm not sure. We were overjoyed because our parents had left us at the movie house and wouldn't be back until some time later. The five of us went to Pumper Nic, drank Pepsi, put ketchup on our food, and twisted our mouths when we spoke. We were free, *dammit*.

We Argentines were always a good colony. At San Telmo market, housewives would ask for a tin of *Woolite*, stressing the first syllable with academic precision, and lengthening it until they finished with a short apicoalveolar sound. In the games we played in the schoolyard, I don't recall ever having suffered a Spanish *zancadilla*, but lots of *tackles*. No one was ever *fuera de juego*, but you were often declared *offside*. And there was no such thing as an *árbitro*: we ourselves were the *referee*. We were always a good colony, although I don't know whether we were good learners.

As for The Beatles, I can still remember the Argentine translation, in a sublimely impossible Spanish, of the single *Please please me*: nothing less than *Por favor, yo*. And who was I, please, singing songs like that in my last year at school.

# 54

"I FIND IT hard to tell you about this past year. To make things worse it's cold here in São Paulo and the sun's been playing hide-and-seek all day, which doesn't help, I guess. What are you doing right now, I wonder? Sleeping? I should be too, really, but it's no use. So I suddenly got this mad idea in my head, this totally crazy idea of talking to the future. I'm going to ask your mom and dad to keep this cassette for you, Andresito, assuming they think it's okay, of course, for 'x' amount of time. We don't know how long that will be. It doesn't really matter. You're one year old now, aren't you? So, it could be five, ten, fifteen years from now, who knows? I hope someday we'll be able to listen to it together. Or that you listen to it on your own and that it'll be of some use to you. Like those treasure chests, right?, the ones that lie waiting at the bottom of the sea, as if they didn't exist, until a diver goes and finds them. Some say that depends on luck, chance or whatever, but I think it happens when it's meant to happen. Those divers deserve to find that treasure, don't you think? Because they were things to be opened in the future. And it's curious, you know, because I've thought and thought about the future, but right now I can't imagine a thing. A void. A noise in front of me. Like this cassette going round and round."

Thanks to an accidental wrist injury and the pain in her right hand, my great-aunt Delia decided to make a recording of her letter to me. I listened to it about twenty years later. My great-aunt Delia, interior designer, and furniture specialist, immersed in the new silence of her empty apartment, set about arranging shadows. Afterward she was going to send the tape to Buenos Aires with someone she knew. My great-uncle Mauricio had gone off to film a documentary, and my cousin Martín had accompanied him. So Delia was all alone, and that night she decided to chat with me, without me knowing it.

"I'm here, in my bedroom" (her voice moves away for a few seconds, becomes muffled but also more intimate, as if she'd lain down on the bed), "I'm here with my cassette recorder, my cigarettes, I've poured myself a drink, which I guess I'm going to need, right?, because I feel, how can I put it" (and here something ever so slight, in her voice and in her breath close to the microphone, cracks: a certain steadiness, a certain valve in her chest), "suddenly I feel all emotional because I'm not speaking to you now but rather, I'm, I don't know, imagining you, I guess, when I'm not even sure if we'll be able to be together again sometime, or if I myself will exist. So this voice, oh, just think of it! Maybe you'll have to imagine *me*."

"I guess," (a lengthy pause and an eloquent sigh) "I guess by now you'll know about the special situation we're living through." (*Special situation*: that oh so careful euphemism. Is this because

I'm still only a year old and she has to be careful what she says to me? Or in case the walls there also have ears?) "Right now, of course, it's all very raw for us, you see?, but sooner or later this will be the past, there's no other way, for better or for worse, it'll be the past. I hope by then we'll be nearer to one another, and that you'll have learnt the details." (*Details*: that's what she calls them.) "And in the meantime, well, I wanted to tell you a few things, talk to you, anyway, about these times, which I'm sure you'll already have heard about, of course. I don't know how you young people will view it, because I guess that now, I mean later on, we'll be a bunch of crazy old folk, right? But despite everything, what I'm saying is every experience is unique. And our experience" (here my great-aunt Delia appears to sit up abruptly in bed and smooth out the covers, or possibly her nightdress, trying to create order before getting properly under way), "is proving quite unique, Andresito, take it from me. It could be that when you see us, or rather hear us, you'll probably have plenty of reasons for reproaching us, and you can point out plenty of mistakes we made. But we also have something to offer you. When we start living our life it's hard to imagine other lives, it's like we're the only ones living. And that's partly why now (yes, now, please), I want to tell you about how things went for us there, in that country I'm not sure you'll still be living in.

"It wasn't easy, you know. As you grow up, and above all lose things, you realize everything you took for granted, goddamn it!, was actually hard-won, and it can suddenly fall to pieces." (Apparently being born has never been easy.) "Trust me, I've known you since you were in your mom's tummy, since you were moving around in there. What makes me most angry is that we only got to see you, to touch you" (her voice catches, trembles, steadies itself), "until you were eight months old. Okay, how long before this side of the tape runs out? Wait, I'm going to check, just to make sure."

Then the first side of the tape does run out. And yet, when I turn it over, after a noise like a hammer blow, like some spectral intermission, can suddenly be heard from a later recording, a few seconds of something astonishing. A conversation, distant as an echo, between my father and me. Between my young father, more or less the same age as I am now, and the babbling child I once was:

FATHER: Recording, recording. Come on, son, say something.

CHILD: . . . *cording, cording.*

FATHER: Sing something.

CHILD: You sing.

FATHER: Come on, sing something for me, and I'll play it back to you.

CHILD: I've already sung!

That was all. Then the other voice immediately returns.

"You puked all the time, Andrés" (continues my great-aunt Delia, afterward, or underneath, whispering, as if she didn't want to wake me after a bad night), "right after you were born, you started puking all the time, I guess day and night you were throwing up that whole situation we were going through, however much of a brave face we put on it. You hardly fed at all, you had trouble sleeping. And we were getting increasingly worried, for you and for ourselves. But the months went by and you pulled through, and we moved to San Telmo, and it was great, you know?, going to live there, so close to each other, even though the neighborhood was pretty run down, I don't know about now, but back then it was, for sure. Your grandma Dorita was horrified!, she didn't want to know, neither did your mom to begin with, partly because she hated old buildings and all that, but it was great to feel, I don't know, that we were living side by side" (like right now, great-aunt, just like right now), "until suddenly, overnight, an edifice, a family, a notion of a country, everything collapses. Good or bad, well, if I'm honest, I'd say it was pretty lousy, but at least the world we were living in still looked fairly stable, if you follow me, then it all came crashing down around us, and we had to settle somewhere else." (Where: the essential adverb for that "x" time.) "And yes, in the end we settled elsewhere. Not everyone could. Among them, of course, a lot of friends."

For another half hour or so her voice continues talking like that, rippling, thinned out by the filter of tiny glitches. Sometimes, you can hear the rattle of a matchbox, a rasping scrape, the crackle of the flame. At others there is the clink of ice in a glass, or liquid hitting the bottom. Then again you sense, or I imagine, that she's drawn up her knees and is clasping her legs on top of the covers, as if the cold were suddenly clasping her from behind. There are also a couple of moments when the sound is different, tiny interruptions preceded by a noise like a hammer blow after which, I could swear, a child burbles a syllable or less, a phoneme, a chip, the memory of a voice. Yet my great-aunt Delia always reappears and takes up her story once more, the story of her family's exile. And the man I would become, the man I am now, listens to her again, while he also smokes a cigarette.

"Yes, it might not have happened" (she concludes), "but it did happen, and here we are. And we're in pretty bad shape, but we have no regrets. What can I say, that would be to deny what we are, what we believed in. And still believe in. Anyway, you must have heard the family stories a thousand times" (don't be so sure, great-aunt, don't be so sure), "but maybe not this one. Let's see if it helps, if later on it makes sense. Sometime. Whenever." (Possibly when that time "x" arrives; the time that never finishes arriving?) "I think this is almost coming to the end. I'd better stop now, I don't want it to cut off suddenly. A big, big kiss. And see you soon, right? I've enjoyed recording this."

FATHER: . . . kay, son. Do you want to say something else?

CHILD: Yes.

FATHER: What do you want to say?

CHILD: I don't know.

FATHER: Well, have a think.

CHILD: I don't know.

FATHER: Then say anything, the first thing that comes into your head.

CHILD: What?

FATHER: A word, for example.

CHILD: Tree!

# 55

A WOOD WAS boring. A sunset was stupid. Listening to birds, a weakness. Lighting a fire? Do me a favor. That was what a city kid like me used to think, until my parents and grandparents bought that small plot of land in Monte Grande.

I've never thought of childhood as a lost paradise. Although I suspect that every childhood has its sacred place, that redoubt in which to escape some hell or other.

We used to go almost every weekend. Loaded up the car and set off. My father would drive in the direction of Ezeiza, then shortly before reaching the airport turn off right down some dirt roads. Along one of them the wooden gate would be waiting for us at the entrance to the small plot of land, and at the back the white, damp little house. Opposite, on the far side of the track, stood a sign with the magic word: *Pamahini*, the name of the adjacent property.

As if it had been transporting a load of springs, as soon as the car door opened my brother Diego would leap out and land on the grass, roll in it, smell it, rub himself against the greenery. I would run to the house, look for my football, and race off. My father had built two goalposts from branches. I played at scoring goals alone until I collapsed exhausted, staring up at the sky. I don't know if I was happy, but it was easier there to know you were alive.

I remember the sunbaked racket of my birthday parties, which we celebrated with my schoolmates. The mystery of nights to the rhythm of grasshoppers. The summer fights with hosepipes. Hunting for toads with mom at the end of the rainy season. The barbecues grandpa Mario and dad cooked. I used to stare at them stirring the charcoal, poking the embers, prick the meat. There was something disturbing about that red midday ritual: fire, blood, red wine. Did *Pamahini* have something to do with it? What sort of forces or gods did that word invoke?

Dreamy urban child, promise you won't forget that last afternoon with your grandfather Mario, when he took you to plant a willow? How strange, burying roots so that they can breathe. Sowing life by getting your hands dirty. Promise me you'll always water that tree. Mom, I want to go in outside!, my brother Diego cried as night fell and we returned to the house for supper. Go in outside: without realizing it, my little brother was pointing out the impossible path to any paradise.

Everything began to change when my father knocked down the lemon tree. It was growing dark, and we were on our way back to the city. My father put the car into reverse. The lemon tree was slender, not very tall. His father Mario had planted it. How was he to see it in the rear view? It was so thin, so low, insisted my mother, trying to console him. Yes, but how could he not remember the tree was there? my father wondered, his face pale.

There was a loud sound. The sound of splintered wood, of an unequal crash. My father braked and got out of the car. In the glow from the rear lights I could tell by his face something serious had happened. He kneeled there out in the open for a while, with the slender trunk in his hands. None of us said a word. We saw him run back to the house, switch the lights on, then come back with some adhesive tape. My mother didn't know whether to get out as well or leave him to it. It took my father some time to return to the car. When finally he got behind the wheel, he didn't switch on the engine, but sat staring at the night through the windshield. My mother spoke to him, but he didn't reply, or replied shaking his head in disbelief. How could I not see it? How come I didn't remember? It was growing cold and we still hadn't set off. Grandpa Mario was no longer standing, and his lemon tree had just been split in two.

Bit by bit, we started going less to Monte Grande. There were robberies in the area. Our house was broken into, things stolen, a door was burned. Some of the neighbors decided to pay people to keep an eye on their properties, although possibly these were the same ones who stole from them. The police were happy to collaborate (with the thefts). Mario's trees had been planted in 1983; since then, most of them had dried out. Only our willow seemed to be in robust health, and continued to grow.

Following a brief truce, there were fresh raids in the area. One of our goalposts was knocked down. After she was left a widow, grandma Dorita seldom went to Monte Grande anymore. Things weren't going well with her *Bichito de Luz* toyshop either, so that, mired in debt, she sold everything off and closed it down. Finally one afternoon I opened a deep cut on my forehead against one of the posts. It was identical to the one my father had suffered thirty years before. It was only then, while I was having stitches put in, that I suddenly managed to decipher the mysterious name *Pamahini*: the beginning of *padre, madre, hijos,* and *nietos,* the Spanish words for father, mother, children, and grandchildren. The pride I felt at my discovery was nothing compared to my disappointment.

Shortly afterward, following the fourth robbery, my parents put the land and the empty house up for sale.

# 56

IT'S TIME TO admit it: my friend The Raven's real name was nothing more than Juan. Juan was blond; I had dark hair. Juan's ancestors were Swedish; mine from all over the place. He was starting to grow tall; I was starting not to be so anymore. He was a River fan; my club was Boca. He had moved to the posh Belgrano neighborhood, whereas I was still living in San Telmo. It was difficult for us to agree on anything. As we grew, we increasingly liked to argue about politics. Since neither of us understood much about it, we both had sensible ideas.

During the 1989 presidential election, The Raven and I collected all the parties' posters, leaflets, decals, and ballots. We got them in the street, tearing them off walls and lampposts, or went to the neighborhood political offices to ask for them. We enjoyed playing at democracy: it was still a novelty for us. The fact was, we both still voted for our parents.

One afternoon we managed after a great effort to pull off a huge poster of the Partido Justicialista party, which we found stuck up next to one for the ultraconservative Unión del Centro Democrático. On a prophetically black background, splendidly side-burned, the candidate and future President Carlos Saúl Menem was smiling at the camera. Beneath his portrait, in stark lettering, we read: *Follow me! I won't let you down!* Neither of us had that poster. The Raven and I looked at each other. We both said at the same time:

"You can have that one."

# 57

"TO OBEY A government elected by the people," as General Onganía had explained at West Point military academy, "no longer
makes sense if that government is supported by exotic ideologies."
Exotic ideologies: that's how Onganía called them, himself a defender of the far more natural principles of his much-admired
Franco. And the general had his reasons, because Argentine uni-
versities, to take but one example, were rife with atheism, Marxism, and psychoanalysis. "The mission of the armed forces," the
impassioned general had insisted, "is also to preserve the morality
and spiritual values of western Christian civilization."

On top of all that, President Illia had seen fit to lift the proscrip-
tion on his own Peronist adversaries and, as if that weren't enough,
he was proposing a law on medicines that was a grave insult to the
pharmaceutical multinationals. The ever-willing General Alsogaray,
who a decade earlier had already played his patriotic part in an attempted coup, went to the presidential palace to put an end to so
much tomfoolery. When President Illia was impolite enough to call

him a usurper, the general's treatment was to prescribe him many kicks up the backside.

Having closed Congress and prohibited political parties, Onganía began the self-styled "Argentine Revolution." One of its most pressing aims, of course, was to put a stop to exoticism in lecture rooms. However, the University of Buenos Aires authorities did not listen to reason, and continued with their pernicious syllabuses.

One Friday in July 1966, a decree was issued declaring all political activity in university faculties illegal. Every president and dean had to follow the hygienic regulations imposed by the Ministry of Education, or quit their posts. To demonstrate the patience of the military authorities, they were given forty-eight hours to consider this. Students, professors, and university authorities immediately occupied campuses to protest at this violation of their autonomy. That same night, without even waiting for the deadline to expire, in a Western Christian burst of speed General Onganía ordered infantry troops to clear all the seats of learning. Every dean was sacked, four hundred university students were arrested, and fifteen hundred lecturers resigned. This was the so-called Night of the Long Batons.

The Colegio Nacional de Buenos Aires high school was linked to the university, and to some extent replicated its debates on a small scale. Its building was on the same block in central Buenos Aires as the faculties of Architecture and of Mathematics, one of the most active not only in scientific research but in student movements. In the green corridors of the high school, my father would bump into members of the magazine *Estirpe*, which prided itself on defending martial, nationalist, and antisemitic principles. Its followers wore loafers, blue blazers and, as true patriots, donned short ponchos for grand occasions. They were often seen with chains coiled round a fist, or sporting brass knuckles. In the classes they were a minority, and always hung about in a pack. My father felt hatred mingled with fear toward them; he had seen them storm into meetings held by the students' union to break them up violently.

My father went to the Colegio Nacional with his sister Silvia, who was two years above him. By chance, among his schoolmates he became friends with a well-read eccentric youngster by the name of Marcelo Cohen, who some years later emigrated to Barcelona and became one of my favorite Argentine authors. In Silvia's class was the girlfriend of one of Marta Lynch's sons; Marta herself was a suicidal writer, almost a character in her own work. My father would often wait for my aunt to enter the school, and then escape to La Puerto Rico or El Querandí cafés. Papa, you're behaving badly and I can see you.

My father was never a member of the Fede (the Federación Juvenil Comunista), although he did attend their meetings because several of his friends belonged to it. Outside the school, the Fede organized clandestine indoctrination sessions. Even during the intermittent periods of democracy, these usually took place in empty apartments or weekend homes in the countryside. There the older schoolmates, known by aliases, led debates, passed on pamphlets, and coordinated revolutionary readings. Despite sharing some of their ideas, my father always worried about the constant repetition of the term "people." Like a sudden vision, pow! "The people." Apparently the people were waiting for them, oppressed, and all they had to do was go out onto the street and become one with them. Maybe that's why my father felt more comfortable collaborating with the Student Union magazine, where he published articles on music. I suspect that, if he had been obliged to choose a collective cause to risk his life for, he would have preferred music.

On the Night of the Long Batons, my father had been to the meeting called by the principal and teaching staff of the Colegio Nacional de Buenos Aires. The vast majority agreed to support the university's official position and therefore to reject the intervention decreed by Onganía's military government. Night had fallen, and my father was applauding the speeches by the more militant lecturers, was enthusiastic about what some of the Fede members had to say, but was also thinking it was becoming time for him to go home for supper.

All of a sudden, a janitor rushed into the assembly hall and went up to whisper something to the principal, who seemed unnerved and muttered a few words into the deputy-principal's ear. He remained seated, but began waving his hands about as if he were sewing an invisible thread. A few minutes later, the meeting was brought to an abrupt close, and word spread among the audience that the police had surrounded the building.

Someone said it would be best for the students to evacuate the school without a fuss, to which many students reacted by shouting that they wanted to stay where they were and make all the fuss they wished. My father didn't know what to do and talked it over with three of his friends. One was in favor of staying and waiting a while longer. The second insisted on going to the entrance and taking on the police. The third recommended they leave cautiously. In the midst of their discussion, a loudspeaker could be heard, coming from Calle Bolívar outside. A metallic voice demanded that everyone inside the building should leave within fifteen minutes, otherwise the forces of order would be obliged to force their way in. This was because the school doors were carefully closed: the only, symbolic show of resistance that had been taken. The metallic voice repeated would they please evacuate the building. And would they please do so in an orderly fashion with heads bowed, because police batons were going to fly.

Even before the fifteen minutes were up, they heard deafening blows on the school's front doors, followed by explosions. The main corridor filled with stinging smoke. Handkerchiefs! somebody shouted, cover your faces with handkerchiefs! Police armed with pistols emerged from the clouds of tear gas. My father and his friends were ordered to face the wall, and they were immediately searched. My father had a coughing fit. A policeman beat him in the ribs. My father wanted to turn and say something, but another blow made him change his mind. A voice shouted at him to obey, but that wasn't easy either: there was so much shouting and confusion it was hard to tell instructions from insults, threats from groans. Close beside him, he heard the police find tacks (often used to puncture police patrol car tires) and marbles (to make the mounted police's horses skid) on one of his colleagues, and pulled him out of the line. My father turned his head, but a gloved fist pushed it back to face the wall. Even so, he managed to catch sight of one of the oldest professors clinging on to one end of his umbrella, and a policeman tugging at the other end. The professor was defending his umbrella as if he were holding on to his dignity, while the astonished officer couldn't reach him with his baton, until after a brief struggle he did manage to smash him on the head with it. Noticing someone with a gun behind his back, my father stopped looking.

After the search, they were all lined up in single file and pushed and shoved toward the exit. But before they could exit the building they had to run the gauntlet of police who, as the students moved forward, smashed them with their gun butts, kicked them, tripped them up, and kneed them. Beyond the school entrance they could glimpse the nightfall outside, more clouds of smoke, and the glow of the street lamps.

Hands above his head, trying not to fall over, my father ran with his eyes half-closed. For a moment, despite the pain in his side and the choking sensation in his throat, he risked looking round. What are you looking at, you sonofabitch, he heard, before receiving a blow from a baton round the head. The voices mingled, and were growing louder all the time. Through a sea of raised arms, but this time not turning his head because he could hear the thud of blows and cries of pain behind him, my father reached the steps down to Calle Bolívar. Feeling he was leaving something crucial behind, that he was heading in the wrong direction, but at the same time realizing it was impossible to go back, he ran down the steps, trying to avoid being knocked over.

From the far side of the street, eyes streaming, he saw horses and police patrol cars with students pressed face down on their hoods, arms behind their backs. He saw it was dark night, saw the submachine guns and the flashes from cameras; heard the explosions, the screams, horses charging and windows smashing. Can I lower my arms now?, my father wondered, still not daring to do so because a policeman seemed to have his eye on him. He walked on stiffly, like someone trying not to look suspicious, and out of the corner of his eye saw how someone was throwing up, and a photographer with a bloody head. He carried on walking, and finally lowered his arms with relief. He turned into Calle Moreno, and when he saw more police, raised his hands again. He quickened his pace. When he reached the corner with Calle Perú, he ran into a pitched battle: the students from the Mathematics Faculty were confronting the mounted police with no chances of success. My father thought of running away at once, but found himself unable to do so. Stunned, as if hypnotized, he stared at the famous Block of Enlightenment, the illustrious surroundings of the Colegio Nacional de Buenos Aires, the cradle of national heroes, etc, now lined with horses and submachine guns. There was blood on the walls, flames from the windows, the gallop of the nation's terror.

Eventually my father retraced his steps and ran toward the subway station. As he went back down Calle Bolívar toward Plaza de Mayo, he came across a line of trucks. Crowded on them were university professors and students, under armed guard. He managed to recognize one, two, three faces before the trucks disappeared. He had to get back home, have a shower, soak his head.

# 58

I COULDN'T GET it out of my head. I had read the news when I got up, and spent the whole day trying to understand it. That evening I asked dad. His reply was terse, hesitant, the mixture of rage and caution of someone trying to explain the ways of justice to his son.

The decree, which had not even been deemed worthy of consideration in Congress, pardoned hundreds of state agents of repression. These included all the military commanders who had not benefited from the laws of Full Stop and Due Obedience. Lieutenant-general Galtieri and the others jailed as a result of the Malvinas War. Also those who had taken part in the military uprisings of the previous two years.

The photograph in the newspaper showed President Menem with crooked mouth, prominent sideburns, one finger raised. The president had confessed he couldn't bear to see a big ugly bird in a cage.

The year 1989 was flying by. On the night of the first pardons, I had a strange dream. A dream that was a memory. A memory I could not have had. But there it was, stirring in my mind, so distinct it couldn't be a lie.

That warm October night I dreamt I was a "subversive." A Montonero, a militant in the ERP (the People's Revolutionary Army), or suchlike. There were two of the others.

"Sing, you Jewish piece of shit."

I was trying to breathe as little as possible: my ribs felt like broken branches. The taste of acid blood was rising from my stomach.

"Turn him on his front."

I could feel them untying my wrists. A few days earlier, I would have been desperate to take advantage of this fleeting chance. Now though I found it hard to even think of it: in my mind I saw the position of my extremities, calculated the distance between me and my two assailants and the cell door; that was as far as my fantasy took me. I could no longer even imagine I was escaping. I was enveloped by a wave of vertigo, as though I was speeding through a dark cylinder so quickly I was in a state close to losing consciousness. They laid me face downward.

"Spread his legs, Flete," ordered the one with the gruff voice.

"No," I managed to whisper, "no."

"Wow! Did you hear that, Condor? The little faggot has found his voice. The gentleman is giving us orders! Maybe he thinks he's still in the movement. You're used to people listening to you, aren't you, shit-face? Did your comrades listen to you open-mouthed? While you recited Lenin to them, was it? Or did you go straight to shooting practice? Look at him, the leader of the masses! A real beauty. The thing is, now I get a good look at you, hooded and everything, even though you've pissed yourself, I can see at once your greatness, I really can. Look at him Condor, the way he raises that little head of his!"

I could hear the one with the gruff voice laugh.

Then a pair of gloved hands parted my buttocks.

I thought they were going to use the electric prod on me again, but this time the sensation was different, less rough but more sinister.

"Go on, Flete. Knowing what he's like, I bet it'll go in easily."

"Please," I said.

The pressure eased for a moment. I heard the man behind me coming closer and whispering in my ear:

"What's wrong, hero? Are you scared it'll hurt? But lefties like you are supposed to love to try anything. And now you don't have the balls for it? What's the matter, you worm? Didn't you lot want to overthrow the established order?"

I'd already learned in there that questions, except when they referred to names or specific facts, were not meant to elicit an answer. With my buttocks clenched and my lips burning with thirst, I simply waited.

"Well?" the one with the gruff voice said impatiently.

"Hold on a minute, Condor," said the one who was on top of me. "Maybe now he'll remember . . . won't you, Che Guevara?"

I let out a groan.

"I can't stand these chickens. Come on, you lump of shit, are you going to tell us or not?"

It seemed to me this question did require an answer.

"But what do you want me to tell you?" I stammered.

There was a clang very close to my head.

"Don't play the innocent, or we'll hang you up again!"

"Start with Cesarini," the gruff-voiced one specified.

I imagined Fatty Cesarini escaping out of the window at his home. Running off with some kind of school satchel on his shoulder. Then I saw him sitting in a plane. Then I saw the plane getting lost in the clouds, and those clouds becoming confused with the vapor from my breathing.

"So why is this sonofabitch smiling now?"

"No idea. But while we're at it, let's have some fun as well."

A piercingly sharp pain shot through my testicles, ran up the marrow of my spine, and blocked my throat. I think at that point I passed out.

A jet of cold water brought me round with a start. I could make out a third high-pitched voice together with the first two. I guessed he was a priest because at a certain moment they called him *Father*. When they realized I had come round, they broke off their conversation.

"Cesarini," the gruff-voiced one repeated.

"Or Gillette," added the other one.

"I don't know any Gillette," I answered without thinking.

The sound of laughter.

"Don't worry, sweetheart, you'll meet him in a minute."

Too late I realized they were going to shave the skin off the soles of my feet. The iron board shifted. I felt something cold brushing my heels. Neither of them said a word, although I could hear them panting. Suddenly, without my seeing it coming, a wave of tears flooded my eyes. Tears that didn't seem part of me, as inevitable as a drain. The dark cylinder spun round several more times, and something inside me finally fell off: there are moments you never recover from. And then, betraying my pride, betraying the cause, betraying myself, I heard my own voice bawling:

"He was a militant! A militant! A militant!"

"Are you sure, you Jewish piece of shit?" the gruff voice asked, as the soles of my feet were slit open.

"Yes."

"Are you completely sure he was a militant and took part in all the activities?" the other one insisted, grabbing me by the hair and shaking my head.

"Yes, yes!"

He let go, and my head bounced against the iron board.

"Excellent: now tell him so to his face," said the gruff voice.

They took off the handcuffs and blindfold. Hauled me upright from behind. I knew perfectly well I shouldn't turn toward them. I remained still, my head spinning, trying to look straight in front of me. Every so often I could hear the priest's high-pitched voice murmuring softly, as if he were praying. For a few moments all I could see were blotches, misshapen lights. Little by little the images began to settle, and I felt my heart turn to a block of ice.

Fatty Cesarini was hanging vertically, hands and feet bound, arms outstretched. He wasn't blindfolded, but his mouth was gagged. His face was a mess, and his body was covered with wounds. He was looking at me. Staring at me. It seemed as though his eyes were about to burst.

"Fatty," I sobbed. "I thought you'd got away, Fatty. I swear I did. What are you doing here, for fuck's sake?"

"Jew!" roared the other voice behind me. "No personal contact is permitted with a subversive. Especially when you're one as well, and on top of that a snitch. Get what I'm saying, scum? All you have to do is hit him."

Despite the bruises on my neck I managed to turn my head sideways.

"What did you say?"

The answer was a knee to my kidney.

"Each time you refuse to obey," warned the gruff voice, "that's what you'll get. Understood?"

When I made no reply, I got an even harder knee in the back.

"Understood," I moaned.

"That's what I like to hear," the other one said. "Now give it all you've got. Kick the shit out of your little comrade for me."

Fatty Cesarini was no longer looking at me. His eyes were fixed far away. He peered into the distance. Maybe into the past. Maybe up into the clouds.

"Kick him, Jew!" ordered the gruff voice, kicking me.

Cesarini and I had met again a few years earlier, on a student march. He was carrying a drum and a backpack stuffed with pamphlets. We hugged one another, laughing fit to bust. We got drunk reminiscing about our school days. Since that meeting we had become friends again.

"Kick him, dammit!"

This time the kick knocked me to my knees. The floor was wet and sticky. Motionless in his shackles, Fatty Cesarini seemed to watch me with a ghastly hint of understanding.

I struggled to my feet. I took a few steps toward him, avoiding his eyes. The two voices merged behind my back in a stream of insults. I guessed the priest must have left because I didn't hear his fluty voice again. A knee to my hip warned me my time was almost up. I don't know Gillette, I thought confusedly. I went even closer. Santos never ever talked, it occurred to me. When I was face to face with Cesarini I imagined for a fleeting moment that I whirled round in a fury, confronted my torturers, and succeeded in escaping. Yet as if I were floating, I raised my right leg and gingerly kicked Cesarini in the tibia. The two voices cheered me on. My friend was panting softly. His stomach was swelling, rolling. Said The Raven: *Never More*, I raved. I still didn't move. I was expecting another blow, but none came. It was as though all of a sudden Fatty Cesarini and I were alone. Elsewhere. The two of us together. Without understanding where it came from, I could feel pent-up anger rising in me. I stepped back and this time raised my knee high and hard. As I sank it into his groin, I felt something soft and pleasant.

Then, clutching the pillow and in a sweat, I woke up.

I recognized the shadows of my bedroom.

But it wasn't a lie. It was still there.

# 59

STUDENTS ARE NEVER sure if they want, should, or are persuaded to enter the Colegio Nacional de Buenos Aires. I had at least four reasons to attempt it: that place was regarded as the best state secondary school in the city; its programs were supervised by the University of Buenos Aires, of which it was part; it was there that my father and his sisters had studied; and it happened to be only a few blocks from my home.

You didn't win entry into it just like that, no señor. According to legend, in the past when entrance was by lot, even Sarmiento himself had missed out. In my day, an entrance course lasting a year had been put in place. This coincided with the last year of elementary school, and consisted of a dozen exams: three in Language, three in Math, three in History, and three in Geography. Each of these counted for fifty marks. After this seemingly interminable journey, the offspring with the highest total entered the shrine's noble doors. That was why since time immemorial, with differing degrees of irony, its pupils simply called it "*The* School."

As if there were not and could not be another one in the entire capital. Adorably pedantic, middle class and free: what you could call a Buenos Aires institution *comme il faut*.

When in 1990 I won my place by a single miserable point, that whole edifice (school, state education, middle class) was beginning to tremble as the result of an earthquake called President Menem. In its classrooms however, French, English, Latin, and some Greek were still taught. My father seemed pleased: there was no doubt I was studying *in nomine patris*.

In the green corridors of the Colegio Nacional I became friends with Ferrando the Beanpole, with whom I saw the "Chino" Tapia play in Boca's stadium one last time. Also with the Croaky Rychter, the most precocious reader of Borges I've ever met, and who missed the most incredible goal I can remember. With the pianist Sarudiansky, who would sometimes accompany me to one of my mother's concerts. With Koutsovitis, who with a surname like that, Old Radick would have said, was destined to make records. With my neighbor Delgado, with whom I walked home beneath a pensive sky. Or with Flores, the first girl I exchanged poems or something worse with.

In my solemn debut as a pupil at *The* school, I got a well-deserved two out of ten on a math exam. In language my destiny began to be foreshadowed: I was given the highest mark for commentary on a text, but a dreadful one for syntactic analysis. There were also computing classes, if that's not too optimistic a way to describe the prehistoric commands we used to type on a black screen, or those square disks whose storage space was inversely proportional to their size. Our gymnastics classes took place a freezing hour away at the sports field in the port: it was there

I tried my hardest to make up for the goals I was never going to score in a Boca Juniors shirt. As for Music, I very much doubt we were ever taught any.

I have a fond memory of two of our teachers: Miss Stein, who had a great knowledge of history, and maybe because of that always had an ironic smile on her lips. And Miss Corbella, who encouraged us to write short stories in the literature classes, and whose gently droopy breasts we could read beneath her white blouse. I was also lucky enough to have chess classes with grandmaster Oscar Panno, who gave lessons in the school basement. I remember his gray eyebrows, heavy with strategies. His amused gaze. And the way his hands sped across the board when he was playing against himself.

But perhaps the most modern of our teachers was in fact the one who taught Latin. Everything about Mr. Silva was slim. He had delicate gestures and a polysemic mustache. He walked with shoulders raised, as if always about to reply: "Who knows?" He talked with polished disdain, drawling the "s" sounds. Even though Mr. Silva was often absent, we quickly learned that his surname could be declined, and he soon won our respect. Forceful without ever raising his voice, Silva returned our jibes with loftily ironic remarks it took us a whole class to understand. He thought Latin was a live language and convinced us it was.

During that year of private astonishment and astonishing privatizations, the government threatened to do away with the school sports field to build a shopping center: the first steps toward the development of Puerto Madero. We students went on strike, made posters, shouted slogans, and stopped the traffic. In the streets a sticky aroma of decrees reigned. *Ego ipse sum lex.* Freed from their cages, big ugly birds were flying like vultures.

I spent my last Argentine summer in the quiet humidity of Entre Ríos province, where my classmate Delgado's family had a little house. We rode bikes, bet our pocket money on cards, and drank Quilmes beer on the sly. That was where I first read Bioy Casares' *El sueño de los heroes* (*The Dream of Heroes*). I learned much later that Mr. Silva died of AIDS the following year.

# 60

AFTER SEPARATING FROM Cacho, my great-aunt Delia began living with Mauricio Berú, a tango documentary filmmaker and the founder of the Asociación de Cine Experimental. Experimental tango was bound to lead to Piazzolla, who became his friend and a recurrent theme in his work. My cousins Hugo and Martín quickly adopted Mauricio as a father. I wouldn't go so far as to call him the real one, but at least he was the tangible one: the character who would never vanish in the middle of the movie.

Hugo, the eldest, was my father's companion at the Scholem Aleichem. They looked surprisingly alike, although this similarity lessened over time, like actors who change their appearance from one role to another. Many family scenes later, my cousin Hugo was studying cinematography in Brussels. Meanwhile in Buenos Aires his brother Martín was showing a peculiar talent for drawing. His character swung between two extremes: a crystal-clear love of games against an opaque background of conflict; a luminous sense of humor and a dark tendency to anguish.

Unsatisfyingly creative. Creatively unsatisfied. Martín Kovensky, my painter cousin.

If Homero was known as the *jettatore,* and Leonardo as the dandy, my great-uncle Rubén Casaretto was the family painter. He had a cordial relation with paint brushes, more communicative than introspective. He taught my mother and my aunt Diana to draw using charcoal and to paint watercolors. Rubén smiled as if there were no other possibility. This became an aesthetic choice and a political conviction: utopia as temperament. My great-uncle Rubén preferred painting in vibrant colors. In fact he himself had high coloring: due to high blood pressure, his face often turned bright red. He enjoyed slow conversation and the company of silence. Thanks to his meticulous patience, he seemed untouched by frustration: there would always be some other opportunity.

One morning in 1977, the year I was born, Delia and Mauricio received an extremely synoptic telephone call. A friendly voice simply said: Get out. They then understood it was true. For some time my great-aunt and uncle had suspected they were being looked for. The net had been tightening around their cinema colleagues, many of whom were militants on the left of Peronism, some of them linked to the Montoneros guerrilla group. (Left-wing Peronism?, my grandparents Mario and Dorita would object during family meals, does such a thing exist? You don't understand anything!, Delia and Mauricio would retort, there's more to this country than middle class! And they would clink glasses.) A few days earlier, some individuals in suits had gone to question one of their closest friends, the poet José Viñals (who, fifteen years later, living in exile in Andalusia, was to be my literary mentor). And now a Ford Falcon had just pulled up outside the home of one of Mauricio's relatives. The voice on the telephone said no more than: Get out, and the two of them left the food where it was, didn't switch off the oven, stuffed clothes, money, and documents into a backpack and rushed out.

Rubén's wife was, as used to be said, a good woman. That is, a dedicated housewife who never challenged her husband's certainties. Porota was strong, talkative and no great lover of the fine arts. And yet she always respected "Rubén's things," as she called, with a mixture of irritation and curiosity, her husband's painterly vocation. If on the one hand she often complained about my great-uncle's lack of ambition, on the other she would find different jobs and even keep him for long periods, provided he went on devoting himself to canvases that were hardly ever exhibited.

Delia and Mauricio went to hide in a house they were lent in Palermo Viejo. They called my cousin Hugo, who was still in Brussels, from a public phone. Then they rang my parents, and asked them to memorize the address: it was better there was no written record. My parents went to visit them that same night. They drank coffee sitting on a mattress on the floor, with the blinds lowered. They discussed plans. It was a brief, whispered visit: everything—the coffee, the hugs, the plans were all rushed. In the end Mauricio and Delia decided to leave Martín in Buenos Aires, while they escaped to Brazil to test the waters. They traveled more than a day in a bus to avoid airports: they had heard about people who had been seen off at the departure gate and had never reached their destination. São Paulo seemed like a good choice, with professional opportunities, the anonymity of a big city, and good communications in case of an emergency. One rainy Friday, my parents and grandpa Mario went down to the port to say goodbye to Martín. They had decided that what was safest for him was to take the hydrofoil to Colonia in Uruguay, because this crossing had lots of tourists and was less checked. They said farewell to my cousin without any great show of affection, wishing him a great weekend in Uruguay, have a good time and bring something as a present, any little thing, it's the thought that counts, until Sunday kid, you'll see what a beautiful city it is, and don't get up too late, eh, make the most of the day, we know what you're like! Shaking with laughter, shaking with fear. My cousin Martín had no problems reaching Colonia. There he was reunited with Delia and Mauricio (the initial panic, the restrained joy, precautionary pretense) and the three of them went on by land together to São Paulo. There one night my great-aunt recorded for me a letter to the future. Mauricio began working on his documentary *Certas palavras com Chico Buarque*. Martín made good friends, learned Portuguese, and managed to dance samba. That was also when his dance of homes began.

All his life, my great-uncle Rubén never moved from west Lanús. He played basketball and went to the club's dances. He lived in a small, rented apartment with his family. To reach it, you had to go down a darkened passageway until you reached an interior courtyard, then climb several floors up narrow staircases. His home consisted of a living-room full of easels and canvases, a kitchen, a tiny bedroom, and bathroom. As far as I am aware, Rubén never went beyond the borders of Buenos Aires province. He never saw any need to. My great-uncle's theory was that to think far into the distance you had to be as still as possible. He wasn't so much a sedentary person as somebody who deeply believed in staying put. He was happy knowing every daily itinerary by heart. Thanks to this he was continually surprised by some fresh detail. In that year of 1977, apart from the worrying rumors he heard from friends, he didn't change his routine one jot.

The apartment Delia and Mauricio had to abandon so quickly was very close to Parque Lezama, where I used to cycle as a boy, and ironically just opposite Avenida Brasil. It was a spacious, architecturally designed apartment with a winter garden and a mezzanine with a cinema projector. The walls were full of exotic masks that told the story of their travels. My father took it upon himself to pack everything up, water the plants, and clean the apartment for possible rental. The first time he entered, he was struck by how everything seemed suspended in time: a coffee cup on the side table with dried coffee grounds; some hairs in the washbasin; a dripping faucet; clothes strewn all over the carpet; a cigarette with ash curled in the shape of a bass clef; their double bed messed up. In the kitchen there was a smell of burning. He opened the oven and, coughing, took out a blackened joint of beef. The fridge was full. For no particular reason, he picked up half a lemon and squeezed it hard, watching it drip. Whenever he visited their apartment after that, my father felt like an intruder doing his work while the noisy masks stared down at him. He emptied drawers, sorted papers, went through closets, archived boxes of films and slides, put away photographs, letters, paintings. It was only a couple of months later that he discovered a plant pot half-hidden on the mezzanine. It touched him to see that despite being neglected for so long, it was still alive. Meanwhile, a survivor in foreign soil, my cousin Martín began to collaborate as a designer and illustrator for *Folha de São Paulo* and *Playboy*.

Besides being a painter, my great-uncle Rubén was a gas fitter. For some years he worked installing and repairing pipes. He was interested in the job because it gave him the chance to talk to very diverse kinds of people, and above all to see inside lots of homes. Every one of them was an unsuspecting treatise on structure and the use of color. Each family had its own way of organizing the space, a different manner of surrounding themselves with objects. Rubén would enter, greet them cordially, and, before settling down to work, pretend to be looking for other gas fixtures in the other rooms. As he did so, he made a mental note of what he saw, and when he got home he would paint something. Could this have been his way to move houses, to travel without going anywhere? If he had to work outside, he was less comfortable but gained in light and perspective. If it was pouring with rain, Rubén would say goodbye to his wife with a: *Chau*, Porota, I'm going to do some Monet water-lilies! It wasn't a bad job, and he had no reason to complain. But when the opportunity arose to teach in a small workshop in east Lanús, my great-uncle leapt at the chance. *Che,* what luck!, his brother Homero congratulated him, let's hope they don't close it down!

Not entirely convinced by a career in Architecture, which he had just enrolled for, my cousin Martín decided to leave São Paulo for New York. There he studied at the Art Students League and let a very interesting beard grow. A photograph from that period shows him laughing on a flat roof, in a roll-neck sweater, surveying the Big Apple's frenetic cubism. And yet it was little more than a year until Martín returned to São Paulo, where he held his first solo exhibition. That was shortly before he returned to Buenos Aires, at the end of the dictatorship. His parents had found stable positions in Brazil, and had decided to stay.

The inheritor of his father Martín Casaretto's political concerns, my great-uncle Rubén felt linked to the workers' movements. At the same time, he was sufficiently clear-sighted to be always skeptical about Stalinism. He had lengthy discussions about it with Grandpa Jacinto. My grandfather tended to justify the Soviet government on the theory of the lesser evil: authoritarian excesses that were of course reprehensible, but on the foundation of an equitable distribution of wealth. Rubén rejected the Soviet regime's legitimacy, arguing that the means always betray the ends. The two men shared the improbable fantasy of visiting Moscow.

I suspect my cousin Martín returned to Buenos Aires just so that he could leave it again by choice. To be able to go without anyone throwing him out. My cousin's feelings of nostalgia had less to do with the idea of going back to places than with the need to get out of them. His first exile seemed to set in motion a wandering mechanism that encouraged not only his love of voyages, but also his habit of moving with compulsive frequency. For Martín, homes weren't so much a place of rest as the seed of a diaspora. On his return from São Paulo he came to stay with us for a while. He would get up early, have breakfast with me, then go up onto the flat roof to paint. Up there he could hear the muffled sounds from Avenida Independencia, and see the reflection of the sun on the aluminum roof covering. Some afternoons I joined him, vainly promising I wouldn't disturb him. I used to love his delirious ramblings, and perhaps he was amused at my efforts to make sense of them. As well as drawing for *El Porteño*, the magazine that the writer Miguel Briante had just founded, Martín painted canvases a bit too similar to Picasso. One of these, showing geometric nudes, was his leaving present. A pencil dedication on the back recommended I look after the birds flitting round my head. For some reason, that image worried me immensely. What birds were they? Where they coming or going? It wasn't long before I copied my cousin. One fine day, after getting hold of some brushes and tubes of tempera, I painted a jumbled mess on the back of his canvas. One night I dreamed that *baba* Lidia came to study it, frowning.

My great-uncle Rubén liked canvases of academic simplicity. His concept of painting was closer to craftsmanship than to any exploration. Despite his declared optimism, there was something vulnerable about his brush strokes. I especially remember one painting, in which a man was leading a young boy by the hand down a deserted path toward a large circus tent. Rather than any childish joy, this scene gave me a rare sense of desolation. Possibly I imagined, because the track was so arid, that there would be nobody in the circus. A father, a son, and an abandoned game. For years, that painting hung in the apartment of my grandparents Jacinto and Blanca. It occurs to me that if I saw it again now, I would grasp something about my childhood that escaped me back then.

Shortly after Alfonsín became president, my cousin Martín moved into a studio in San Telmo. Every so often the restless ghost of his father, my great-uncle *Okay*, slipped in through the window. He would glide around the room as though waiting for someone who was late, then disappear again. At first these visits disturbed Martín, but he soon began to feel that more air than fear entered through the window. It was at this time that my cousin had his first exhibition in his native city. He helped design the magazine *Crisis*, and drew for *Tiempo Argentino* and *Fin de Siglo*: three titles that suggest a story. He had the idea of organizing a collective show in a laundromat in the city center (the creative process: get things dirty, wash them, spin them, get them dirty again). He got to know writers of his generation like Martín Caparrós or Alan Pauls, whose books I came across years later. When hyperinflation arrived and Alfonsín's government fell apart, most of his projects collapsed. Delia and Mauricio suggested he return to São Paulo. He would listen to them, admit they were right, and didn't leave. A brief interlude in Cuba brought on another attack of nomadic nostalgia, and so Martín returned to Argentina. He met his first wife, a photographer called Laura, and went off with her to the hills in Córdoba province, possibly to live with the window open.

Bearing in mind their economic situation, my great-uncle Rubén and Porota decided to have only one child. Their daughter was given a name suggesting an entire rainbow of colors and also the center of the gaze: Iris. Her mother wanted to teach her to embroider so that she would learn a trade; her father wanted to teach her to draw so that she would feel she had company. Both of them were convinced of the great utility of their intentions. The summer after their daughter was born, they went to spend a week at the beach so that Iris could breathe in sea air. I wonder what a memory recalls if it sees the sea before it can name it. A paint brush can be an oar.

After spending a while in the hills of Córdoba building strange electromechanical objects, my cousin Martín returned to the place he was always leaving. Back in Buenos Aires, Martín saw the birth of his eldest daughter, Violeta. A synesthetic name. The newborn had little time to breathe the air of her native city: after taking part in a show organized by Miguel Briante, my cousin decided to go back to São Paulo. Even though I was unaware of it at the time, my parents were also starting to make plans to leave Argentina. In one of Briante's stories that I read years later, I underlined a phrase that continues to intrigue me: "Here and there sounded the same." A paintbrush can be a root.

# 61

WE MET AGAIN by pure chance. Almost three years had gone by since we had last seen each other. I was on my way to grandma Dorita's apartment on Calle Libertad, when a flash of bronze sent my head spinning. She was walking along absentmindedly, as if she was going over a song in her mind. She didn't look at me, but I saw her. Getting closer. It was her. Ariadna. My hand took the decision before I did, and by the time I tried to react it was already touching her shoulder. Ariadna raised her head, brought her reddish eyebrows together, screwed up her black eyes and beamed like someone uncovering a flashlight blocked by fingers. She barely said hello before linking arms with me. Then we walked on toward her place, as if that was where we had arranged to meet.

We weren't adults, but something had defined our bodies and refined our movements. Ariadna invited me in. I went down those corridors once more: this time they seemed shorter. We settled on a sofa. Drank tea from the same cup. Her parents would be back late. Her sister had gone out. Ariadna slipped off her shoes. I stared at her hard heels, already on their way. We talked for hours. My voice didn't tremble. I was still afraid, but now it was a challenge. As if in a trance, I revealed from memory my postponed feelings. I told her everything I had kept silent summer after summer. I confessed I had dedicated kitsch poems to her that I had the misfortune still to remember, such as one that opened: "When a redhead happens, it's everlasting sunset," then going on to list mineral miracles, red hailstones and a shameful etc. Ariadna listened to me with tinkling freckles.

That evening I learned two things. First, that from early childhood Ariadna had felt the same as I did in secret, had shared my impotent silences, and hoped for the same signs from me as I was hoping for from her. And that, if her parents had decided to return from the United States, it was thanks to the "stability" that President Menem's "modern policies" had brought to Argentina.

Moderately at first, but increasingly louder as I responded with enraged objections, Ariadna tossed her locks and explained how "fan-tas-tic!" it would be if our country adopted the U.S. dollar as our currency. And to make sure everything "worked well," she was very much in favor of the privatization of the entire state, or what was left of it.

When night fell we said goodbye, with a twisted grin that looked very much like a broken mirror.

# 62

WHERE IS THE enemy lying in wait: outside or inside? What use is a border: so that no intruder will cross it, or to have somewhere to flee to? Out on the balcony of our apartment, surrounded by the warm plant pots, I could see tanks traveling up Avenida Independencia. No one in the neighborhood stirred.

In the early hours of December 2, 1990, a group of rebel soldiers with painted camouflage faces got inside the Regimiento de Patricios; someone had collaborated with them from inside. A lieutenant colonel and a major were heading there to dissuade the mutineers. There was an exchange of gunfire in which the two of them died. Meanwhile, more rebels were taking over more army headquarters, the Naval Prefecture, a battalion in Palomar, and the tank factory in Boulogne, the town where my mother had spent part of her childhood. A third group of mutineers commandeered tanks, jeeps, and trucks, and drove in a convoy toward the capital.

Who were these rebels? No one knew for certain. Lieutenant Aldo Rico swore that he had nothing to do with this particular

coup attempt. Colonel Seineldin, imprisoned for a previous uprising, at first expressed surprise, then threatened to kill himself, and
finally admitted his responsibility. Many didn't believe him, seeing
this as an attempt to stamp his authority on the rebels. Who was
carrying out a coup against whom? Whose were the planes flying
over our heads?

The tanks continued on their way up Avenida Independencia.
My mother, chain-smoking as she stood in front of our TV, shouted for me to close the balcony windows.

President Menem stressed that democratic sovereignty was
non-negotiable and declared a state of siege. He ordered the uprising be put down ruthlessly, and added a patriotic etcetera. And yet
a few weeks later, the president himself decreed a second round of
pardons that led to mass murderers such as General Videla, Admi-
ral Massera and General Viola being set free. For my parents, this
was the last straw. The Regimiento de Patricios: the same military
barracks where my aunt Silvia had been abducted and tortured.

The operation to stifle the revolt had begun early that morning.
Many neighbors awoke to the clanking of tanks and the roar of
planes. I had gotten up early to study Math: I had a retake exam,
my last chance to avoid spending the summer immersed in equations. While I was preparing my breakfast, my mother came into
the kitchen in despair. Soon afterward she, my father, and I were
in front of the TV: explosions, gunfire, journalists with cameras on
their shoulders running crouched along a wall, reporting breath-
lessly into their microphones. My little brother Diego played in
circles round us.

A few hours later, the streets of San Telmo were occupied by
loyal commanders. We heard that the most violent combats were

taking place opposite the Casa Rosada presidential palace. There was also fighting opposite the main Post Office. I was shocked to think of flames and gunfire on the corner where so often I had gotten off the Number 22 bus to go and swim at the YMCA. We changed the channel: the images were repeated over and over, until we were unsure if the shooting was the same or a new outbreak, if the attacks were from before or happening right at that moment.

At one point it was announced that there was fresh fighting to regain the tank factory in Boulogne and the Regimiento de Patricios. This gave me a start: I remembered my friend The Raven, who lived very close to those barracks—I used to pass them in the number 152 on my way to his home. I called him on the phone: no answer. I tried several times. I grew alarmed. My parents observed me and, in some dreadful way, saw themselves reflected.

The evening was shrinking. Every so often armed trucks passed beneath our building, or we heard a plane flying low over the roofs. My brother Diego raced my old Matchbox toys up and down the corridor, trying to join in the general melee. Although I had been strictly forbidden to go out onto the balcony, I tried to glimpse whatever I could. Finally The Raven called. He told me his parents had sent him to his grandparents' just in case. We tried to talk of other things, but it was odd to mention soccer, books, or girls at that moment, and to say see you soon, I'm off to watch the tanks.

On TV meanwhile it was reported that a retreating convoy had crashed into a Number 60 bus. The Palomar battalion had just been retaken with mortar fire, and the Regimiento de Patricios was surrounded by loyal artillery. Other reports were more disturbing: they insisted that a column of rebel tanks was approaching Buenos Aires from the coast. Later we learned that the bridges they would have to cross had been blown up, and that the column had been bombarded by I don't know what kind of planes. Some details were filtering out. Among the rebels, for example, were seven officers who had been pardoned the previous year.

The army headquarters fell at the same moment as night. About nine o'clock that evening, almost all the channels announced the uprising was practically over. I remember that, at that very moment, I was leafing through an article in *El Gráfico* about the supposed links between the Italian mafia and Maradona, who had just been suspended for drug abuse. "God was a drug addict," a Neapolitan neighbor lamented.

My parents were preparing dinner; I could hear their still tense whispers. The TV was still on; the news was the same, and the apartment was a mess. I hadn't done any studying all day. I felt exhausted. Flat out on the sofa, I turned my head every which way. I looked at the balcony, the telephone, and my math books. I thought about getting up.

# 63

THE IDEA WAS to transfer to different Latin American countries a project that the violinist Yehudi Menuhin, my mother's absolute idol, had created years earlier in the United Kingdom. *Live Music Now* offered music to those forcibly deprived of it: the terminally ill, psychiatric patients, homeless old people, orphans, prison inmates. And it was played in places where there were no concerts at all: hospitals, asylums, reformatories, prisons, psychiatric units. The opposite of charity, it was meant as a political initiative. To deserve music meant becoming a citizen again.

In Buenos Aires, the project was called "Presence of Music," and my father was one of the people contracted. His job consisted in getting together chamber groups, organizing their programs, and presenting their performances. On the agreed date, the musicians would meet at Retiro or Constitución stations and travel to the place chosen for the concert. They would have a look at it, try to acclimatize, set up their music stands, start to tune up. They considered the sound they made, their echoes inside and outside.

Shortly afterward, their audience would arrive. Or more accurately, their audience was brought to them. The recitals were relatively formal: that was partly the aim. My father could, and sometimes had to, modify the program, or intervene with some commentary. As well as reacting to the public's unexpected behavior, he would reassure the musicians with discreet gestures in code. He had constantly to keep his eye on the medical staff and the guards. Generally, no one did anything threatening. But that array of attentive, alarmed or moved gazes was always present, and even became part of the repertoire.

In 1990 and 1991, I often went on these visits with my dad. I felt they helped me discover the hidden side of the city, its concealed inhabitants. In Hospital Neuropsiquiátrico J. T. Borda for instance, I recall that a trio with two guitarists and a violinist were performing. They played Falla, Aguirre, Paganini, Bach, and Atahualpa Yupanqui. After the recital, as the musicians were leaving, my father stayed to talk to one of the doctors. All of a sudden the doctor said he had to go and see a patient, told us how to find the hospital exit, and disappeared. Dad and I started to explore the asylum. Unable to remember his directions, on several occasions we entered and left a yard where the patients were playing at climbing on top of each other, or wandering around with a lost look in their eyes. We met inmates who had attended the concert and applauded, giggling. My father stopped to talk to them, asked their names, gave them hugs: he was overplaying naturalness in order to feel it. Every time we set off again, we suspected we were heading in the wrong direction. Throughout all this, until we met another doctor who offered to accompany us, I had a disturbingly close sensation, as if no one in there was that different, or that we ourselves were two madmen searching for the way out.

Much more frightening was our visit to the psychiatric unit of a prison. At first Dad had refused to let me go with him, but I'd insisted so much he relented. We had to get a special permit for a minor to enter. My father was surprised at how calm I seemed, although I don't know if he realized that my calmness disappeared as soon as we were inside.

The barred gates closed one after another behind our backs. The noise of them clanging shut produced an echo that seemed never to fade, trapped like us in the prison corridors. We went into an area with cells; I think I felt a mixture of intrusion, panic, and guilt. That place didn't seem to be anywhere, and yet at the same time the presence of the state was everywhere. Where were these walkways lined with prisoners: far outside or far inside our country? And where were we walking? Along the outer fringe of the innermost side, or along the interior of somewhere outside everything? Naturally, doubts such as these came later, because the only thing that was blatantly obvious at that moment, as we walked past the cells, was the smell. A fetid smell that almost had a shape, that could be touched. A smell of damp, filth, sweat, excrement, and sick-making brews. That, and I don't know why, a dull weight of repentance, as if we too had done something terrible and were on the point of confessing it.

We reached a multipurpose room. The musicians, a string quartet, began to get ready. The audience soon came in. There must have been fifty inmates, all of them with psychiatric illnesses, plus half a dozen guards surrounding the chairs. My dad told me to sit next to one of the guards in the front row and not to move.

I remember being surprised the prisoners didn't wear striped uniforms. Following the concert (Haydn, Mozart, Boccherini, some Habanera) several of them came up to the musicians to talk to them, and above all touch them, feel their arms, their backs, those fingers that could do so many things. Among them was a young, clean-looking man. Unlike the others, there was nothing odd about his attitude. His gentle gestures suggested a certain refinement. My attention was caught by the way he took hold of my father's hand and held it between his, as though trying to communicate something that had nothing to do with words.

As we were heading for the prison exit, Dad told me the man had talked to him about Bartok. His comments had been those of a knowledgeable music lover. He had confessed to my father that this brief concert had been the happiest moment he could remember in there. Then he had asked the guards for permission to take my father's hand. And, not letting go at any moment, he accompanied us to a secure area where my father, the string quartet and I went on while he said farewell, repeating all our names from memory through the bars. Dad told me he had noted an extraordinary energy in the man's fingers, a restrained strength and depth similar to those of many instrumentalists. He asked one of the prison authorities what such a man had done. Without batting an eyelid, the guard replied that he had stabbed his wife and two daughters. Instinctively, my father stared at his hand in horror. I felt slightly dizzy.

In another prison a wind quintet performed. I don't really remember the program, but I do recall the female flute-player. Even though she had dressed as chastely as a nun, the libidinous gazes of the inmates were plain to see. After the applause, one of them tried to approach her, but a guard stopped him. My dad went to talk to the prisoner, but he insisted on saying hello to the flautist. And he wasn't going to leave, he emphasized, until he had seen her, if only for a second. My father went to find the flautist, who was dismantling her music stand and putting away her scores. He explained the situation. She looked at him anxiously. The prisoner hadn't moved, and was still standing next to the guard. My father signaled discreetly to a second guard, who came over to accompany the musician to the prisoner. When she was close to him, she asked his name, forcing herself to smile. The prisoner said nothing, simply staring at her with his lips pursed. The first guard stepped forward, ready to lead the man away. At that moment, the inmate handed the flautist a poem he had just written on the back of the program. With that he gave a bow, and went off quietly with the guard.

In another prison psychiatric unit for women, a recorder trio played with a guitarist. Although we had been warned about unruly reactions and even possible harassment, the inmates sat like vegetables throughout the concert. Their eyes were staring into space, and they barely responded to my father's explanations. Their applause sounded as if it was in slow motion. Later we learned they had been drugged to avoid any untoward incident: the prison authorities usually seemed more concerned to present an image of order than for the audience to learn something. In the middle of the concert, one of the women suddenly stood up and asked to speak. My father indicated she should wait until the end of the piece. She sat down again, but a few seconds later the same thing happened. At the third repetition of this, Schubert's music was interrupted and the inmate was invited to come up to the front. She did so with a bemused look. When she reached the musicians, she smoothed down her dress and announced she was going to sing one of her own songs. She glanced at my father out of the corner of her eye, and he nodded. Then the woman began to sing in a pleasant voice, without often straying off key. Her fellow inmates and the musicians applauded. She acknowledged this several times, seeming undecided whether or not to return to her seat, reluctant to leave the center of the stage. Her song was about birds in the air.

I was surprised to learn that almost all the drugs circulating in the prisons were brought in by the inmates' families. It was a known fact that many of them took advantage to do deals during their visits. Their imprisoned relative would act as intermediary: a gram of coke for a quantity of dollars far higher than the street price; medication in exchange for a gold ring; a twist of marijuana for what they received for the rest. Of course, the guards participated in all these transactions. In exchange for a commission on every small deal, they looked the other way and allowed the merchandise in.

When we went to an old people's home in Burzaco, I was struck by the icy cold inside. The musicians' fingers were paralyzed. More than once the music had to be interrupted because one of the old people had a coughing fit and had to be attended to. They all applauded like children, swapped enthusiastic comments, and smiled toothless smiles. Another concert took place in a center for homeless mothers. It was an inhospitable place, with almost no furniture. Almost none of the women stayed still during the concert: a few of them would get up to rock their crying child to the rhythm of the music; others went to a small table at the back of the room to change a diaper; others simply raised their old clothes, uncovered a flaccid breast, and started feeding their baby while humming.

But if I had to keep the memory of only one of those recitals, I would perhaps choose the one in the reformatory.

The building looked nice enough, and was surrounded by gardens. But as soon as we entered, we saw iron grilles and rows of cubicles that were not so different from ordinary cells. My father, the two guitarists and I were led down a fairly wide corridor, with some natural light. Almost at once we turned a corner into a darker, more airless passageway. Then we came to a small room with tables, chairs, and an iron grille at the far end. We thought this must be where the concert would be held. But the guard carried on until he came to a halt in front of the iron grille. He slid it to one side, revealing a narrow, gloomy passage. We went through, and the grill closed behind us. Through the bars, the guard just said: If you need anything, call for me. And before we could respond, he went to sit down in the other room. For the first time since I had been going with my dad, I could see real confusion and alarm in his eyes. No one had warned him it would be like this. All distance had been removed: there the four of us were, inhabiting the reformatory.

When our eyes became accustomed to the lack of light, we saw all the cubicles had their doors open, and someone was standing on each threshold. These silhouettes slowly approached, then sat on the floor in front of us. I estimated that they were boys aged between fourteen and seventeen. Serious, tough faces. They might have had more or less the same number of birthdays as me, but they were not my same age. I thought they would probably regard me as completely ridiculous. Bowing my head, I sat next to my dad as far away as possible from them, my back pressed against the iron grille.

My father cleared his throat, rubbed his hands, and greeted the audience. The guitarists took out their instruments. Then he risked a joke, and some of the youths laughed. The guitarists began to tune up. There was an expectant silence. And then the music spoke. They played Argentine tunes: milongas, vidalitas, gatos, chamamés. They asked the inmates where their families were from, and played something from that region. They took them back home. The young inmates kept demanding encores. I understood then that music was not so much a place as a means of transport.

# 64

IN MY MEMORY there's a musical score. From before I was born, on the threshold of the belly of this world, I listened to music. My mother went to rehearsal with a brimming stomach and impatient feet. I shifted inside her, dancing awkwardly to the conductor's rhythm, trying to find the best position to listen from. And within the warm walls of my house of flesh the orchestra's instruments, my mother's breathing, and my future thoughts all mingled. What do we think before we're born? Could it be like one long muted note? Or like a bar rest, similar to a bow floating above the strings, about to land? Or perhaps a sonorous silence, one of those silences full of meaning?

A month before my birth, mom had to abandon a concert because of my insistent percussion. The critical moment came during Strauss's *Don Juan*, a piece he composed at twenty-four, exactly the same age as my mother. The symphonic poem's dynamism and contrasts apparently aroused my desire to get in on the act. Those were the strangest sixteen minutes of my mother's musical career.

At some passages she thought she was going to have to push back her music stand and give birth onstage. That wouldn't have been so bad, after all. And it would have made a completely different start to this story.

My first memories of movement, or the first movements I remember at home, were those of a quartet. This consisted of my mother, a violinist called Marcela, a pianist called Lucrecia, and a French cellist called André. The four of them used to meet each week to rehearse. I would launch my tricycle along the corridor and invade the room like a roll of drums. Startled, the other musicians would look round as my tricycle sped past their legs and the music stands, then left the room. My mother would shrug, smile resignedly, and say to them: Where shall we go again from?

Childhood was also listening to my dad's concerts with the Filiberto orchestra, or attending his music classes. My father gesticulating in front of hundreds of children, like someone directing an entire choir of his own family. Or holding his oboe, ready to blow. Or sitting beside a lamp, head down, shaving the reeds. My father whistling loudly, my mother humming with her tobacco voice. An orchestra spinning round on the record player; the radio flooding the kitchen. My brother a meter tall, and Mr. Beethoven as his partner: at the age of four, Diego was in the habit of dancing naked as soon as he heard a symphony start up.

When the staves became crossed and everything began to sound off-key, my mother wanted to say farewell to her country with a record, a record of her country. Shortly before flying to Spain in the autumn of 1991, she shut herself in a studio with the pianist Diana Schneider. There the two of them, Galán and Schneider, recorded a short album called *Argentina. Su música.* A title that, as I write it now, seems more ambiguous than I remembered: Argentina's music? The music that an instrument called Argentina produces? Argentina and someone else's music: in this case the two of them?

Looking at my copy of that record, mom, and reading your dedication ("to my beloved son, in the hope this will be a memory in sound of his old mama") it suddenly seems as if you were no longer there, and I weep for you in the future, and am sorry, like all children, that I haven't returned every gift. Listen, that's you playing. And, in the silences, I hear you breathing.

I remember you and dad up against the loudspeakers, head down and eyes closed, choosing the takes. You discussed tuning, phrasing, reverberations. I watched you, wanting to join in, with no tricycle and no opinion. How much love and how much fugue you brought together on that record, mom. How much you offered a country that hurts and calls you back.

The first side starts with five pieces by Gianneo: a dreamy vidala, a festive Inca song; a light-hearted chacarera; a slightly nasal lullaby, like falling asleep with a head cold; and the final joy of a zapateado. Then come two criollo airs by Aguirre that hesitate somewhere between singing and lamenting. What came next? Ah yes, the oblique milonga by Ginastera. And the last track, without doubt my favorite, the tango *Escualo* (Shark) by Piazzolla. Its aquatic leaps, its brusque silences. That Bartok sound with a touch of Aníbal Troilo and a drop of Milt Jackson. Piazzolla, that foreign patriot.

The second side sees Cobián's drunks stagger past. Then those drunkards sober up with a sonatina by Gil. I confess, Mom, that I don't like the introduction: you sound tired, almost on the way to the airport. Then the cielito brightens and is more cheerful. The sonatina's third movement is a swaying rondo that ends up at the feet of Juan José Castro. This last piece leaves a dense, worried gesture in the air, a violin escaping by playing scales chased by a piano.

Mom, you traveled the country from north to south with your instrument; you plowed grooves in a record that was a map. Meanwhile, that corner of the planet went on spinning round a hole, spinning and spinning until it was scratched.

And, in the silences, I hear you breathing.

# 65

AT THE COLEGIO Nacional de Buenos Aires we had to choose our representatives for the school council. We *had to,* because voting in Argentina is mandatory. There were different lists and the candidates' campaigns lasted weeks: posters on the bulletin boards, leaflets on desks, photocopied flyers, decals, placards, speeches in the corridors. There was an almost vengeful electoral euphoria in the air. We first year students felt part of something that, even if we didn't fully understand it, filled us with pride. We listened, read, debated. We overdosed on terms like representativity, struggle, change, assembly, claims. Those words were sweet in our mouths; they whetted our appetite.

Beanpole Ferrando and I were our class delegates, the eleventh division, which sounded like an air force squadron lost in battle. Fascinated, we attended meetings with the older delegates and, very occasionally, dared raise our hands to express a timid opinion that was listened to with a mixture of parliamentary indulgence and paternal indifference. At first I imagined that the hall where we met would be a hubbub of conflicting ideas and passionate voices. I soon learned that the opposite was the case: in these assemblies everything was extremely disciplined. When the veteran representatives spoke, a ritual silence descended on the room. What an orderly organization we have, Ferrando and I congratulated ourselves. It didn't occur to us that perhaps that was the problem.

As with the majority of educational centers, at that time the Colegio Nacional de Buenos Aires was dominated by the Franja Morada, the youth section of the Unión Cívica Radical. Still influenced by my family's political preferences, or perhaps with a desire to support the party that President Menem had recently defeated, at first I leaned toward them. But it wasn't long before I became aware of petty cheating, double talk, and shady deals that prefigured future irregularities beyond our classrooms. Disillusioned, I joined those who supported a new list with no links to any party. This was the LIBRE, Línea Independiente con Base en la Reacción Estudiantil (Independent Group Based on Student Reaction).

Printed in bright colors, LIBRE's leaflets were incisive and well-argued. Their speeches sounded different, combative rather than bureaucratic: a tune anxious to become reality. All their slogans encouraged the students' critical faculties. With unerring precision, they denounced every single mistake and contradiction of the current representatives. "How long are we going to put up with them?" their placards appealed to us.

In our eleventh division there was a companion who was active in LIBRE from the outset. His name was Nazario and he was keen to provide us with information. We often consulted him when we had a doubt or demand about the way the school functioned.

He would listen closely to us, purse his lips in solidarity, and then pepper his reply with a profusion of pertinent facts. Nazario's talks were more in depth than for electoral purposes. His reasoning was strongly based on political theory; he knew the legal ins and outs, and analyzed the newspapers with enviable expertise. That was why, despite Nazario's discretion when it came to asking for our vote, many of us knew that year we would elect the LIBRE in the certainty we were contributing to the transformation of the school's structures. We also enthusiastically took part in collections and fundraising events: we had to match the resources of the established student groups.

At the start of the following year, despite knowing I wouldn't complete it, I continued going to school: my way of resisting no longer belonging to the country. I took notes just like the others, my classmates treated me as one of them, and for a while it seemed to me as though I would always be living on that frontier: about to leave, but remaining. A month before we were to fly to Spain, I came across Nazario sitting at his desk during one recess, studying a little notebook and anxiously chewing a pencil. As soon as I went over to greet him, he snapped his notebook shut, smiled, and asked me how the preparations for my trip were going.

A couple of days later, Croaky Rychter told me Nazario had been appointed treasurer of the LIBRE. I was slightly surprised at this, because Nazario and I often chatted together, and he hadn't mentioned it. A short while later, I heard rumors that the LIBRE accounts were being tampered with, and small sums disappearing. I was astonished to discover that quite a few of my classmates knew about these suspicions; it was obvious I had already begun to withdraw from the school without realizing it. At first I thought this must be nothing more than slander. But my companions' opinions gradually convinced me that, at the very least, there was something dubious about Nazario's behavior. When I tried to sound him out about his role as treasurer, all I got from him was a troubling, conspiratorial smile.

Whenever I bumped into Nazario in the corridor, or saw him immersed in his little notebook, I desperately wanted to demand an explanation. I was held back by my companions' air of calm, even those who had voted for the LIBRE, and also something of a sense of guilt: after all, I had supported the list as well. I wonder now if we all felt the same and decided to say nothing. Nobody protested out loud or seemed very surprised. You're not doing anything either, was the very sensible retort from Croaky Rychter.

I never succeeded in confirming what was really going on with the LIBRE accounts. The last time I talked about it with someone, a week before I left the school, the succinct response was:

"They learned quickly."

# 66

THEY CAME LOOKING slightly wary, cast a more or less interested eye over our things, and then went away again. Some bought, others didn't. The corridor of our apartment on Avenida Independencia was crammed with bits of furniture, clothing, books, toys, ornaments, pictures (including the portrait by Spilimbergo that had once belonged to *baba* Lidia), an array of tools and kitchen utensils. The scattered summary of our lives. An inventory after a storm. Strangers came and went. The Argentine state was up for sale; so was our home.

My father had asked me to get rid of everything non-essential. I had replied that everything in my room was essential. All he said was that, in that case, I should choose three or four things, and he would take all the rest. I'm inclined to think those renunciations ended up being extremely healthy for my collecting mania, one of the clearest signs of panic. But at that moment, my brother Diego and I were busy observing the bustle of intruders trampling everywhere, deciding how much of our memories they would take away with them.

One lady bought my Casio keyboard and several things grandma Dorita had brought me from her old toyshop. She had a pale, friendly face, replete with grandchildren; that consoled me a little. But I can't recall the face of the boy who went off with my collection of horror stories—those black books published in Barcelona that I used to read avidly: in my drawer I kept a list of the comments and absurd marks I gave my favorite authors (statistics, that symptom of an allergy to doubt). Studying this civilized looting of our possessions, I suddenly remembered my Lithuanian great-grandmother, who kept her most precious things in little bags that she put in boxes and then inside other bags.

If those losses were stupefying for my brother and I, who were still at school, I can only guess how painful it must have been for my parents to sacrifice a whole lifetime's possessions. Who knows? Perhaps a lot, or perhaps very little. When we dispose of things we once adored, there must be a powerful reason that wisely allows us not to worry about them. So I suppose that as they watched their entire household being carted away, my parents were thinking of the modest sums they were receiving, and the voyage drawing closer by the day.

A lot of pain; very little. Over all the time the sale lasted, I caught only two glimpses of it: my parents' discreet tears as their German piano disappeared down the stairs on the porters' shoulders, and their silent embrace while a man in blue overalls measured the piles of books we had laid out by our door. They were being bought by the meter. Some of the titles were the same as those with which, thanks to my friend The Raven, I had first started to read. And yet the best possible destiny awaited them: the shelves of a second-hand bookshop on Calle Corrientes.

When the man in the blue overalls finished measuring our library, my mother went into the kitchen without a word to smoke a cigarette. My father stayed to bargain with him. I think this was the first time I realized parents can feel far more defenseless than children. Fifteen years earlier, mine had been forced to burn some of their books; now they only had to sell them off. No doubt, this was progress.

# 67

UNAWARE I WOULD never see him again, or that the Pazzo Telmo ice cream parlor would soon no longer exist, I went to say good-bye to my friend José Luis. I told him about our yard sale and he came to take a look. He bought the video player and the washing machine. It was the first time the ice cream man came to visit me, rather than the opposite. Then back at the parlor we played our last game of chess.

We each bet two kilos of grapefruit ice cream. The game lasted all afternoon. I defended myself from his attacks better than ever before. Patiently, I conquered the center of the board. I respected my pawns as if they were kings. At the end, we celebrated my longed-for victory. The one I had wanted for such a long time. I said to him: Unlucky. I made fun of him for a while, and we laughed. His attitude was the same as ever. We didn't mention my journey, and he didn't ask anything about it. We didn't give each other a hug when we parted. We merely waved goodbye.

On my way home, with a bag full of ice cream tubs, I went over his moves in my mind. And I had the feeling that José Luis had let me win.

# 68

IN *THE* SCHOOL there was a basement swimming pool which, I imagine, its coaches considered *The* swimming pool. To get your diploma from the Colegio Nacional de Buenos Aires it was essential to have passed a swimming exam. If you didn't, the fact that you got top marks in academic subjects didn't count: either a student could swim, or they sank. This Olympian requirement, which we students regarded then as absurd and unwarranted, now seems to me one of the few sensible measures in our educational system.

I can remember our first swimming exam: I recall us all there at the side of the pool with our uncertain pubescent bodies. What an explosion of imminence, all that beauty on its way! The boys' lanky, slightly shaky legs. The timid smudges under the armpits. The swarm of girls' feet. Budding breasts, others fully fledged, some still absent. Astonishing to see us abruptly half naked, no longer shielded by lessons, trembling shoulder to shoulder from cold, desire, embarrassment or all three, above the azure waves.

In the male sector we were seriously disappointed to find that Fanego, whom many of us had a crush on, had preferred not to expose herself to our indiscreet gazes: realizing that in the second round there would be fewer spectators, she ducked out of this one, claiming to have a last-minute head cold. We were consoled by Rodríguez's athletic thighs, the surprise of my friend Flores's early breasts, or the sudden buttocks of Arcidiácono—a phrase that made his rear-end seem vaguely mythological. For their part, the girls giggled at the sight of our torsos and soaked groins. Especially Nazario's, who seemed to have learned it all too quickly, and Hoon Kim's, a Korean classmate we used to make cruel fun of until the day we saw him with no pants.

In my case, I was fortunate that the one thing I had learned at the YMCA was to swim. All those years of training were finally put to good use. For some of my friends however, this test was an insurmountable obstacle. This was the case with López, who from the outset had insisted he could not float and had a phobia about chlorine. Although he had sworn to his parents that he would at least try, the first year he turned up at the swimming pool he was in sneakers and jeans, ready to cheer us on from the balcony. He intended to turn down every request to take the exam until forced to do an intensive course or kill the swimming instructor. However, for the exam in the autumn of 1991 everything changed, giving López an unexpected opportunity.

I was about to emigrate to Granada, and wanted to say farewell to my friends in some special fashion. I, who was going to drop out of the eleventh division in only a few days. I, who had therefore nothing to fear from the school's rigid disciplinary system . . . Nothing, except for the official record with my grades, and the certificate of good conduct as a student: indispensable documents for validation to enter a Spanish high school. Since I didn't realize this, it could be said that on that morning, without knowing it, I put my academic prospects on the line for López. Or maybe I was somehow aware of it, and this was my attempt to sabotage the future awaiting me far from my friends.

When I entered the locker room, I saw one of them: Croaky Rychter, who was somewhat wearily tying up his trunks. He cleared his throat and asked me how things were going. I said well, so-so. He asked why. I answered that as he knew I had to leave the country. And I added: What a drag, no? He answered with a shrug: Or what good luck, who knows.

That morning I was López. I had had a haircut exactly the same as the one on his ID card. I had memorized the number, and, just in case, his date of birth and address. Yes, that morning I was a perfect López. I left the locker room imagining I had another head on my shoulders. I lined up, feeling a mixture of sadness, theatrical euphoria, and a desire for revenge against something I couldn't define. From the balcony ten or so of my classmates, including the real López, were relentlessly shouting my new name: Go for it, López! Give it all you've got! Break the fuckin' backstroke record! You're the best, López! Go on, swim, swim, don't stop! Keep it up, López! Catch a catfish, champion! López! López!

I swam from one end to the other at top speed, my arms and legs flailing desperately, fleeing my name and my uprooting. The voices bounced off the damp walls of the Colegio Nacional de Buenos Aires swimming pool (López! López!), and slowly disintegrated, mingling with my panting breath and the quiet depths of the water.

# 69

I THREW THE jigsaw puzzle of the motorbike rider and the ring of fire out of my bedroom window. I watched as the box, with my forbidden magazines inside, plunged down into the vacant lot next door. After so many years, the rider had finally managed to complete the slowest of leaps.

# 70

NOW I HAVE a letter and a restless memory. My grandma Blanca's letter, the letter of her life, and its slightly faded lines. From the moment I first read it, I felt I owed her the debt of continuing it, of completing it. My grandmother's handwriting slips, "I'm going to try to please my beloved grandchildren," then she corrects herself at once: "by telling them my little story," like an elderly ballerina determined to stay straight despite her aching back. "I knew both my grandmothers: one was Latin American, the other French." That's how her family novel begins, and is now traveling within mine. Characters imagining what they remember, remembering what they imagine.

It was her uncle Luis, who used to drop in to Juliette's apartment to bring magazines to the reclusive Louise Blanche, who also gave my grandmother her first piano. "The first so longed-for piano," she emphasizes almost erotically. It was this same Uncle Luis, rather than her father Martín, who checked her school reports to see what grades she had. Or who ran to visit Blanca whenever she fell ill. "I'll love him as long as I live," writes my usually very reserved grandma. And this affirmation of hers becomes the greatest declaration of love not only to my great-great-uncle Luis, but also to life: in writing those lines at over eighty, Blanca was still aiming to live a good few more.

Apart from playing the piano, Blanca, just like my other grandmother, loved to play at theater. Pure theater: how families are. Blanca turned the stories from the Sunday newspapers into plays. She also liked to buy, with the change left over from her the shopping, the famous illustrated stories by Calleja. "They were stories with morals that enchanted me." How wonderful is syntax: was she enchanted by the stories or by the morals? When it came down to it, Grandma Blanca, just like her husband Jacinto, always thought that the only unbearable torment is to fail to do what one ought. Maybe that's why the true torment for my studious grandmother must have been not to have completed her studies. And if she didn't do so, it was for theatrical reasons.

Blanca had begun her secondary studies in Escuela Normal 3 on Calle Bolívar, in the heart of San Telmo neighborhood. The same school where, sixty years later, my brother Diego spent his only school year in Argentina. Or possibly not the same one: in my brother's day, the school roofs were falling to pieces and the teachers were constantly on strike. When our grandma went there, the building was in perfect condition and was prestigious among state schools. But it was far from where she lived in Lanús. Before dawn Blanca had to walk along nine dark streets to the train station, travel to Constitución, and from there at daybreak walk as many streets again. As a result, she quite frequently arrived a few minutes late, and was given a black mark on the attendance sheet.

At the end of the year, the sleepy Blanca had too many black marks and found she had to retake exams in every subject. Unfortunately, she didn't have the heart to do so. For a young girl to want to have a secondary education was almost an oddity back in those days, and her enlightened father didn't insist much. It was then that my grandmother didn't do what she ought to have done. "I admitted defeat, gave up my dream of being a teacher, and sought consolation in the piano," Blanca admits in her letter. In fact, it was pure theater that made her arrive late at school: she would stay up late at night going to the rehearsals and performances at the Confraternidad center founded by her father. And the next morning she would reach the station platform at a run, only to see her train disappearing in the distance.

Among the students who attended the classes that my great-grandfather Martín gave at the Confraternidad center, there was one who at times seemed more interested in the teacher's daughter than his lessons. His name was Jacinto, and he was to become my grandfather. "Since we were children," my grandma explains with a mixture of mischievousness and shyness that might not exist nowadays, "Jacinto found ways to be at our house a bit more by teaching one of my brothers the violin." Soon afterward, no excuse was needed.

Referring to the domestic duo they were to become, Blanca adds: "the love of music meant we never stopped practicing our instruments, in the hope that we could make up for the lack of talent by a wealth of dedication. I still apply that principle, so that even now, at eighty-one years old and with rheumatic hands, I don't let a day go by without practicing." Luckily those rheumatic hands also served to write some of the most precious words I've ever read.

Disciplined even in their leisure, for decades my grandparents were prudently content with their small house, their hundred books and their hundred records. The one great fear for them was to fail to do what they ought. Perhaps because of that, when she was already over fifty, Blanca decided to study her mother and grandmother's native tongue. Her aim was to be able to enjoy the prose of her beloved authors, from Voltaire to Camus, Stendhal to Simone de Beauvoir, in the original: all the things my great-grandmother Juliette had never been able to read. She achieved this goal at the same time as she saw the birth of her first grandchild, my dearest cousin Ernesto, my childhood playmate.

Apparently, this renewed interest in studying upset my grandfather. As a result, out of a mixture of empathy and vigilance, he began to attend the same classes as Blanca. I've no idea whether my grandmother was pleased by this. All I know is that it didn't take her long to abandon the French academy, claiming that she had reached the level she wanted to.

Among Blanca's books, I found an old copy of *Portrait of a Man Unknown* by Nathalie Sarraute, published by Gallimard in the year I was born. On the frontispiece I was astounded to discover that my grandmother had not signed with her father or her husband's family name, as she so often did, but with that of her French mother: "Blanca Pinault." I suspect that Grandma Blanca's secret biography is silently scattered among the underlinings and comments in her books. Some of them look like passages from discussions she never had with our family.

In *The Fall* by Camus for example, this underlined sentence stands out: "One sentence will be enough for modern man: he fornicated and read newspapers." Or this other one: "The satisfac-

tion of being right, the joy of self-esteem, are powerful impulses."
In *The Age of Discretion* by Simone de Beauvoir, she underlined
the following lament about motherhood: "I am the one who
shaped her life. Now I watch it from outside, a distant witness.
That is the shared destiny of all mothers, but who has ever consoled themselves by saying that their destiny is a shared destiny."

As well as the piano, teaching, and French, my grandma almost
secretly entertained a fourth dream: to sing opera. She did take
some singing lessons for a while, despite the fact that "I already
had other responsibilities as I was married, and so it was out of my
reach. First duty, then pleasure," Blanca writes, and I'm no longer
sure if the irony is hers, or an ironic echo my words take on as I
transcribe hers.

What my grandmother did find pleasure in was initiating my
aunt Diana to music; she went on to become a piano teacher. My
grandfather meanwhile took it upon himself to start my mother
on the violin. "As you will know," writes Blanca with contained
emotion, and her hand seems to tremble a little more than usual,
"the most important pupil Jacinto taught was his daughter."

In the final paragraphs of her letter, told in much less detail,
Blanca outlines my grandfather Jacinto's activities after his retirement. Walks, records, tea. A few violin pupils. Yoga on the
rug. Rereadings he noted mentally, never in pencil. Blanca ends
her letter abruptly: "Among his other pupils, only one showed
his appreciation. This grateful student, whom he used to visit at
home, had a terminal illness and he knew it. He was a doctor by
the name of Augusto."

This is how, mentioning a doctor attended by his violin teacher,
my grandma preferred to end her story. Ought I to remain silent

now, as my schoolmate Santos did, to match my grandmother's silence? Or should I do what I ought to do, out of loyalty to her principle, and complete the story?

# 71

I LOOKED FOR the last short story I had written, "The Chest of Drawers," dated April 1991. Out of curiosity, I tried changing some words, adapted some turns of phrase, conjugated the verbs again, just to see how they sounded. Would I ever be able to speak from the other side? And if I learned how to, would I then be able to return to my earliest words? Would I be able to retrace my palate with the tip of my tongue? The two extremes of my imminent voyage left me stuttering.

I was used to reading Spanish magazines and books, some of them sent from Madrid by my aunt Silvia, so it wasn't hard for me to try out these variants. They were small details, or maybe not: perhaps that moment of linguistic uncertainty was my first attempt at survival. The shore was about to move. Even though it was the same, my language was about to be transformed: a mother and a foreign tongue forever. Would my memory also change? Now I come to think of it, possibly my memory was just about to begin. I recalled my great-grandfather Jonás, who had abandoned

Yiddish to become Jewish in Spanish. Or my great-grandfather Juan Jacinto, who had become a Galician with a Buenos Aires accent.

I took that last story I had written out of my luggage. An adolescent tribute to Poe, it was about a character who finds his own heart beating in a forgotten drawer in his house. Someone for whom, in short, what is most his becomes foreign to him. I suddenly thought of an alternative title. I scribbled it on the story: "From the Other Side."

# 72

BOTH GRANDPA JACINTO'S parents were from Spain. From Galicia, my great-grandfather Juan Jacinto Galán, and from somewhere in La Mancha, my great-grandmother Isabel Redondo. Juan Jacinto had emigrated to Argentina at a very early age: that was why, it was said, he had lost his accent. Or perhaps it was something more amphibian: a rapid assimilation at school of his adopted way of speaking, and the habit of practicing his original intonation at home. Maybe he couldn't keep to only one shore and, depending on who he was speaking to, switched between the two sound patterns, inhabiting a bifurcating language. Great-grandpa, how I'd love to listen to you even for just a minute, in some phantom recording, to read your accent between the lines, to weigh up your vocabulary, savor your pronunciation.

To absorb a foreign way of speaking. To take root in the absence of a home. That was my Spanish great-grandfather's fate, and mine as well, a century later. So that in some way Juan Jacinto foreshadowed my voice, or its two variants, but in reverse order: in the opposite way to him, I spent my childhood in Argentina and my adolescence in Spain. Since both lands are supposed to share the same language, it might be thought this displacement wouldn't bring with it a linguistic crisis as acute as emigration to a country speaking a different tongue. Yet in the latter case the native language can become a haven of certainty, a bastion of identity faced with all that's foreign. When on the other hand the move alters the same language one thought of as one's own, what is called into question is the basis of how one talks to oneself. That is, the condition of writing.

This process was aggravated by the age at which we made our respective emigrations—an age of change and self-doubt. In order to relate to my new schoolmates in Granada, I spent my whole adolescence translating myself from Spanish to Spanish, from one south to another. Searching for equivalences, comparing expressions, thinking each word from both sides. Over time, this split learning came to be the only way for me to approach my language. I'm no longer in the habit of speaking as I once did: I've grown used to a different pronunciation, and I've acquired a Spanish accent which sometimes strikes me as odd. When the occasion arises, I'm still able to rescue my lost way of speaking. I'm not the same speaker, but I can recall my other words, which also define me.

Just as when my brother Diego started school he soon acquired the genuine diction of an Andalusian neighborhood, so my great-grandfather Juan Jacinto so perfectly adopted a Buenos Aires tonality that he ended up sounding like a tango lowlife from Barracas or a character from an Evaristo Carriego poem. Juan Jacinto used to like to tell the story of one of his former girlfriends who, unaware of his origins, confessed to him casually one day that not even if she were drunk or crazy would she marry someone from Galicia, because they were all stupid. My great-grandfather's response was a model of concision: "Well then sweetheart, we'd better say goodbye."

However, it didn't take him long to find a wife in Buenos Aires, and in fact she was Spanish. My great-grandparents Juan Jacinto and Isabel made an asymmetrical couple. He was fairly tall and a convinced anarchist. She was short and a devout Catholic. They fell in love with that fury that seduces opposites. They fought and made up with an ease akin to genius. Their son, my grandfather Jacinto, was born over Christmas in 1913. Unfortunately, he had no memory of the father he came to resemble in so many respects. My great-grandfather lost his life shortly afterward, still in his twenties, as a result of a badly treated infection and an absurd medical mistake. He would remain forever young, forever absent.

I keep his battered ID card like a holy relic. It was issued and filled out in the city of Buenos Aires over a century ago. His number, as far as the paper allows one to guess, was 371187. "I certify that Don *Juan Jacinto Galán*, who states that he is *married* (states? did the conjugal reality of each individual depend only on their testimony?) and an *employee* (what kind, I wonder?) by profession, who *yes* can read and write (this very option is the map of an age), is born (to be born isn't the same in the present and past tenses) in the town of *Coruña,* province of *Coruña,* in the nation of *Spain,* height 5 feet _____ inches (did my great-grandfather refuse to be measured because he was smaller than he had claimed?), skin color *white,* hair *medium brown, beard and mustache id* (possibly mustache idem, idiosyncratic, ideological, idiotic?), nose *straight,* with a *horizontal* base (this is starting to sound like a description by Zola) an *average-sized* mouth and ears (so, in proportion at least). Visible distinguishing marks ____." None: my great-grandfather was invisible.

The booklet concludes with a red stamp that crosses the certificate diagonally: "This document confirms identity only." Some adverbs are a whole novel.

After losing her husband, one of the first things my great-grandmother Isabel did was to give Jacinto a late baptism and, a few years later, oblige him to take communion. "I found your father when he already had his own ideas, but you won't escape the Lord." Jacinto kept his mother happy, but never actually took communion. He hid the wafer in his mouth the whole time and then, without anyone seeing, he spit it out in the street.

Isabel soon remarried. The family moved to Lanús, where Jacinto's stepfather had a small plot of land. My grandpa's elementary school teacher lamented the move. Suspecting her favorite pupil would find it difficult to continue studying, she offered to pay his fares from her own pocket. Perhaps out of wounded pride, Isabel rejected this generous offer, and that was the end of my grandfather's education. The couple decided the time had come for their boy to earn his daily bread, and so found him a job delivering it.

This deplorable decision may be interpreted like an act of revenge on my great-grandmother's part. Revenge for a childhood spent in a tumbledown house in Castile, brutal beatings by her father, an early flight from home, a hazardous Atlantic crossing, and numerous jobs as a cleaner when she was still only a little girl. So now Grandpa Jacinto went out on his bicycle at first light, did his bread round, and when he got back home served his mother her breakfast in bed. Her burgundy-colored bedroom was always in semi-darkness. Her dressing table was decorated with saints' images and plaster statues, and there was always a lighted candle on it.

Sometimes my great-grandma Isabel asked Jacinto to help do her hair; this was the moment he feared more than any other because it meant he had to go in search of her combs, which were stuck in an old braid of her hair. The long, dry braid she had worn the day of her wedding to her deceased first husband, and which she still kept tacked to the wall.

My grandfather Jacinto learnt a lot with his job on the streets. That if you didn't hide the bike carefully in the house entrances, your bread could be stolen in the blink of an eye. That trustworthy clients didn't ask you for anything on trust. Or that people respected you less in short trousers. But Jacinto kept a secret: every evening, after finishing all his chores, he would play the violin for a while. And went on doing so for the next seventy years. "So that not everything was duty," my grandmother Blanca writes, "as fate would have it he found the violin and a teacher who taught him for nothing."

Indeed, thanks to a family acquaintance, my grandfather started taking free lessons. This small providence led Jacinto to do the same with other people throughout his entire life. That violin teacher, whose name was Petraglia, "taught him all he knew, which was a lot." Was it a lot that Petraglia knew, or was it a lot for a teacher to offer his modest knowledge to a pupil? My grandma's sense of humor has always been almost imperceptible. Jacinto made rapid progress and, after several temporary jobs, decided to look for a stable position that would allow him to devote more time to the instrument.

My grandfather started work as an employee of the Corporación Argentina de Carnes (Argentine Meat Corporation), where the daily timetable was slightly less onerous, and his pay slightly higher. I can still hear him saying, just like when he was trying to teach me to play the violin: "Little by little, little by little." Around that time he became part of an orchestra led by the violist Bruno Bandini, a name worthy of a crime thriller. Several young people who were to become notable soloists also passed through that orchestra. For example, a certain thin, mustachioed oboe player by the name of Di Grimaldi, who was to be my father's teacher.

To perfect his style, Jacinto also took classes with Señor Vezzeli, famous for his relaxation techniques. Those lessons, which it seems were far too relaxed, didn't last long. "That maestro," my grandmother notes with a hint of malice, "was in the habit of talking more than teaching." Only someone who knew the all too measured Jacinto can imagine how unbearable this waste of time must have been to him.

Meanwhile, my great-grandmother Isabel couldn't understand why her son was wasting his time precisely on music. Just as earlier she had refused to go to his wedding ceremony to some young pianist in the disgraceful civil registry, now she couldn't understand how any sensible person could save up for years to buy a wooden box and a hairy stick. "Do you reckon that blessed violin is going to earn you some money one day, my son?" she would reproach him, "or do you really think you can live off that nonsense?" My grandfather would listen to her biting his tongue, preferring not to answer. Besides, it didn't matter. He had his four strings, a harmony he could trust. There was a kind of musical chord to his life: the sides of beef stamped by the Corporation; the taut touch of his violin; Blanca's soft, tuneful skin.

In his rare moments of leisure, Jacinto read Marx, José Ingenieros, and Sarmiento, from whom he learned to detest *caudillismo* in general and Peronism in particular. That was why, when he considered his daughters were old enough, he hastened to teach them music and give them Sarmiento's *Facundo*, the *Communist Manifesto* and Ingenieros' *Hacia una moral sin dogmas* (Toward an Ethics without Dogma). This last title didn't prevent Jacinto, when my mother announced she was getting married, from warning her: "No synagogues, churches, or mosques. If it's not a civil ceremony, daughter, I'm not going to your wedding."

Little by little: the last job my grandfather had was with the Ford motor company. For some time he had been broadening his commercial knowledge, studying English, and learning how to use Comptometer calculators. In fact, Jacinto spent the next twenty-eight years, four months, and seventeen days of his life between Ford and Comptometer. In all that time, according to everyone, my grandfather never missed a day of work. To be precise, there was one particular occasion when he didn't go to the factory: he thought he had a head cold coming on, and decided it was more productive not to go out to avoid it getting worse. Apart from that anomalous day, neither before nor after Jacinto suffered the slightest illness until he was quite elderly.

Equally meticulous about his small pleasures, my grandfather lived rereading the same hundred books and replaying the same hundred records. Someone who does what he ought to, he repeated tirelessly, never feels any agony. He went from home to work and work to home. He went to bed early, and he got up early, even on Sundays. He always remained on the outskirts of the city: in Lanús, Boulogne, Florida. As well as the more affordable house prices, he did not like noisy urban centers. He was reserved with his neighbors and could be gruff with people he didn't know. He rarely went out or met friends. "All my friends," he would say, "are here," pointing to his library. He never smoked, and didn't particularly enjoy sweet things. He drank half a glass of red wine with his meals. What he did do was cut himself huge, disproportionate slices of cheese. Cheese was perhaps the only extravagance he allowed himself.

Unlike many of his colleagues, it was only when he retired that Grandpa Jacinto felt young: a whole life growing old at work before finally having the freedom to play. He could spend his days practicing his instrument as much as he wanted. He joined the Juan José Castro Conservatory orchestra, which of course was still being led by Old Radick. Despite his adamantly strict nature, my grandfather allowed himself a few demonstrations of fondness for which I'll always thank him. Such as traveling almost an hour and a half to San Telmo to teach me violin, just as he had done with my mother in his own home. After his retirement, I remember it was common to find him listening to a record, holding Grandma Blanca's hand.

Until he was eighty, my grandfather Jacinto was in the habit of taking energetic daily walks, making love exactly twice a week, and doing half an hour of yoga every afternoon. He considered these three things, and especially the second, as an essential part of everyone's inner balance. He walked along very erect, giving the impression he was playing the violin as he went. When we visited him, he would occasionally take me to a park alongside some railway lines, and we would play soccer while we watched the trains go by. I would defend and he would shoot. He kicked the ball mechanically and accurately. Not too hard, not too soft.

If during his twenty-eight years, four months, and seventeen days of service for Ford all he ever had was a mild cold, then over the next fifteen years my grandfather's health remained remarkable. On the one occasion he agreed to have a check-up, the doctor asked for the tests to be repeated because he thought the results had been mixed up with another much younger patient. This confirmed Jacinto in his view of the uselessness of medicine.

The passing of the years only served to increase my grandfather's skepticism, his acute sense of loneliness and his contempt for the political class. He continued to reread his favorite books, but with less enthusiasm. Toward the end he dedicated himself to destroying them systematically, as if this were the last phase of some strange hermeneutic method. When it was Borges's turn, he declared he was getting rid of them because he had discovered their trick; he disposed of all of them apart from *Other Inquisitions* which my grandmother begged him to keep. He burned Balzac last of all, and didn't spare any as a keepsake. A Balzac book, he declared, should never be on its own. Instead of throwing them away, one day my grandfather gave me a selection of Gogol. If you're so interested in short stories, he said, you're going to have to read *The Cape*. He also gave my brother, for when he was older, an illustrated version of Cervantes's *Exemplary Novels*. That was a special gift: he had inherited it from his father, with whom he had never been able to talk about books.

During this same period of healthy retirement and physical exercise, my grandfather was able to devote himself more consistently to teaching. Even if, as Blanca insisted, "the most important pupil Jacinto taught was his daughter." Shortly after this, my grandmother's letter ended with those brief final lines: "Among his other pupils, only one showed his appreciation. This grateful student, whom he used to visit at home, had a terminal illness and he knew it. He was a doctor by the name of Augusto." It was with someone else's illness, a doctor attended by his old music teacher, that my grandmother Blanca brought her tale to an abrupt end. And yet she remained silent about another death much closer to her. I can understand her, but I feel I ought to round off this part of the story, the novel of her memories that is now traveling inside mine.

Her letter has expanded. I've seen it grow with the same fascination as that with which my great-grandfather Jacobo watched buildings going up, how their appearance gradually changed and how their structures grew. And to do that, to complete Blanca's letter, I have another doctor's notepad. Tall, narrow sheets of paper. All of them headed: Dr. Mario Neuman, Associate Professor of Anatomy, head of Surgery at the Policlínico Ferroviario Central, Mondays, Wednesdays and Fridays, telephone appointments on 983-5112, the telephone that no longer exists, Medrano 237, First floor A, next to the front door. Let's open it wide now.

For the first time in his life, when he reached eighty my grandfather Jacinto began to suffer from dizzy spells and headaches. His reflexes and energy were gradually waning, his gaze seemed less focused. His steps looked less assured. His character turned even more sour; he was not used to any weakness. He had to give up his daily exercises, going out on his own, and finally, playing the violin. That was the last straw.

Not wishing to investigate exactly what his illness was, nor doing much to search for a remedy, Jacinto preferred to choose his own ending, just as he had chosen every part of his life.

He sat down to write three letters. One for Grandma Blanca, another for Aunt Diana, the third for my mother. He hid them for a while. Every so often he would reread them—I'm certain to shorten them—and then write out the new version. There were almost no books left in his library, and only a scattering of photographs.

One afternoon, when my grandmother had gone out to the market, he left the three letters on the table. Then he took off his clothes—fearlessly, I imagine, convinced yet again he was doing what he ought to, and began to slowly fill the bathtub.

# 73

WE WERE ALL lined up taking one another's photos. Anyone seeing us might well have thought that we were on an excursion to the airport. It was as though we had been intending to go to our old plot of land at Monte Grande, but had continued on past it, this time arriving at Ezeiza airport.

My schoolmates were laughing politely at the jokes I felt obliged to make to hide my anxiety. Half our family wished us good luck. My grandma Dorita couldn't speak: Aunt Ponnie held on to her just in case. Let's spare the tears and things like that. It was hard to give The Raven a final hug. My father hadn't slept for days because of all the paperwork and the sale of our apartment. Smaller than his luggage, my brother Diego was pushing a suitcase with both arms. Hands were waving rapidly, the escalator was moving up slowly.

*Chau*, Delgado, look after San Telmo for me. Come on, come on, my father kept saying. *Chau*, Beanpole Ferrando, make sure Boca are the champions. My suitcase wouldn't fit on the moving step so I had to balance it with my foot. *Chau,* Sarudiansky, write me if you play at the Teatro Colón someday. I stroked my brother's head. *Chau,* Croaky Rychter, what do you think of Bioy Casares? The escalator was whirring, as if we were about to take off. *Chau,* Cesarini, please forgive me. I tried to ease the weight of my hand luggage. *Chau,* Santos, teach my grandma Dorita how to speak again. It was starting to be hard to make out the ones I was waving to at the back. *Chau,* Nazario, I'm afraid you'll go far. I couldn't see them all now. *Chau,* Flores, every so often send me a happy poem, they're the most tricky ones to write. Was the escalator going faster all of a sudden, or was it just my impression? *Chau,* Ariadna, because we got together too late. *Chau,* Gabriela, because we never got together. By now only the ones waving from the foot of the escalator were visible. *Chau,* Iribarne, can we play cards by airmail? My father looked at me from deep in his dark-lined eyes, trying to smile. *Chau,* José Luis, remember it's always got to be grapefruit. I thought about turning my back on them or closing my eyes. Then I remembered my old schoolmates Emsani and Mizrahi: didn't you want two worlds? Now all I could see were indistinct feet. *Chau,* Raven, thanks for the library. Only a few steps left on our escalator. *Chau,* ancestors, imagined bloodlines. The last step flattened out. *Chau,* characters, *chau.* And we picked up our bags to avoid the clanking escalator.

It was noon one day in April 1991.

Stiff on its hinges, time shifted.

# 74

"HEAR, OH MORTALS, the sacred cry!" the national anthem begins.
Memory tomorrow will be a new hinge.

# 75

THE SKY STRETCHED out, searching for its color.

Beneath it, my Grandfather Mario's skinny torso folded and straightened as he dug with the spade.

I was helping him: that's to say, watching him.

"Grandpa, have you nearly finished?"

"What's wrong? Are you tired already, you layabout? I'm the one doing the digging!"

"Let me dig then."

"I already told you: you might hurt yourself. Give me some more dirt, my boy."

"Here."

"Thanks, my boy."

"Grandpa."

"Yes?"

"And can't you hurt yourself?"

"Me? No."

"You sure?"

He stopped digging and looked at me. He was a bit impatient, but smiled. He wiped away the sweat: a smudge of black soil stayed on the middle of his brow. Wrinkling his nose, he raised his eyes to the horizon.

"Oh, alright. Take the spade. Hold it tight. Put this hand higher. No, not there. That's right."

"And now?"

"Now you plunge it straight in. You push down, put your foot on the edge for a moment, then pull the tip backward."

"Like this?"

"More or less, my boy, more or less."

"Don't laugh!"

"How light you are."

I dug two or three small spadefuls, then handed the spade back. Mario was breathing heavily, his voice a little hoarse.

"Is the young master satisfied?"

"Come on, Grandpa, let's plant the tree."

"Be patient. The hole still needs to be a bit bigger. And we have to straighten out the roots and put some manure in. Go and fetch me that bag, will you?"

"Okay."

"It's heavy, isn't it?"

"No, not a bit."

"So why have you gone all red?"

"Because it's so hot, Grandpa."

"You're a little monkey."

"What a horrible smell, Grandpa."

"What, from the bag of manure? You know what's in there, don't you?"

"I'm not sure, it looks like . . ."

"It is what it looks like!"

"Really?"

"Pass me the gloves, please. And turn the hose on."

"Okay."

"Get a move on."

"Grandpa."

"Yes, my boy?"

"How long do these trees last?"

"Don't worry, this one'll last for ages."

As he combed out the roots, my grandfather Mario poured water on them. Then he slipped on the gloves with a surgeon's dexterity. He wrinkled his nose even more, his breathing became harsher. The sky almost, almost fell apart.

"Hurry up my boy, it's growing late on us."

*Granada, 2003.*
*Rewritten and expanded, 2014.*
*Revised, 2021.*

# LIST OF FAMILY CHARACTERS
# IN ALPHABETICAL ORDER:

ABRAHAM, GREAT-GREAT-GRANDFATHER. Husband of Great-Great-Grandmother Lea. Father of Great-Grandmother Sara. Grandfather of Grandmother Dorita and of Great-Uncle Cacho. Great-Grandfather of Víctor, the narrator's father, and of aunts Silvia and Ponnie.

ANITA, GREAT-GRANDMOTHER. Second wife of Great-Grandfather Jonás. Step-Grandmother of Víctor, the narrator's father, and of aunts Silvia and Ponnie. Daughter of Doña Genia.

BEILE, GREAT-GREAT-GRANDMOTHER. Wife of Great-Great-Grandfather Itzkjok. Mother of Great-Grandfather Jonás. Grandmother of Grandmother Dorita and Great-Uuncle Cacho. Great-Grandmother of Víctor, the narrator's father, and of aunts Silvia and Ponnie.

BLANCA, GRANDMOTHER. Wife of Grandfather Jacinto. mother of Delia, the narrator's mother, and of Aunt Diana. Sister of great-uncles Rubén, Homero, and Leonardo. Daughter of great-grandparents Juliette and Martín.

CACHO, GREAT-UNCLE. First husband of Great-Aunt Delia. Brother of Grandmother Dorita. Uncle of Víctor, the narrator's father. Father of cousins Martín and Hugo. Son of grandparents Sara and Jonás.

DELIA, MOTHER. Wife of Víctor, the narrator's father. Mother of Diego, the narrator's brother. Daughter of grandparents Blanca and Jacinto.

DELIA, GREAT-AUNT. Wife of Great-Uncle Cacho and subsequently of Step-Great-Uncle Mauricio. Mother of Cousin Martín and Cousin Hugo.

DIANA, AUNT. Sister of Delia, the narrator's mother. Mother of Cousin Ernesto. Daughter of grandparents Jacinto and Blanca.

DIEGO, BROTHER. Son of Delia, the narrator's mother, and of Víctor, the narrator's father.

DORITA, GRANDMOTHER. Wife of Grandfather Mario. Mother of Víctor, the narrator's father, and of aunts Silvia and Ponnie. Daughter of grandparents Sara and Jonás.

ERNESTO, COUSIN. Son of Aunt Diana. Grandson of Blanca and Jacinto.

GENIA, GREAT-GREAT-GRANDMOTHER. Mother of Step-Great-Grandmother Anita. Step-great-grandmother of Víctor, the narrator's father, and of aunts Silvia and Ponnie.

HOMERO, GREAT-UNCLE. Brother of Grandmother Blanca and of great-uncles Rubén and Leonardo. Uncle of Delia, the narrator's mother. Son of great-grandparents Juliette and Martín. Married to Lali.

HUGO, COUSIN. Son of Great-Aunt Delia and Great-Uncle Cacho, and of Step-Great-Uncle Mauricio. Brother of Cousin Martín.

ISABEL, GREAT-GRANDMOTHER. Wife of great-grandfather Juan Jacinto. Mother of Great-Uncle Jacinto. Grandmother of Delia, the narrator's mother, and of Aunt Diana.

ITZKJOK, GREAT-GREAT-GRANDFATHER. Husband of Great-Great-Grandmother Beile. Father of Great-Grandfather Jonás. Grandfather of Grandmother Dorita. Great-Grandfather of Víctor, the narrator's father, and of aunts Silvia and Ponnie.

JACINTO, GRANDFATHER. Husband of Grandmother Blanca. Father of Delia, the narrator's mother, and of Aunt Diana. Son of great-grandparents Juan Jacinto and Isabel.

JACOBO, GREAT-GRANDFATHER. Husband of Great-Grand-mother Lidia. Father of Grandfather Mario and Great-Aunt Lía. Grandfather of Víctor, the narrator's father, and of aunts Silvia and Ponnie.

JONÁS, GREAT-GRANDFATHER. Husband of Great-Grand-mother Sara and subsequently of Step-Great-Grandmother Anita. Father of Grandmother Dorita and Great-Uncle Cacho. Grandfather of Víctor, the narrator's father, and of aunts Silvia and Ponnie. Son of great-great-grandparents Itzkjok and Beile.

JUAN JACINTO, GREAT-GRANDFATHER. Husband of Great-Grandmother Isabel. Father of Grandfather Jacinto. Grandfather of Delia, the narrator's mother, and Aunt Diana.

JULIETTE, GREAT-GRANDMOTHER. Wife of Great-Grand-father Martín. Mother of Grandmother Blanca and great-uncles Rubén, Homero, and Leonardo. Grandmother of Delia, the narrator's mother, and Aunt Diana. Daughter of great-great-grandparents Louise Blanche and René. Sister of Great-Great-Uncle Luis.

LEA, GREAT-GREAT-GRANDMOTHER. Wife of Great-Great-Grandfather Abraham. Mother of Great-Grandmother Sara. Grandmother of Grandmother Dorita and Great-Uncle Cacho. Great-Grandmother of Víctor, the narrator's father, and of aunts Silvia and Ponnie.

LEONARDO, GREAT-UNCLE. Brother of Grandmother Blanca and great-uncles Homero and Rubén. Uncle of Delia, the narrator's mother. Son of great-grandparents Juliette and Martín. Married to Normita.

LÍA, GREAT-AUNT. Sister of Grandfather Mario. Aunt of Víctor, the narrator's father. Daughter of great-grandparents Lidia and Jacobo.

LIDIA, GREAT-GRANDMOTHER. Wife of Great-Grandfather Jacobo. Mother of Grandfather Mario and Great-Aunt Lía. Grandmother of Víctor, the narrator's father, and of aunts Silvia and Ponnie.

LOUISE BLANCHE, GREAT-GREAT-GRANDMOTHER. Wife of Great-Great-Grandfather René. Mother of Great-Grandmother Juliette and Great-Great-Uncle Luis. Grandmother of Blanca. Great-grandmother of Delia, the narrator's mother, and of Aunt Diana.

LUIS, GREAT-GREAT-UNCLE. Son of great-great-grandparents Louise Blanche and René. Brother of Great-Grandmother Juliette. Uncle of Grandmother Blanca. Great-uncle of Delia, the narrator's mother.

MARIO, GRANDFATHER. Husband of grandmother Dorita. Father of Víctor, the narrator's father, and of aunts Silvia and Ponnie. Son of great-grandparents Lidia and Jacobo.

MARTÍN, GREAT-GRANDFATHER. Husband of great-grandmother Juliette. Grandfather of Delia, the narrator's mother, and of Aunt Diana. Father of grandmother Blanca and great-uncles Rubén, Homero and Leonardo. Son of great-great-grandmother Chazarreta and great-great-grandfather Passicot.

MARTÍN, COUSIN. Son of Great-Aunt Delia and Great-Uncle Cacho, and of Step-Great-Uncle Mauricio. Brother of Cousin Hugo. Married to Laura and subsequently Ana. Father of Violeta.

MAURICIO, GREAT-UNCLE. Second husband of Great-Aunt Delia. Step-father of cousins Martín and Hugo.

PABLO, COUSIN. Son of Aunt Silvia and Uncle Peter. Grandson of Grandmother Dorita and Grandfather Mario.

PETER, UNCLE. Husband of Aunt Silvia. Father of Cousin Pablo.

PONNIE, AUNT. Sister of Víctor, the narrator's father, and of Aunt Silvia. Daughter of Grandmother Dorita and Grandfather Mario.

RENÉ, GREAT-GREAT-GRANDFATHER. Husband of Great-Great-Grandmother Louise Blanche. Father of Great-Grandmother Juliette and Great-Great-Uncle Luis. Grandfather of Grandmother Blanca. Great-grandfather of Delia, the narrator's mother, and of Aunt Diana.

RUBÉN, GREAT-UNCLE. Son of Great-Grandmother Juliette and Great-Grandfather Martín. Brother of Grandmother Blanca and great-uncles Homero and Leonardo. Uncle of Delia, the narrator's mother. Married to Porota. Father of Iris.

SARA, GREAT-GRANDMOTHER. First wife of Great-Grandfather Jonás. Mother of Grandmother Dorita and Great-Uncle Cacho. Grandmother of Víctor, the narrator's father, and of aunts Silvia and Ponnie. Daughter of great-great-grandparents Abraham and Lea.

SILVIA, AUNT. Sister of Víctor, the narrator's father, and of Aunt Ponnie. Mother of Cousin Pablo. Daughter of grandparents Dorita and Mario.

VÍCTOR, FATHER. Husband of Delia, the narrator's mother. Father of Diego, the narrator's brother. Son of grandparents Dorita and Mario.

ANDRÉS NEUMAN (1977) was born in Buenos Aires, where he spent his childhood. The son of Argentine émigré musicians, he grew up and lives in Granada, Spain. He has taught Latin American literature at the University of Granada, was selected as one of *Granta's* "Best of Young Spanish-Language Novelists," and was included on the *Bogotá-39* list. His novel *Traveler of the Century* won the Alfaguara Prize and the National Critics Prize. It was shortlisted for the International Dublin Literary Award, and received a Special Commendation from the jury of the Independent Foreign Fiction Prize. His novel *Talking to Ourselves* was longlisted for the 2015 Best Translated Book Award, and shortlisted for the 2015 Oxford-Weidenfeld Translation Prize. His collection of short stories *The Things We Don't Do* won the 2016 Firecracker Award for fiction, given by the Community of Literary Magazines and Presses with the American Booksellers Association. His most recent titles translated into English are the novels *Fracture*, *Bariloche*, and *Once Upon Argentina*; his selected poems *Love Training*; and the praise of noncanonical bodies *Sensitive Anatomy*. His books have been translated into twenty-five languages.

Nick Caistor is a prolific British translator and journalist, best known for his translations of Spanish and Portuguese literature. He is a past winner of the Valle-Inclán Prize for translation and is a regular contributor to *BBC Radio 4*, *Times Literary Supplement*, and the *Guardian*.

Lorenza Garcia has lived for extended periods in Spain, France, and Iceland. Since 2007, she has translated over a dozen novels and works of non-fiction from French and Spanish.